DEATH
FUND

DEATH FUND

THE ALEX GREENE SERIES: BOOK ONE

Stina Hemming

ICE QUEEN PRESS

Printed by ICE QUEEN PRESS. Toronto, Canada.

ISBN: 978-1-73873-684-3 (paperback)

This book is dedicated to my parents,
proud Viking descendants
albeit from different sides of the Baltic.

Prologue

Contrary to popular belief, the securities regulatory system in the United States is there to support Wall Street—not to protect investors. Sure, so-called market participants on Wall Street are "policed" by the Securities and Exchange Commission, known as the SEC, but that's because "money goes where money is safe."

To maintain a robust capital market, you need a robust regulatory regime. No one's racing to invest in the Russian or Brazilian markets—and for good reason: the risk is too great. But the North American markets are not risk free either. The SEC tends to be a step behind the systemic corruption and fraud that proliferates on Wall Street. When it comes to scams, aka "new products," the SEC is pitted against a trillion-dollar financial market hell-bent on avoiding the more draconian aspects of securities regulation. Skilled attorneys maneuver their way through a complex and often incomprehensible labyrinth of rules to discover "solutions" for their clients, and when a client wants to raise a billion bucks for a new product that will take the investment world by storm, attorneys will find a way to get the offering to market. *Death Fund* is about one of those new products, something known in the business as "life settlement funds," and the attorneys who facilitate it.

Chapter One
Marseille, France
September 2019

The midnight surveillance operation at the Port of Marseille-Fos had gone very wrong for investigator Alex Greene and Max Pound. They were on a remote dock when a massive explosion rocked the area.

Alex and Max were at the old seaport investigating a $400 million insurance claim made by the owners of the *Sinop*, a Russian container ship insured by Alex's employer, Basel Re. Armed pirates had hijacked the ship after it left the Port of Ningbo in China, and the ship's owners reported losing contact with the captain somewhere off the coast of Yemen. When the *Sinop* was finally located, anchored off Alula in Saudi Arabia, the entire cargo—450 million tons of personal protective equipment, or PPE—was gone.

It had been the second claim by the same company in as many months for piracy on the high seas, so Karl Guttmann, Head of Claims for Basel Re, called in Alex to check out the client's story. Alex and Max flew to Marseille from Paris to investigate. They were met by the captain and his first officer of the *Sinop*, who escorted them around the ship, never leaving their sides.

After two hours of examining every nook and cranny, Alex called it quits.

Sure enough, the PPE was missing. No surprise there.

What was surprising was the lack of any evidence of a hijacking. The captain and the first officer had been very vague on the details. They claimed to have not seen the pirates approaching from the stern side, so when the heavily armed bandits boarded the ship, it was too late to initiate emergency procedures. Cooperating had been the only choice. Fortunately, the pirates did not keep anyone for ransom.

They had set the captain and his crew adrift on lifeboats, and no lives were lost. Unfortunately, the captain could not prove his story. The ship's security cameras were not working, and the crew members were unavailable for interviews; they had all been sent home after the harrowing ordeal.

All very convenient, Alex thought.

After touring the vessel, Alex made a few inquiries around the port and got lucky. One of the security guards, after accepting a significant contribution to their family's summer vacation fund, gave Alex a lead: a few days earlier, shipping containers containing the PPE were unloaded from the *Yalena*—another cargo ship owned by the same Russian company—into a heavily guarded warehouse on the wharf. According to the guard, the *Yalena* had docked at midnight to offload its freight, and the ship left port before daybreak the next day.

Alex reported the intel back to Guttmann, and he sent her a sample of the universal product code for the stolen PPE with instructions to check out the warehouse. The area's open layout, however, made it impossible to breach security without being seen, so she and Max returned after midnight that night and spent the next four hours watching the warehouse from behind a wall of containers at the water's edge, waiting for an opportunity to approach the warehouse.

Alex and Max were still waiting when the explosion occurred. The blast pitched Alex's 140-pound frame into the air, hurling her across the wharf's uneven concrete surface and propelling her perilously close to the inferno. Alex struggled to stand up but could not and, ears ringing, head throbbing, crawled away from the burning debris toward the adjacent parking lot with a low fence. Panic surging through her chest, and fighting nausea and dizziness, Alex pulled herself up and—peering through the blackened ash and glowing embers floating all around—frantically called out for Max, her voice lost among the wailing alarms bursting through the fiery chaos.

Alex finally spotted Max's thermal imaging goggles near the edge of the water, but Max was nowhere in sight. Fearing the worst, Alex walked unsteadily to the side of the pier and looked into the swirling seawater. If Max had fallen into the water, she could not save him.

Suddenly, she heard coughing and a barely audible call of "boss, boss."

"Max!" *Thank God, he was alive.*

She walked unsteadily toward him. He was lying inches from the dock's edge. Alex leaned over and said, "Hang in there, Max, you're going to be okay."

Max half-opened his eyes and, blinking against the blood streaming down his forehead, whispered, "I think I broke my leg."

Gathering all her strength, Alex grabbed Max by his underarms and dragged him to safety. It took all the strength that she could muster to pull him just a few yards.

"Sit tight, Max. I'll be right back."

Alex hobbled to the parking lot and the blaring sirens. The emergency response vehicles were arriving. She flagged down a couple of paramedics and led them to Max.

Alex refused medical treatment, and after Max was safely inside an ambulance, she returned to the wharf. She had to inspect the scene: the timing was critical. Any chance of an independent investigation would be gone after the local authorities took control, and Alex still needed hard evidence to link the *Sinop*'s stolen cargo to the PPE stored in the warehouse—or whatever remained of it.

As she walked toward where the port security and local police were congregating, Alex noticed remnants of medical masks in the rubble on the ground. Most were too damaged for identification purposes, but she found one with the code intact. She compared the serial number on the tattered mask to the serial sequencing that Guttmann had sent her for the missing cargo.

The codes matched! The PPE in the smoldering warehouse was from the *Sinop*. Alex knew that although the damaged mask would not be enough for a successful criminal prosecution, it would be enough for Basel Re to refuse the claim. Prosecuting the Russians was not her job; saving Basel Re money was. She smiled to herself. She had resolved the insurance claim in record time, and the commission would be substantial.

Alex stuffed the burnt mask into the back pocket of her ripped jeans and ignored the police officer calling after her as she walked away from the carnage.

She had what she needed.

Chapter Two
Paris, France
October 2019

"Kiai!" Alex Greene's bamboo sword vibrated as it struck her opponent's weapon. Behind the slits of her kendō mask, Alex grinned as she aggressively pushed against the mat, her bare toes digging in like blades. Alex always felt her best whenever pummeling an adversary—whether for sport or for work.

"Good defense, Hanna!" Alex called out as the young student fended off the attack. With an eighth dan ranking, the highest possible, Alex was not easy to impress.

Seeing Hanna hesitate, Alex bellowed, "Keep focused!" To make her point, she raised her bokutō sword over her shoulders in the practiced Katsugi waza technique and drove Hanna to the mat with a thump.

Hanna got up and bowed. "Thank you, uchidachi."

Alex bowed in return. "Thank you, shidachi." She took off her mask and exhaled as sweat ran down her forehead. "Excellent workout, Hanna."

"Thanks, Auntie Lexi."

Alex had been very pleased when Hanna, her ward, showed an unexpected interest in martial arts at the age of twelve. To support Hanna's training, Alex added an impressive dojo to their Parisian apartment for sparring practices.

Alex glanced at her cell phone as they left the room.

"You'd better get going, Hanna, or you'll be late for school."

"Yes, yes, I know," Hanna said impatiently.

"Sophie will drop you off," Alex said.

"I don't need a ride," Hanna countered.

Alex gave Hanna a dirty look. Hanna was becoming more and more belligerent and had added truancy to her toolbox of activities designed to irritate Alex. She had developed a habit of joining her friends at the Place Monge after being allowed to take the Metro on her own, which resulted in showing up either late or not at all for her classes. Worse still, she had recently been picked up for shoplifting on one of her "days off." Luckily, Hanna got off with a warning, and no charges were laid by the local Prefecture of Police.

Her behavior was inexplicable to Alex—Hanna had a generous allowance for such expenses. When Sophie, Alex's housekeeper, suggested that it was a cry for attention, Alex spent her entire Saturday entertaining Hanna: shopping along the Avenue des Champs-Élysée, followed by lunch at Epicure. It hadn't changed her penchants for everything *haute* .

"You've got thirty minutes," Alex said.

"Fine." Hanna huffed and brushed past her down the long hallway toward the kitchen.

Alex went back to her quarters and stripped off her gear, and glanced at herself in the wall of mirrors that dominated her dressing room.

Her face still bore the cuts and bruises from the explosion in Marseille, but overall, she was aging well. Her auburn hair had only recently started to gray, and her flat stomach belied the fact that she eschewed traditional exercise, which she found excruciatingly boring.

Life had been good to Alex. American by birth, she'd spent most of her adult life in Paris, working as a securities investigator. Those investigations invariably included an element of physical danger, and Alex had learned to defend herself by whatever means necessary—a lesson she intended to pass on to Hanna. Martial arts training was just the start.

After her shower, Alex slipped into a cashmere hoodie and track pants and walked barefoot to her kitchen on the other end of the apartment. Alex had decorated the large space with cream-colored walls, terracotta floors, and distressed cupboards and shelves to complement her collection of antique copper pots and Limoges china. It was her favorite room in the apartment, even though she didn't cook and rarely entertained.

Alex made herself a café au lait and walked down the wide hallway to her study. She sat on the sun-warmed chaise lounge by the patio door and scrolled on her laptop through several English, French, and American daily newspapers.

The sound of her cell interrupted her morning ritual. She fished the phone out of her pocket and checked the screen.

"Hi, Karl, what's up?" A call from Guttmann could only mean one thing—a new investigation.

"Hello, Alex. How are you?"

"Fine, thanks. Almost back to my old self."

"And Max, how is he doing?" Karl asked.

"A lot better," Alex replied.

Max had been diagnosed with a minor concussion after the explosion, and luckily, he had not broken his leg.

"That is good news."

"Yes. Now, how can I help you, Karl?" Alex asked.

"I have a new investigation that may interest you. It should be lucrative."

"I need to confirm whether Max is available. I promised him time off." She would not take on an assignment without Max, and Karl knew it.

"Understood. Come into the office tomorrow at four and I'll brief you," Karl said.

Alex wasn't sure she was ready to start a new investigation either, but she'd hear what Karl had to say.

Chapter Three
Steubenville, Ohio
October 2019

Charlie Yusky had aged beyond his thirty-five years—poverty will do that to you. But when he looked in a mirror, Charlie could still find traces of the high school football star his wife, Julie, had fallen in love with all those years before, even though crow's-feet edged his blue eyes, and gray laced his dark-brown hair. Even more disturbing was the beer belly that Julie lovingly teased him about.

He and Julie had married right out of high school, and it had been a match made in heaven. Charlie adored Julie and that had never wavered. Julie was the homecoming queen in their senior year in high school and he had promised to make all Julie's dreams come true, and he still would. Charlie was Julie's rock and her trust in him was unwavering. They had built a life together and had two daughters and a house in the suburbs to show for it.

Things had been tough since being demoted from his millwright position after the steel plant moved its steel production offshore. The steel plant was outside of Steubenville, a small city in Ohio with fewer than twenty thousand residents. Steubenville, the hometown of Dean Martin, had seen better days, and Charlie considered himself to be a lucky man: he still had a job as a security guard that kept his family's head above water. But only barely—they struggled every month to make the mortgage payments on their two-bedroom ranch, which they'd bought new fifteen years ago. Charlie and Julie had taken advantage of the developer's low monthly interest rate and zero-down offer to finance the purchase of the house.

They were proud of their home, but Charlie didn't know how they were going to pay the balloon interest payment coming up at the end of the year.

One late night on his way home from work, a commercial surging from the tinny speakers of his beat-up Toyota pickup caught Charlie's attention: "We'll pay cash for your insurance policy. Take that special trip with your family or pay off your credit cards! Get your cash within forty-eight hours. Call us at 1-800-765-3457. That's 1-800-PROSPER. It's easier than you think!"

Charlie had a substantial life insurance policy as part of his benefits package at the plant. Maybe he could cash it in, like the ad said.

"What have I got to lose?" Charlie mumbled.

The next morning, after Julie went to work and their two daughters left for school, Charlie called the 1-800 number. A friendly representative named George asked Charlie about his age, general health, and the payout amount on his term life insurance policy. George's tone perked up when he learned Charlie was in his thirties, in good health, and sitting on a million-dollar policy.

"This is your lucky day, Mr. Yusky," George said. "Normally, we only deal with older individuals or people who have terminal illnesses, but given the size of your policy, you may be eligible. Can I send someone out to talk to you?"

"Sure," Charlie said, pleasantly surprised at how fast things were happening.

"Excellent, Mr. Yusky," George said. "I'll get back to you with a date."

After hanging up, Charlie searched for "life settlement funds" on the internet. According to Wikipedia, life settlement funds bought life insurance policies from people like him with money from investors. The investors made money when the insureds died. Charlie shook his head and chuckled. He had no intention of dying any time soon.

Then Charlie Googled the Prosperity Fund's website. There were two prominently featured tabs on the website: one for policyholders wishing to sell their policies and the other for investors wanting to invest in the fund.

Charlie clicked on the "For Policyholders" tab and read: "Cash now with no strings attached. Follow our simple approval process, and you will get cash based on the total amount of your policy. We will take over your premiums, saving you even more money."

Next, Charlie clicked on the "For Investors" tab: "Invest in the Prosperity Fund and double or triple your money when the policyholders die."

He scratched his head and read the rest of the page. Charlie understood very little about investing in the stock market, but betting on death gave him the creeps.

Charlie got a call back from George, who said all Charlie would have to do was complete an online health history questionnaire, and a representative from

Prosperity would meet him the following Monday at 10:00 a.m.

Charlie sighed, relieved that Julie would be at work. She would only fret if she knew what he was considering.

When he pulled into the Howard Johnson's parking lot the next Monday, Charlie was taken aback by how rundown the building had become. The HoJo, as the locals referred to the hotel, was in a dilapidated mall that had also seen better times. The mall's anchor stores were long closed, and everything else in the area looked shuttered, with papered windows and doors plastered with legal notices.

Weird place to meet, Charlie thought.

Charlie parked his dusty truck and walked across the littered parking lot into the HoJo's lobby. He immediately spotted the Prosperity Fund representative sitting in the coffee shop. The man was too well-dressed to be a local and looked as if he'd just stepped out of a department store window—totally out of place in the shabby surroundings.

Charlie walked up to the table. "I'm Charlie Yusky. Are you from the Prosperity Fund?"

The man put down his cell phone and stood up to shake Charlie's hand. "Yes, I'm Nick Martin. Pleased to meet you."

Taller than Charlie, Nick Martin was maybe six-foot-two or six-three, and he looked in good shape with a full head of dark-brown hair. Charlie would have pinned the guy in his late thirties.

"Sorry I'm late," Charlie said as he sat down.

"Not a problem, Mr. Yusky. I used the time to check my emails."

A waitress came by and, without asking, filled Charlie's mug with watery black coffee. She hesitated for a moment, and Nick asked Charlie if he wanted some breakfast.

Charlie said no, and the waitress was gone as quickly as she had appeared.

Charlie made a feeble attempt at small talk, asking Nick where he was staying. But even Charlie knew that Nick would not be spending much time in Steubenville.

"I'm not planning to stay overnight," said Nick. He explained that he had an afternoon flight out of Pittsburgh. Then they got down to business.

"You're interested in selling your life insurance policy to the Prosperity Fund?" Nick asked.

Charlie nodded.

"If you agree to go ahead, Charlie, the Prosperity Fund will pay you cash for your policy," Nick continued.

Great. "How much cash?" Charlie asked.

"That depends on your age, health, and payout under your policy."

He sounds like he could do the pitch in his sleep, Charlie thought. "Will my family get *any* money if I die?"

"Another excellent question, Mr. Yusky. You've been doing your homework," Nick said solicitously, making Charlie blush. "If you sell to Prosperity, the fund becomes the new beneficiary."

He continued, holding Charlie's gaze. "When you die, your family will not be paid a death benefit. All the money goes to the Prosperity Fund."

"I don't know," Charlie said, looking away and hesitating. "What if something happens to me? Who'll take care of Julie and the girls?"

"I totally understand your concerns," Nick said. "I have a family myself. How old are your girls, Charlie?"

"Bekka is twelve, and Kaylie's ten," Charlie answered.

Nick leaned forward and asked, "Wouldn't you like to have money for the girls now, instead of after you die?"

That made sense to Charlie. His family needed the money now, not in fifty years.

Nick pulled a pile of papers out of his briefcase. "Mr. Yusky, I reviewed the health questionnaire that you filled in online, and I'm pleased to offer you fifty thousand dollars for your policy. Normally, the fund requires a medical report, but I'm making an exception for you."

Charlie's mouth dropped open. "What do I have to do to get the money?"

"You'll have to sign a few documents. That's all," Nick said. "Let's go over them together."

After explaining each page to Charlie, Nick returned the documents to their original envelope and slid it across the sticky table to Charlie.

"If you want to go ahead, sign wherever you see a red tab. And don't forget to get a witness—this can be anyone who knows you and watches you sign. Then, just FedEx the documents back to me in the included prepaid envelope."

Charlie said nothing. *It seems so easy.*

Sensing Charlie's hesitation, Nick put his embossed business card on the table. "Here's my card. Take your time and call me if you have questions."

Charlie read the card. "You're an attorney?"

"Yes, but I'm also a licensed insurance broker." Without further explanation, Nick stood up and dropped a twenty-dollar bill on the table. "It's been a real pleasure meeting you, Charlie, but I've got a plane to catch. Just remember, you can always buy another life insurance policy for your family, so don't worry too much."

Charlie watched Nick leave the coffee shop and finished his coffee. He wasn't sure what Julie would think of him selling his insurance policy, but they needed the money. Better to have $50,000 today. Who knows how long he would live, and if he lost his job at the steel mill, could they even afford the monthly premiums? He stood up and scooped Nick's card off the table, eyeing the twenty on the table. *The guy sure is a big tipper.*

Chapter Four
Paris, France
October 2019

Max Pound pulled up in front of Basel Re's offices on Avenue Perronet Sud to drop Alex off for her meeting with Guttmann. He jumped out and opened the back door of the black Mercedes-Benz S65 AMG for Alex and asked, "Want me to come upstairs with you?"

Dressed in his "work uniform"—an Italian navy Hugo Boss suit, matching tie, and light-brown Santoni loafers—Max would easily blend in with the business crowd in the busy building, but Alex didn't need him for security, and she certainly didn't need him to participate in the meeting with Guttmann. Max and Alex's relationship had persevered over the years because Max understood his role in their relationship: to support Alex in any manner that she deemed appropriate and keep her safe. The high comp and interesting assignments didn't hurt either. Working with Alex had made Max very rich over the years; not as rich as Alex, of course, but Max was okay with that.

"No. You can wait in the car. I'll text when I'm done."

"Yes, ma'am," Max said.

Alex crossed the concrete plaza and entered Basel Re's office tower in the La Défense District, one of Europe's largest business districts. Alex walked briskly across the glass-and-steel lobby, the heels of her knee-high black Alexander McQueen moccasin boots clicking on the polished concrete floor, and her dark-gray Christian Dior cape gliding behind her. She pressed the button for the thirtieth floor and, moments later, stepped into Basel Re's reception area.

"*Bonjour*, Marie," Alex said to the young receptionist. "I'm here to see Monsieur Guttmann."

Marie looked up from behind the sleek Winston table and said pleasantly, "*Bonjour*, Madame Greene. I'll tell Monsieur Guttmann you are here."

Alex was well known in the Basel Re offices. She had been saving the company from fraudulent payouts in the capital markets for nearly fifteen years, first as their attorney and now as an in-house investigator.

A moment later, a smartly dressed woman approached Alex at the front desk.

Alex smiled. "Madame Roy, it's nice to see you again. I hope your family is well." Jeanne Roy was Guttmann's longtime assistant.

"We are doing very well, thank you for asking," Jeanne said. "I have a new grandchild. Jacques, my youngest, had a baby boy with his girlfriend, Chantal. We are very pleased."

When they arrived at a large metal door, Jeanne knocked lightly before ushering Alex inside.

Karl rose from behind his desk and gave Alex a traditional kiss, planting air kisses on each of her cheeks. "It's good to see you again, Alex. Please take a seat," he said, motioning toward several leather chairs grouped around a glass-topped coffee table.

Jeanne asked, "May I bring you something to drink? A coffee or a glass of water?"

Alex replied, "No, thank you."

"How about something stronger?" Karl asked as Jeanne shut the door.

"I like the way you think," Alex said. "Make mine a vodka on ice—Grey Goose, if you have it."

After they toasted to business, Alex said, "I wasn't expecting a call from you so soon after the Marseille case. I gave Max some time off, and I've started a new round of renovations on my apartment."

"Ah, yes. No doubt with the cash from your success at the Marseille-Fos Port. Believe me, I heard a few choice words from our CEO about your compensation on that file. Please try to make it look more difficult next time," Guttmann said, and they both laughed.

"And I hope someday to see that apartment you're always renovating," Karl teased.

"Only if you are very good," Alex said, her eyes flashing playfully. "Now, what have you got for me?"

"It's a new file I am sure will pique your interest. Tell me, Alex, what do you know about life settlement funds?"

"Securitizing life insurance policies through a fund structure is not a new concept. A life settlement fund is like a hedge fund, but instead of the fund investing in shares of companies, it buys insurance policies. Returns to investors are based on mortality rates. Not brain surgery," Alex snapped. "I also know that insurance companies don't like them, and for a good reason: the funds play havoc with actuarial calculations on life insurance policies that have already been underwritten."

"Admittedly, it is outside of our normal risk profile to underwrite life insurance policies held by a life settlement fund," Karl said curtly. "But after extensive due diligence and a huge discount, Basel Re has underwritten all of the policies currently held by the Prosperity Fund, and we have a problem."

"Due diligence or not, buying all of the policies held by the fund is a risky move," Alex said.

"Let me finish," Karl said, irritation edging his voice. "Prosperity has a different business model from other life settlement funds. As you know, most of them purchase the policies of elderly or terminally ill people where there's a high probability of death in the short term. This fund buys the policies of young, healthy adults with lower mortality rates. That means that there is less likelihood of Basel Re as the insurer being on the hook for payouts in the short term and maybe never, if the insured lives past the term life insurance age limit."

Alex jumped in. "Agreed that's better for Basel Re, but it's worse for investors in the fund. The lower death rates means lower returns. Doesn't make sense from an investment point of view." Alex swirled her vodka and paused for a moment. "I sure as hell hope you did your due diligence on this one."

Karl frowned. "We didn't have to. The Prosperity Fund is on the verge of a multi-billion-dollar listing on the New York Stock Exchange. Houghton & Willis, a top-tier law firm in Boston, represents the fund, and the offering is being underwritten by a major

American brokerage firm, so extensive due diligence has already been done."

"Yet here I sit," Alex said, raising an eyebrow. "What's gone wrong?"

Worry clouded Karl's face. "Over the last few weeks, the Prosperity Fund has made several claims where the death was accidental."

"What are you suggesting?" Alex asked.

Karl adjusted his glasses. "I am not suggesting anything, but the trend is a bit odd. We need you to investigate."

"What's Basel Re's exposure?" Alex asked.

Karl shifted in his seat. "Difficult to estimate. We are talking about forty million dollars in claims at this point, but the numbers could increase. Are you interested?"

Alex did the math in her head. Forty million in claims would mean a very big payday. "I am interested. But let me confirm with Max." She paused. "We would need to borrow one of Basel Re's jets."

Karl nodded. "Of course."

Alex finished her vodka and stood to go.

Karl escorted her to the door. "Always a pleasure." He followed up with the obligatory kiss.

Alex texted Max as she waited for the elevator. *Good news. A new file and a company jet to play with. See you outside in five.*

Chapter Five
Paris, France
October 2019

Alex briefed Max on their new assignment on the drive back to her apartment in late afternoon traffic, and when Karl confirmed by text that a Gulfstream G550 could be waiting for them at Orly at six the next morning, he was in.

As Max pulled up in front of Alex's building, she leaned forward and said, "Pick me up at four-thirty sharp. I'll also have work for you this evening, so stay close to your laptop."

Max turned and gave a mock salute. "Yes, ma'am."

The concierge gave Alex a friendly "*bonjour*" as she crossed the art deco lobby to her private elevator. Alex stepped out of the elevator into the foyer of her fourth-floor apartment, and the first thing she noticed was silence.

She threw her cape on the Louis XIV chair by a console table of the same vintage and headed down the long hallway to her kitchen. The expansive hallway featured some of her best art pieces, including works by Frédéric Bazille, William Kurelek, and Picasso.

Basel Re paid for that art, and with each successful investigation, Alex expanded her collection. Alex had an eye on a Dina Vierny sculpture that was coming up for auction in the next few weeks. The comp on the Prosperity Fund file would be more than enough to buy the multimillion-dollar item.

The expansive kitchen and informal dining area was Alex's favorite room in her apartment and normally the hub of activity in her family. Today it was empty. Alex knocked on the door to Sophie's quarters, but there was no answer. *Sophie and the kids must be out.*

Sophie and her son, Olivier, lived in an adjoining apartment to Alex's, and they—along with Hanna—were a part of Alex's untraditional extended family. It was a family that had developed despite Alex's best intentions to maintain a solitary, single life.

Alex had expanded her family after her sister, Meagan, showed up unannounced one afternoon with two-year-old Hanna in tow. Within the hour, Meagan was gone, leaving Hanna in Sophie's care. Alex had tried to find Meagan, but Meagan did not want to be found. From then on, Sophie was the primary caregiver for Hanna, and Hanna still affectionately referred to Sophie as *Maman*. Alex had been *Auntie Lexi* since Hanna could speak. And that was just fine with Alex; she didn't have a maternal bone in her body.

Alex pulled out her cell and dialed Sophie's number. After a few rings, Sophie answered. "*Oui, allo.*"

"It's me. Where are you?"

Sophie replied, "We're on our way to Laouz for dinner with my cousin Fared and his wife. Afterward, we are going over to my aunt's apartment in the Barbès district. We spoke about it this morning."

"Of course, of course, it slipped my mind," Alex said. Alex's focus on domestic matters had never been great, and she often treated Sophie's chatter as white noise. She made a mental note to try to start listening to what Sophie said to her. "I'm leaving for Boston first thing in the morning for work."

"Will we see you before you leave, *madame?*"

"I doubt it," Alex said.

"I'm afraid there is nothing prepared for your dinner."

"Don't worry, I'll go out," Alex said. "Please say goodbye to Hanna and Olivier for me."

After Alex hung up, she went to the wine fridge, opened a bottle of Sancerre, and poured herself a generous glass. She took the wine to her study and spent the next few hours reviewing the information that Guttmann had sent her on the Prosperity file.

She started her online research with Prosperity's filings on EDGAR, the public database of the US Securities and Exchange Commission, or the SEC. The fund was in the throes of an IPO, or initial public offering, with the endgame of a listing on the New York Stock Exchange. The fund's manager was a company incorporated in Liechtenstein, and someone named Vladim Bulgarin was its sole shareholder, officer, and director.

The Prosperity Fund had gotten off to a good start after analysts gave the fund a strong "buy." Prosperity managed to presell the entire $750 million offering, which attracted a waiting list of prospective buyers. The promise of a 20 percent per annum return and a return of capital in three years was enough to get investors' juices running. The market was always greedy for new products, and the Prosperity Fund, which monetized human life, fit the bill. *Investors are so damned gullible.*

The Prosperity Fund's preliminary prospectus, designed to entice mom-and-pop investors into handing over their hard-earned cash, had been filed six months earlier. Investor cash would be held in escrow by the investment bankers and not released till the prospectus went final, which should have happened months ago. Alex wondered why the final filing had stalled.

An online search of blogs and chat rooms revealed that the fund was struggling to build its asset base. Only a handful of US states allowed the purchase of life insurance policies by third parties, and the Prosperity Fund was having difficulties sourcing policies with the right mortality profile.

Alex checked the preliminary prospectus posted on EDGAR again. The mortality tables in the document were for older and/or terminally ill insureds, resulting in higher return projections for investors. But according to Guttmann, the Prosperity Fund was picking up policies of young and healthy individuals, probably for cents on the dollar. *What the hell was going on?* Then it hit Alex: Prosperity was artificially inflating its fund's asset base to make it more marketable to investors and the investment bankers on Wall Street.

Next, Alex checked out the website for Houghton & Willis. The firm was headquartered in Boston and employed over a thousand attorneys worldwide. Houghton's sweet spot was Russia and Eastern Europe. According to social media, one of Houghton's co-founders was a Russian-born national who'd changed his name upon first arriving in America.

Pyotr Holodov became Robert Houghton. The word on Wall Street was that Houghton and the firm maintained strong ties to the Russian regime. Rumors even swirled that the managing partner of Houghton's Moscow office was also the mistress of a senior politician close to Putin.

The firm website identified the partners and associates active on the Prosperity file. All appeared to be squeaky clean, except for Mihkel Ivanov, a Russian national who had immigrated to the States after a stint in Houghton's Moscow office. A simple Google search revealed that Ivanov had been sanctioned by the United Kingdom's securities regulator, the Financial Conduct Authority, or the FCA.

At the time, Ivanov was on the board of several Russian companies listed on the Alternative Investment Market, a submarket of the London Stock Exchange. When all six Russian companies were delisted over allegations that they were laundering cash for members of the Russian mafia, the FCA commenced an enforcement action against Ivanov personally. The FCA found Ivanov in absentia not to be a "fit and proper person," and he was banned from acting as an officer or director of a listed company in the UK.

Nick Martin, the team leader on the Prosperity transaction, was also featured prominently in the press release. Martin was clearly punching above his weight when he'd joined the prestigious firm after graduating from a second-rate law school ten years earlier. But even more surprising was Martin's meteoric rise to partnership at Houghton. Martin had made equity partner shortly after joining Houghton's and was named the head of the firm's life settlement group later that same year.

According to Martin's LinkedIn profile, he had worked summers as a licensed insurance agent for a life settlement fund while he was in law school. Alex, on a hunch, cross-referenced that fund, and lo and behold, she found it was one of Ivanov's life settlement fund clients at the time.

Alex swirled her glass of Sancerre. If Mihkel had brought Martin in and promoted him, it didn't bode well for Martin's integrity; he could be as dirty as Ivanov.

The one bright light on the Houghton team was a securities attorney named Paul Field. According to his LinkedIn profile, Paul was a retired naval aviator who had flown F-14 Tomcats off the flight decks of aircraft carriers for a living before going to law school. Paul, a poster child for a successful securities attorney, had joined the SEC after law school, and after several years working his way up the SEC food chain, he left to join Houghton.

Field's stint at the SEC marked him among the superstars of the Boston securities bar and gave him added credibility with SEC staff.

Alex put in a call to one of her contacts at Interpol for intel on Ivanov, Bulgarin, and any related associates.

After reviewing what she could find online about the regulatory framework around life settlement funds, Alex fired off an email to Max with instructions for further research.

In addition to being her bodyguard and driver, Max was her go-to guy for research and electronic surveillance. He'd been a member of France's Foreign Legion, and after his honorable discharge, he claimed his

French citizenship. His dual citizenship—American and French—came in handy when he joined the Directorate of External Security, the French equivalent of the CIA. There he provided counterintelligence to the French government. After five years, he'd been ready for a change and jumped at the opportunity to work with Alex.

Max, having never met a system or computer he could not hack, had proven to be invaluable to Alex. It also didn't hurt that he looked like a young Brad Pitt!

Chapter Six
Steubenville, Ohio
October 2019

Selling his life insurance policy to the Prosperity Fund was a no-brainer for Charlie Yusky. Even with Julie's telemarketing job, they were always broke, and the cash would change all that. He could pay off their maxed-out credit cards and Julie's car loan. There might even be enough money to pay the balloon payment that was coming due on their mortgage.

Charlie decided he was in.

He followed Nick's instructions to the letter and was relieved when the money showed up in his bank account a week later. He took the night off work, and when Julie came home, Charlie announced he was taking her and the girls out for dinner. Julie resisted, reminding Charlie that they were strapped for cash and tapped out on their credit cards, but Charlie insisted. With the $50,000 he could give Julie the life that she deserved, one that was free from worry. That was something to celebrate!

They hit the local Olive Garden around 5:00 p.m. as the evening rush was starting. Julie loved the bottomless soup bowl and salad bar. The girls always got the fettuccine Alfredo, and Charlie enjoyed the parmigiana. He even ordered a beer and talked Julie into a glass of the house white wine.

After dinner and dessert, the girls fell asleep early, and Charlie and Julie enjoyed a moment of quiet before bed.

"Our money problems are history. Wait till—" Charlie began, but before he could get his good news out about the incoming cash, tears welled up in Julie's eyes.

"I heard from Dr. Boldt's office," she blurted. "Bekka needs braces. Your dental insurance won't cover them, and we have no more room on our credit cards."

"Don't worry about Bekka's braces," Charlie said with a big grin. "It's all taken care of."

Julie gave him a puzzled look. "What do you mean?"

Charlie showed her Nick Martin's business card and explained, as best as he could, how the Prosperity Fund worked. "I don't get it. What are we going to do if you die? Will we get any money?" Julie asked.

"That's crazy. I'm not going anywhere," he said. "Now we can pay for Bekka's braces and a whole lot more."

Julie shook her head. "I'm worried."

"Don't worry. Besides, like the guy said, I can always get another insurance policy."

They spent the $50,000 in a few days. Bekka's orthodontist was paid in advance. Then they paid down the credit cards and Julie's car loan. Charlie also bought a one-carat solitaire ring for Julie—something he couldn't afford when they first married. Julie cried with joy when she opened the box, and Charlie knew he'd have paid double for the ring. Charlie plunked the rest down on the mortgage.

Two weeks after the payout from Prosperity, Charlie's old insurance company sent him a letter by registered mail saying that he would not be eligible for another policy with them.

"That's okay, babe," he told Julie when she fretted. "There are plenty more companies. This is America."

Charlie called his local insurance broker in Steubenville the next day. His broker didn't think it would be a problem for Charlie to get another policy either.

"I've got another insurance company in mind," he told Charlie. "Someone will call you later today about a medical examination. Just a formality."

Within forty-eight hours, Charlie met with Dr. Patel, the insurance company's doctor, and underwent a full physical examination, including a series of diagnostic and blood tests.

Charlie waited for the call from his broker to give him the green light on the new policy, but it didn't come. Instead, Charlie heard from Dr. Patel's office. The nurse asked Charlie to come in and go over the results with the doctor.

When Charlie arrived for his 3:00 p.m. appointment the next day, the receptionist escorted him into Dr. Patel's office.

"Thanks for coming in, Mr. Yusky," Dr. Patel said, directing Charlie to sit down on a chair beside his desk. "When was your last physical?"

"I've never had one," Charlie answered.

"I wondered," Dr. Patel said, and he took off his glasses and rubbed them on his white jacket. "I'm sorry to give you the bad news, Mr. Yusky. You have a leaky heart valve. The medical term is a mitral valve prolapse. Usually, there's no known cause, and it's certainly nothing to worry about at your age. But—"

"But what?" Charlie asked.

"Your application for insurance has been denied. Insurance companies are very sticky about these preexisting conditions." Dr. Patel put his glasses on. "I'm really sorry."

"You mean I'll never get insurance again?"

"It is unlikely," Dr. Patel said, shaking his head.

Charlie sat back, dumbfounded. *How am I going to explain this to Julie?*

It was after midnight when Charlie got off shift and drove down the Ohio Turnpike. He was stressed about telling Julie about his leaky heart valve and hoped that she would be asleep by the time he got home.

He didn't notice the Hummer coming up beside him until it rammed him, slamming his truck against the concrete embankment. He felt the powerful force of the impact—and then nothing else.

Charlie's pickup crumpled like tinfoil.

A trucker discovered the accident a few minutes later. There was no sign of life inside Charlie's truck when the ambulance and police arrived, and it took several hours to remove Charlie's body from the wreckage.

Julie had already called 911 several times by the time the state troopers showed up on her doorstep. After finding the courage to answer the door, she collapsed into the arms of the officer before he could give her the bad news.

Chapter Seven
Paris, France
October 2019

After finishing her review of the Prosperity file, Alex cleared her upcoming social calendar—not that she had much of one. Her job made it difficult to maintain close relationships. She was always flying off somewhere, breaking promises, and standing people up. But she preferred it that way. She had few friends and no spouse; most of her sexual relationships were transitory one-night stands. Alex was fluent in French, Spanish, and Italian, but she could say "let's fuck" in any language.

Alex went to her bedroom, took out a small carry-on from her walk-in closet, and packed a few things, including her Luger. She looked at her watch; it was nearly nine, and she was starving. Alex decided to head to her favorite neighborhood haunt, Café des Initiés, where she often ate her evening meal. The food was great, and the quiet of the small restaurant was often a refuge from the normal day-to-day chaos of home.

Now that Olivier and Hanna were older, their activities often spilled into Alex's apartment; both kids preferred Alex's state-of-the-art entertainment system to Sophie's. Alex did not object unless she had a lover over, and then everyone knew her apartment was off-limits.

For how much longer would her private life stay private? Alex had managed to maintain some separation from

Sophie and the kids by housing them in an adjoining apartment to hers. But things were changing, and Hanna had recently asked for a bedroom in "Auntie Lexi's" apartment. Sophie and Alex had discussed the move and agreed that it would be premature. Alex was often away, and Hanna, strong-willed and independent, still needed direct supervision. But Hanna was determined to have a bedroom in Alex's apartment, and to keep her happy, Alex agreed to the request, but only after a major renovation that would involve adding an ensuite and walk-in closet to Hanna's bedroom.

Alex expected the renovation would take months—maybe years; the French trades were notoriously slow, especially if no pressure was brought to bear. That would give Alex time to get used to the idea of Hanna being underfoot, and Hanna time to understand the game rules for sharing Alex's space.

Alex put on a pair of designer jeans, an oversized sweater, and a large cashmere scarf to ward off the October chill. After dabbing on her favorite Chanel lipstick, she pulled a brush through her thick, shoulder-length brown hair and walked the three blocks to the restaurant.

Café des Initiés was crowded when Alex arrived, but the maître d' quickly ushered her through the busy restaurant to her usual window table facing the Place de Écus.

Her regular waiter, Fabien, poured her a glass of one of her favorite white wines—a 1988 Léon Beyer Comtes d'Eguisheim, a crisp Riesling from Alsace—and asked, "Would you like a menu this evening, *madame*?"

"No menu tonight, Fabien. I'll have the grilled branzino and a green salad," Alex said and took a sip of her wine. She looked vacantly out the shuttered windows at the pedestrians hurrying past the restaurant in the light rain, trying not to think about her upcoming trip to the US.

Traveling to the States always brought back unpleasant memories of her childhood. Alex had grown up in New York City, and it had been a long time since she had seen any of her family. Her mother and grandmother had died several years before, and it had been decades since she'd had any contact with her father. Not that it mattered—he was as good as dead to her. She also rarely thought about her sister, Meagan. Alex had long ago applied for and obtained a private adoption order for Hanna from the French courts. She had given the statutory notice to Meagan and other "interested parties," but given Meagan had been a no-show and no objection came from any party, the court granted the order—no questions asked. The legal and court fees had been staggering, and with surprisingly little paperwork. Meagan had not bothered to leave Hanna's passport or birth certificate when she left her all those years before, but Alex's French avocat had managed to overcome that obstacle with a sworn statement from Alex.

After her meal, Alex opted for a cognac. She was sipping on the glass of Camus Reserve when Fabien placed the bill on her table.

"*Pardon, madame. Monsieur* at the bar has paid for your wine."

Alex looked past Fabien and spotted an attractive man sitting at the bar. His collar-length, graying hair perfectly matched his distinctly Parisian style: a sports jacket over a white shirt and jeans. *No socks,* she noted, eyeing his loafers.

He smiled broadly and held up his glass toward her. Alex could not recall seeing him before in the restaurant.

She smiled back and motioned for him to join her. He did not hesitate and was across the room in a few moments.

"*Bonsoir,* please let me introduce myself," he said, gently shaking Alex's hand. "My name is Hugo Babin."

Alex wasn't looking for a hookup that evening, but what the hell, she'd bite.

"Lovely to meet you, Monsieur Babin, and thank you for your kind offer. Will you join me for a cognac?"

"Of course, and please, call me Hugo," her new friend said as he sat beside her. "Please forgive my forwardness, but I observed you sitting alone and was intrigued."

The oldest pickup line in the book. "I don't mind." Alex smiled.

"Do you come here often?" Hugo asked.

The second-oldest pickup line, Alex thought. But he carried it off with grace.

She motioned to the server. "Fabien, please pour a cognac for my new friend."

"Here is to this beautiful October evening and my good luck at having met you," Hugo said as he raised his glass.

Alex's mouth curved into a broad smile. Clever and charming. She clinked glasses with Hugo. "Cheers."

They spent the next hour talking about living in Paris and their respective professions, and by the time they'd finished their third cognacs, Hugo was fondling the inside of her thigh under the table.

Alex checked her watch; it was nearly 11:00 p.m. She had an early morning, but tonight, she wanted to play; she found Hugo very, very sexy.

Alex whispered in his ear, "Do you live close by?"

Hugo turned his head, his lips grazing her cheek, and said, "Let's get a cab."

They walked out of the café onto the street, and Alex pulled him in close. Taking his face in her hands, she gave him a soft, lingering kiss. As she leaned in, Alex could feel the warmth of his erection against her crotch.

She gently pulled away and flagged down a taxi; when the cab pulled up, Alex opened the door for Hugo and jumped in after him.

Chapter Eight
Boston, Massachusetts
October 2019

Nick Martin sat back in his leather chair and gazed out the floor-to-ceiling window of his thirtieth-floor office in downtown Boston. The coveted corner office had a full-on view of the Atlantic Ocean, which was unusually calm today. Nick's law firm, Houghton & Willis LLP, occupied the top ten floors of the State Street Bank Building on Franklin Street. His office had been redecorated when he'd made partner, but it had too much wood for his liking. The style was a recommendation of a high-priced interior decorator, Stacey Patrick, whom the firm used. Stacey was something of an institution in downtown Boston: her good looks and short skirts had made her very popular with certain managing partners of several larger law firms, including Houghton's.

Nick had to admit that Stacey was not without her charms: she was older than he was, but she had a body like a twenty-year-old. He had discovered that when she showed up at his office late one evening with a celebratory bottle of champagne in hand and only La Perla lingerie under her Burberry raincoat. Naturally, Nick had obliged her, and they had fucked on his new antique wood conference table.

He wished he could introduce Stacey to his wife: some tutoring from Stacey might improve their nonexistent sex life.

Not that Nick deserved more attention from his wife. He'd worked night and day to develop the firm's life settlement fund practice, and it was taking a toll on his family and his relationship with Laura. He was rarely home before midnight and too often gone again before Laura and his two daughters awoke. Most of his communications with Laura these days were by text.

Nick did well enough at the firm, and they had a multimillion-dollar house in Weston, the hoity-toity town outside Boston, to show for it. Yet Laura always said she would happily live in a smaller house in exchange for more of his time and attention. *Laura doesn't get it. It's all or nothing at the firm.*

Nick looked at the framed photos of his family on his desk. He wanted to be a father and husband again and he would be, once the Prosperity transaction closed.

Nick was just back in his office after a grueling seventeen-day road trip across the eastern United States. He had met with fifty policyholders and signed up dozens of them for Prosperity. The trip to Steubenville had been his last stop.

Prosperity had been having trouble finding insurance brokers who would source policies for them. The insurance industry was dead set against the life settlement business and prohibited their agents from working for the funds. They viewed life settlement funds as a form of gambling, seeking out insureds who are sick or infirmed and gambling that they will soon die, leaving the fund with a financial windfall. So Nick reactivated his insurance broker's license and hit the road.

He had forgotten the names of most of the policyholders he'd met, but the look in their eyes—equal parts desperation and hope—haunted him.

Nick had seen that look in Yusky's eyes.

Nick knew that Yusky didn't understand the implications of selling his policy; Yusky just wanted the cash. *Like pigs to the trough.*

Going on the road and signing up new policyholders for the fund was above and beyond what most attorneys would do for a firm client, but without Nick's direct intervention, the Prosperity Fund would be dead. Nick hoped the management committee would notice.

A knock on Nick's open door quickly brought him back to reality.

"Hey, Nick, can I speak to you for a minute?" Paul, one of his partners, stood in the doorway with a wry grin.

"Sure, but it'll have to be quick," Nick said, motioning for Paul to come in to his office. "I have a meeting with Mihkel in a few minutes."

"Good timing then," Paul said. "You can tell Mihkel I'm not working on the Prosperity file anymore."

Nick looked at Paul, shocked. "You're our main contact with the SEC. If you left now, it'd be a disaster for the fund. You gotta know that."

Nick had recruited Paul to work on the Prosperity Fund over Mihkel's objections. Paranoid about prying eyes, Mihkel permitted only a small, tight-knit group of attorneys to work on his files, but Nick convinced Mihkel that Paul's close relationship with SEC staff was critical to the fund's success.

"I said it, and I meant it: I'm out. I've never been comfortable with the life settlement fund business. It's creepy, and so are Mihkel's fucking KGB clients."

Nick did a double-take. *Where is Paul getting this KGB shit from?*

"Paul, the Prosperity Fund is a client of the firm; you can't leave them in the lurch."

"Just watch me, buddy."

"Why quit now?" Nick asked.

"Look, I'm not prepared to put my reputation with the SEC on the line for Mihkel's death funds and his dodgy Russian clients."

"At least, erm, at least give me time to line up a replacement," Nick stammered.

"Okay. You've got forty-eight hours, but in the meantime, I'm pens down."

"Do you have time for dinner tonight at Morton's?" Nick asked. He knew Morton's Steakhouse was one of Paul's favorites, and he hoped he could talk some sense into Paul.

Paul, reading Nick's mind, shrugged and said, "Sure, but I'm not changing my mind about the Prosperity Fund."

"I know, I know, but can we at least talk about it at Morton's? My treat," Nick offered.

"Sure, what the hell. Let's do seven," Paul said, and he disappeared down the hall.

Turning back to his work, Nick groaned when he saw the Halloween notification on his screen. *Shit*, he thought. He called Laura and gave her the bad news.

"Nick, you promised the girls you'd take them out," Laura complained. "You know I can't manage the front door *and* take the girls trick-or-treating."

"I'm so sorry, honey. I have to stay downtown—"

"That's what you used to say when you were with *her*," Laura interrupted, sliding that knife in and twisting it.

"I have a business dinner with Paul," Nick said, ignoring Laura's jab.

"Oh," Laura said, slightly mollified. One of her favorites, Paul had been to their home enough times that the girls called him "Uncle Paul."

"We're going to Morton's. I'll be home in time to tuck the kids—and you—into bed." Nick hoped his flirting wouldn't go unnoticed by Laura, and it didn't.

"Oh, all right. Say hello to Paul for me," Laura said. "See you later, I guess."
***

The two-minute notification for his meeting with Mihkel rang on Nick's computer. He looked at his watch. *Shit!* He jumped up and rushed out of office.

As he passed his assistant's workstation, he said, "Kristen, I'm going up to see Mihkel."

Kristen looked up. "Noted." Kristen had two virtues that were prized in a legal assistant: discretion and efficiency. As an athletic thirtysomething, she wasn't hard on the eyes either.

"Thanks," Nick called out over his shoulder as he hurried down the hallway. He paused at the door of Jennifer Rose's office, but she was on the phone. Their eyes locked when he knocked, but she quickly looked away. He had just ended an affair with Jennifer, and the feelings were still raw—on both sides.

Jennifer, an attractive blonde, was a legal wunderkind who'd moved up Houghton's hierarchy almost as fast as Nick had—but without a Mihkel on her six.

After a yearlong liaison consisting of "afternoon delights" at the Boston Harbor Hotel and the odd hookup at Jennifer's condo, a family friend had spotted them cuddling and kissing at a Back Bay restaurant. The friend reported the sighting to Laura, and Nick ended the affair. It had broken his heart, but Laura had made it clear: it was either Jennifer or his family. It had been awkward at work ever since.

The last office before the elevator belonged to Stefan Popescu, who had been at the firm nearly as long as Nick. Stefan was on the Prosperity Fund's team, but he was never in his office. *MIA, as usual.*

Stefan had a reputation for being lazy and had been passed over for partnership several times. He survived at the firm because Mihkel protected him. Mihkel owned Stefan, heart and soul; Stefan was the only person working on the Prosperity file reporting directly to Mihkel. When Nick complained, Mihkel told him to mind his own fucking business. *And Nick did.*

Nick was impatiently waiting for the elevator when he heard his name and turned to see Tina from HR approaching with a millennial in tow.

"Nick," she said, "this is Peter Keyes. Today is Peter's first day at the firm. He'll be working with Karla on her life settlement files, and Mr. Ivanov asked me to introduce you."

"And Peter," Tina, turning to Nick, casually said, "this is Mr. Martin. He's the head of life settlement."

"A real pleasure, Mr. Martin," Peter said, stepping forward and energetically pumping Nick's hand.

A cloud spread over Nick's face. *That's fucking special.* No one had consulted him on the new hire.

Not one to miss a nonverbal cue, Tina hissed under her breath, "If you don't like it, talk to Mihkel," and she ushered Peter away.

Chapter Nine
Boston, Massachusetts
October 2019

The thirty-third floor of the Houghton suite of offices was the home of the fabled management committee, the pinnacle of success at Houghton & Willis LLP. With its mahogany paneling and expensive artwork, the place was designed to intimidate visitors, to let them know they were at power central. A life-size oil portrait of the law firm's co-founder, the legendary Robert Houghton, dominated the reception area with a brooding expression and a glare that seemed to follow you.

Stepping out of the elevator, Nick averted his eyes from Houghton's portrait and steely gaze before traversing the wide hallway to Vivian Curlon's workstation. After thirty years, Vivian was a fixture at Houghton & Willis, but Nick thought that she must have fallen out of favor to have been assigned to Mihkel, who was notorious for his bad manners and ill-temper.

Vivian looked up from her screen and smiled at Nick. "Hello, Mr. Martin. Mr. Ivanov is tied up for a few more minutes. Can you please have a seat?"

"Of course." Nick sank into one of the nearby leather chairs and mindlessly leafed through a copy of *Forbes*.

Tied up? Vivian had a way with words. If the rumors were true, Mihkel was more than likely up to no good with Molly—one of the assistants from the typing pool on the thirty-first floor. Molly, twentysomething and all legs, was the latest in a long line of legal assistants Mihkel had taken a shine to. The law firm had a strict policy that prohibited attorneys from "consorting" with support staff, which Mihkel honored in the breach.

After ten minutes, the mahogany door to Mihkel's office swung open, and sure enough, out stepped Molly. She called back demurely, "I'll get right on it, Mr. Ivanov."

I bet you've already been right on it, Nick thought.

He shot a look at Vivian, the impassive gatekeeper. If anything was amiss, she did not let on. Houghton & Willis paid her well for her discretion.

"Mr. Ivanov is ready to see you now, Mr. Martin."

"Thank you, Vivian," Nick said and headed in.

Mihkel, standing behind his desk, was adjusting the buckle of his belt, buried under his huge gut. Years of wining and dining clients had aged Mihkel beyond his fifty-odd years. His five-foot-nine frame carried at least an extra hundred pounds of soft, sloppy fat. His tailor couldn't keep up with his ever-widening girth, and his Saville Row suit strained at the seams.

Mihkel didn't even try to button up his jacket. "You're late," Mihkel said, tightening his tie.

I'm late? That's precious, Nick thought.

"Sit down."

Nick obliged and said, "Got sidetracked by Paul Field." After a short pause Nick continued coldly, "I also ran into Tina and the new hire, Peter Keyes, on the way up."

Mihkel pulled a Don Arturo from a wooden box on his desk, trimmed it, and bit down on the end. He lit it with a single match strike and puffed thoughtfully until the tip of the cigar glowed amber. In-office smoking was a no-no, but Mihkel wasn't one to play by the rules.

"That's good. You've met our newest drone," Mihkel answered, flopping into his chair.

"Yeah, Tina said Peter will be working with Karla Murphy on life settlement files. What did she mean by that, Mihkel?" Nick asked.

Mihkel answered curtly, "We need some fresh blood in the life settlement practice. Karla has stepped up. She wanted her own associate, so—"

"What the fuck, Mihkel? I'm the head of the group. None of this was discussed with me."

"Calm down. The Prosperity Fund needs your full attention. Besides, Murphy's keen to work with me, and I couldn't say no—not after I nearly burned her tits off! Peace in the valley and all that."

Karla Murphy wants to work with Mihkel? What the fuck was that about? Everyone knew there was bad blood between the two of them since last year's Christmas party.

Karla's story was that Mihkel had approached her outside the restroom with a glass of champagne in one hand, a burning cigar in the other, and a rock-hard penis in his pants. He tried to grab Karla's breast with his cigar-wielding hand, and Karla's polyester-blend blouse—and bra—burst into flames. Mihkel had thrown his champagne at the flames, which, miraculously, doused the fire.

Mihkel, of course, had denied grabbing Karla's breast. He claimed she had tried to rub up against him, and while pushing her away, he accidentally lit her blouse on fire.

Mihkel told the management committee that Karla should thank him—because he had saved her from a lifetime of scars! *For fuck's sake!*

Houghton's management committee had convinced Karla to drop her formal complaint. There were no witnesses, and it was Mihkel's word against hers. As a consolation prize, they gave her a $10,000 gift certificate to Saks with the suggestion that she upscale her wardrobe and avoid polyester in the future.

"So, where'd the new file come from?" Nick asked.

"Remember that life settlement fund manager we pitched for new work a few months ago in Houston? They finally contacted me and they're moving all of their life settlement work to Houghton's."

Nick could feel the blood rushing to his head. "You're fucking kidding me. I did the pitch, and Murphy gets the file?" He was going to blow. Mihkel was doing an end-run on him.

Mihkel jabbed his stubby forefinger at Nick and said, "Martin, stop being such a fucking pussy. This is how it's going to go down. Karla is going to do the fucking Houston fund, and you're going to finish up the Prosperity Fund."

"Karla has no fund experience. Who's going to supervise her?" Nick scowled.

"Karla doesn't need supervision. It's a vanilla fucking fund. The firm's done it a dozen times before;

the policyholders are seniors and people with serious health conditions," Mihkel said, dismissing Nick's concerns with a wave of his hand. "You know the drill: diabetes, heart disease, respiratory issues, the usual. Mickey-fucking-Mouse. You gotta trust me on this one."

"Trust you? That's a good one," Nick spat out.

"Just shut the fuck up. Karla's doing the Houston fund, and Peter's going to help her. End of story," Mihkel spat back.

A new email notification caught Mihkel's attention, and he turned and tapped his keyboard with his right index finger. "Hm, good news. The mortality tables for the Prosperity Fund are going in the right direction. Deaths are up over last week."

"What else do you expect from a death fund?" Nick grumbled, recalling Paul's words.

Mihkel looked back at Nick. "Your road trip is paying off. One of the new insureds, Charlie Yusky, just cashed in his chips."

"Yusky?" Nick's eyes widened. "He's dead? I just met with him—what happened?"

"Don't know, don't care. The important thing is that it was accidental, so that's double the payout. If we get others popping off like Yusky, maybe the SEC will shut the fuck up about this Ponzi bullshit." Mihkel blew smoke at Nick. "Get Paul to run the revised mortality tables past the SEC."

"Uh, erm," Nick stammered. "I wanted to talk to you about that. Paul says he's done with the fund. We need to find a replacement."

Mihkel almost spit out his cigar. "What the fuck? Paul's not going anywhere till he sorts out the Ponzi bullshit with the SEC. Once he's done that, I don't give a shit what he does."

Nick hesitated a few moments and then said, "That's not all. Paul's been saying some wild stuff—like the fund's backers are former KGB members."

"That fucker." Mihkel lowered his voice. "Do you want me to deal with him?"

"No, no, I'll take care of it—I'm taking him to dinner to talk him down," Nick said.

Mihkel's eyes darkened. "Paul better not make any trouble for the Russians. Believe me, he does not want to fuck with those guys."

Mihkel waved Nick away with his cigar. "Now get the fuck outta here. And shut the fucking door."

Nick shook his head. *Mihkel is such an asshole.* Nick left Mihkel's office, leaving the door open—his one small act of defiance.

Nick went back to the thirtieth floor, knocked on Karla Murphy's door, and walked in without waiting for a reply. Karla was sitting at her desk with her new protégé, Peter Keyes, across from her, and she quickly replaced her look of surprise with one of annoyance. Nick thought Karla might be half-attractive if she put some effort into it. Her short, dark hair and square, black-rimmed glasses gave her a bookish appearance, and her ill-fitting, off-the-rack jacket and skirt didn't help either.

"My door was closed for a reason. I'm busy," Karla said tersely.

"I need to talk to you," Nick said, turning his gaze to Peter, "in private."

Karla nodded in Peter's direction, and he got up and scampered out of Karla's office, closing the door behind him.

Nick turned back to Karla and said in a steely voice, "I know what you're doing, and it's not going to work."

"What are you talking about?" Karla answered.

"Mihkel told me about the Houston file," Nick said.

"So what? Mihkel gave me a file. We both know he's the one who controls the life settlement practice."

Her tone surprised him. He started to say something, but Karla was on a roll.

"Nick, you can't really blame Mihkel, given what's going on with the Prosperity Fund, can you?"

Who was talking to her about the Prosperity Fund? Nick wanted to punch the stupid, insolent bitch in the face, but that could get him arrested. Instead, he took a deep breath and said evenly, "I'm still the head of the life settlement group. Can you update me on what you've done so far?" If Karla thought she had him by the fucking balls, she was mistaken.

"Right now?" she asked.

"Yes, right now."

Karla's update wasn't anything he didn't already know. He wasn't going to tell her that it was his pitch in Houston that brought in the file. *That would be humiliating.*

When Karla finished, Nick sat forward and said, "Sounds like a vanilla fund structure. You'll find precedents in the document management system. I'm available to assist."

Responding to Nick's change in tone, Karla said, "Thank you. I know I have a lot to learn. Mihkel's given me a huge opportunity with this file, and I don't want to disappoint him." She smiled.

Nick suppressed a dry heave at Karla's transformation. *It made him sick.* The bra fire had been the source of endless jokes—all at Karla's expense. But Karla seemed prepared to forget all that for a fucking file. Nick wondered what else she would do for new work.

Chapter Ten
Boston, Massachusetts
October 2019

Nick was still fuming when he returned to his office after meeting with Karla Murphy. He didn't know what was worse: Mihkel cutting him out of the Houston file or Karla taking on a file that she knew should have gone through him. But he couldn't really blame Karla; he would have done the same in her position. Mihkel's actions were another thing. Since joining the firm, Nick had relied on Mihkel for work. If Mihkel stopped feeding him files, he was fucked. He had none of his own clients.

The Prosperity Fund offering had been great for Nick's timesheet. He'd been racking up billable time—at $950 an hour—for nearly nine months. With fifteen-hour days, seven days a week, the Prosperity Fund's billings alone ensured that he'd made his yearly quota of two thousand hours. But the offering would soon be completed, and Nick would need new work to meet his budget for next year—work that Mihkel was now pushing to Karla.

Nick let out a heavy sigh and opened his Outlook. There was a line of red alerts, and he started at the top. He responded to a few emails before he came to one from Jennifer: *Can we speak?*

Nick responded immediately: *Sure.*

A few minutes later, Jennifer was sitting in Nick's office, file in hand. She didn't look happy.

"What's wrong?" Nick asked.

"It's the Prosperity file."

"What about my fund?" Nick asked defensively.

"I've come across something you should know," she said, looking very concerned. "You're not going to like this, but I've been researching state and federal laws that would support the Insurance Council of America's opposition to these funds. I found an old piece of federal legislation, the Viatical Act of 1935. Sound familiar?"

"Viaticals?" Nick asked. "That's the old name for life settlements, right?"

When Jennifer nodded affirmatively, Nick raised his hand and stopped her from saying anything further. "I'm going to stop you right there. You know very well that I can't discuss our life settlement practice with you, and you can't discuss your Insurance Council client with me. What are you even doing here?"

Jennifer's client, the Insurance Council of America, had retained Houghton's to find enough dirt on the life settlement fund business to shut it down. When the Council had originally approached Jennifer to develop a legal brief for lobbying federal and state regulators to outlaw life settlement funds, Houghton already had a longstanding and successful practice representing the life settlement industry. The retainer with the Insurance Council created a clear conflict for Houghton & Willis. But rather than turn away a new client, the law firm created a virtual barrier between the attorneys working on the two files. The whole concept of the wall was a neat bit of legal fiction, designed to sucker clients into thinking that attorneys in the same firm could represent parties with opposing interests. The wall meant shit, but whoever had come up with the concept was a freaking genius.

"Do you think I don't know that?" Jennifer said incredulously. "I am risking my career by being here."

He felt the room swim slightly, and he knew this could not be good news. "What does the Viatical Act have to do with the Prosperity Fund?"

Jennifer frowned. "You didn't know about the Viatical Act? I'm not saying the legislation was easy to find. It didn't show up in any online searches. I only found it in a paper search at the Boston Law School Library."

"Can you just answer my fucking question? What does the Viatical Act have to do with my fucking fund?" Nick shot back.

"I'll tell you what it has to do with your fucking fund, you asshole," Jennifer said, studying Nick's face. "The Viatical Act states that the beneficiaries of a life insurance policy must give permission before a third party can buy that policy. I checked the Prosperity Fund's public filings on EDGAR. Your preliminary prospectus mentions state legislation requiring consents but it doesn't mention the 1935 Act. It also states that Prosperity is in compliance with all applicable laws. I'm not a securities attorney, but that sounds like a material misrepresentation to me."

"So, what's the big deal? We'll amend the prelim to add the Viatical Act and we'll get the consents." As soon as the words were out of his mouth, Nick knew that he had said too much.

"You didn't get the consents? What the fuck, Nick? The Viatical Act states that if the consent is not obtained, the sale is void ab initio."

Nick felt his chest constricting. Void ab initio was Latin for void from the beginning. If Jennifer was right, the sales of the life insurance policies that he brokered to the Prosperity Fund were invalid, full stop. *How did I miss that?*

His mind raced. He had worked on dozens of other life settlement funds. Had the consents been obtained for those funds?

White sparkling dots flashed in Nick's line of vision. He rapidly blinked his eyes, trying to maintain control.

"But, erm, state laws don't have the void ab initio provision," Nick blurted out, having no idea if he was right.

Jennifer folded her arms and said, "Nick, we both know that federal law trumps state law."

Nick took another deep breath. His head felt like it was going to explode. "Can I keep that?" he asked, looking at the folder Jennifer was holding with *Insurance Council of America* prominently featured on the tab.

"No, but I printed a copy of the legislation for you," Jennifer said. She placed the open file folder on Nick's desk, pulled out a stapled document, and passed it to him.

A letter on the firm's letterhead to the Insurance Council caught Nick's attention. It looked like an opinion letter. Jennifer quickly closed the file.

"Thanks," he said, sweat dampening his collar. "Can you keep this to yourself until we figure out a work-around?"

The look on Jennifer's face was hard. "I can give you twenty-four hours, no more. Then I need to report the conflict to the management committee."

"Why would you need to report anything to the management committee?" Nick asked, his face flushing and heart racing.

Jennifer pursed her lips. "You screwed up, Nick—don't you get it? This has created an irreconcilable conflict for the firm. I can't see how we can properly represent either the Prosperity Fund or the Insurance Council. It's up to the management committee to decide the next steps, but my recommendation will be that both the Prosperity Fund and the Insurance Council get new attorneys."

Nick didn't know what to say. Jennifer was right on the law, but how could they fire Prosperity? The firm was into Prosperity for tens of millions in legal fees that would be paid when the Prosperity prospectus went final. Terminating the retainer before that time would be a financial disaster for the firm and Jennifer knew that. Why was she being such a bitch? There was a real possibility that the management committee would follow Jennifer's recommendation to terminate both clients. Nick knew that this was not a risk that Mihkel would take.

He blurted out, "You, erm, you said yourself that the legislation was hard to find." It sounded lame, but he had nothing else.

"But I found it," Jennifer said, lowering her voice. "And I'm taking a colossal risk by telling you this before I go to the committee."

Jennifer's face crumpled. "I still love you, Nick, and I'm not trying to ruin your life."

"And I've never stopped loving you," Nick replied, embarrassed at his self-serving declaration of love.

Jennifer responded with a yearning look, tears welling in her eyes.

"Have you told anyone else about this?" Nick asked as casually as he could.

Jennifer brushed her tears away with the back of her hand and stood. "You've got twenty-four hours," she said and walked out of Nick's office.

Trying not to panic, Nick picked up the three-page-long Viatical Act and read it. The preamble stated the legislation had been introduced during the Great Depression to protect the public from unscrupulous insurance agents who bought policies for next to nothing. Part I set out a clear requirement that beneficiaries must consent to the sale of the life insurance policies, and if the consent was not obtained, the sale was void ab initio.

This is a nightmare.

Nick stood and started pacing the floor of his office. If Houghton's had missed the consents on all the other investment funds, the policies would revert to the original beneficiaries, and the life settlement funds would not be entitled to the death benefits. Worse still, all of the offering documents used for those funds, including the Prosperity Fund, would contain a material misrepresentation, entitling investors to get their money back.

It was negligence and Houghton would have to notify the clients and their own insurers. The firm's $250 million in professional negligence insurance wouldn't even begin to cover the damages awarded in the lawsuits that would inevitably follow.

Nick thought he was going to pass out. He dropped to his hands and knees on the carpeted floor of his office, let his head hang between his shoulders, and took some deep breaths to calm down. It was several minutes before he was able to get up and return to his desk.

Nick quickly pulled up a list on his computer of the life settlement funds he had worked on over the years—all forty-two of them. It didn't take long for him to find the consents for the forty-two funds. Each directory had a file folder labeled *Beneficiary Consents* with PDFs of the consent forms, signed by the insureds, their beneficiaries, and the insurance broker.

He checked the Prosperity intranet. There it was—the file folder labeled *Beneficiary Consents*. He opened the folder and saw that it contained consents for all of the sales except the ones where Nick was the broker of record. He had royally fucked up. If this got out, he was finished at the firm. He needed a cleanup plan, and he needed it fast.

Nick searched the Prosperity Fund intranet for "Viatical Act." A memo dated a few days earlier from Stefan to Mihkel popped up. Nick raged as he read it. Stefan knew about the Viatical Act and the void ab initio provision. Stefan also knew that Nick did not get the required consents. Instead of telling Nick, he had written this memo to Mihkel. What was going on? Was Mihkel setting him up?

Nick printed off the memo and deleted any trace of it from the Prosperity intranet. He raced up to the thirty-third floor and, ignoring Vivian's protests, marched into Mihkel's office.

"You bastard! You buried this!" Nick shouted.

"Buried what, you asshole?" Mihkel barked back.

"I'm talking about this memo—addressed to you," Nick said, and he slammed the memo down on the desk so hard that the framed picture of Mihkel's wife toppled over.

Mihkel sat stone-faced for a few seconds, and then he picked up the memo and flipped through the pages. "Calm down, Nick. How did you get this?"

"I found it on the Prosperity intranet."

Mihkel held up his hand. "Stop. I don't even know what the fucking intranet is."

"You don't know that we have a password-protected internal intranet site where we store all the documents for the Prosperity file?" Nick asked. "I find that hard to believe."

Mihkel chuckled. "You know me. Vivian answers all my emails."

Nick was furious. "Bullshit! Why didn't you tell me about this?"

"What the fuck are you talking about?"

"The Viatical Act, Mihkel! It requires that the Prosperity Fund obtain consents from beneficiaries before buying the fucking policies. If you fail to do that, the sale of the policy is void ab initio. Void from the fucking beginning. That's what I'm fucking talking about!" Nick shouted.

"Lower your fucking voice," Mihkel barked back. "Who gives a shit about a fucking piece of legislation?"

"Well, I'll tell you who gives a shit: Jennifer Rose. She knows all about the Viatical Act, and she knows we didn't comply with it. And guess what, Mihkel? She's going to the management committee with it, and you're going to have to fire your Russian clients."

"Why are you talking to Jennifer? Are you still fucking her? For fuck's sake, she's on the other side of the fucking Chinese wall. What the fuck did you tell her?" Mihkel bellowed. "Now *I* have to clean up *your* fucking mess."

"My mess? My mess?" Nick bleated. "Stefan should have made sure I got the consents."

Ignoring Nick's whining, Mihkel said, "This is all about payback. Everyone knows you fucked Jennifer, and then you dumped her. Now she's going to fuck you up."

Nick stood, slack-jawed. *What a fucking Neanderthal.*

"Don't worry. Uncle Mihkel will take care of things."

Nick took a deep breath and said nothing. If there was anyone who could make this problem go away, it was Mihkel. Nick had no choice but to let Mihkel work his magic.

"Just say thank you and keep your fucking mouth shut. No one else needs to know about your fuck-up," Mihkel said, and he twirled his cigar as he stared out the window at the gathering storm clouds. Mihkel was thinking, and that was dangerous.

"Look, I'll deal with Jennifer," Nick said cautiously. "I'll ask for two weeks; that should give us enough time to get the consents. She'll listen to me."

"No, Nick, *I'll* handle Jennifer. Did she tell anyone else about the Viatical Act?" Mihkel asked.

"I don't know," Nick replied.

"Know what I think?" Mihkel spat out his words. "Jennifer told Paul. That's why he's jumping ship."

Mihkel sat back and glared at Nick. "And for Christ's sake, get Paul under control, or I will. Now get the fuck outta here."

Chapter Eleven
Boston, Massachusetts
October 2019

At five minutes to seven, Nick stuck his head into Paul's office and said, "Take your umbrella, buddy. It's pissing down rain."

Paul looked up from his screen and said, "Give me a few minutes."

"That works. I need to use the gents. I'll meet you at the elevators."

Five minutes later, Paul and Nick stepped out of the office tower into the cool late-autumn rain. They opened their umbrellas and walked the two blocks to Morton's in record time.

They were settling into their booth at the steakhouse when their waiter stepped up and said, "Good evening, gentlemen. May I get you something from the bar?"

Nick looked at Paul. "I gotta get home early, so no starter martinis."

Then Nick turned to the waiter. "Please bring us a bottle of the Beringer Cab Franc, and I'll have the prime rib steak, rare. And a Caesar salad."

"The same," Paul said.

"Certainly," the waiter said.

"Let's get this over with so that we can at least enjoy our meal," Paul said. "I'm off the Prosperity file, and I'm not changing my mind. Don't test me on this one."

"Okay, okay. I get it. But at least hear me out," Nick replied.

The waiter reappeared with the bottle of Cab Franc and opened it. After trying the wine, Nick nodded, and the waiter poured two generous glasses.

Nick picked up his and said, "Cheers."

Paul followed suit.

"Let me make this simple," Nick said. "I spoke to Mihkel, and he wanted me to tell you that dropping the Prosperity file is not an option—"

"Nick, I told you I don't care what Mihkel—"

"Pardon the interruption, gentlemen," the waiter said, wheeling a squeaky pushcart tableside.

The two lawyers watched as the waiter whipped up a dressing for the salad with oil, a raw egg, and anchovies. Usually, Nick found this process an endearing throwback to another time, but tonight—as the minutes ticked down—the intrusion irritated him.

"Can you move any slower, bud?" he mumbled at the waiter.

Paul frowned at Nick.

The waiter set the salads in front of them with a flourish, but before Nick could get a word out, Paul asked, "So when were you going to tell me about the Viatical Act?"

"How the fuck do you know about the Viatical Act?" Nick choked. He grabbed his glass of water and took a long drink.

Paul sat back. "Jennifer told me."

"Nice," Nick said sarcastically. "What exactly did she tell you?"

"She told me everything. You set me up, buddy," Paul said.

Nick shook his head. "How did I set you up?"

"I relied on you. You're the insurance expert. Why didn't you get the consents?"

"I didn't know about the legislation." Nick looked down at the untouched food on his plate.

"Too fucking bad," Paul hissed. "It was your responsibility to get the insurance law right, and you fucked up."

Nick put down his fork. "Paul, please, we'll get the consents, back-date them. We just need you to manage the SEC in the interim."

Paul shot him a dirty look. "You should have gotten the fucking consents. I'm not covering up for you and the firm."

Nick and Paul were silent as the waiter cleared their salad bowls and presented them with two-inch-thick rib eyes.

"Please, Paul," Nick pleaded after the waiter left. "Your timing sucks. I'm trying to do the right thing here. If I can't fix this, the firm could be sued for hundreds of millions of dollars."

"Sure, the firm may get sued, but you're the one who fucked up. Not me. Jennifer is right. This is one for the management team to resolve. And you need to report yourself to our insurers ASAP," Paul said as he cut into his rib eye. Red juices ran out from the meat onto the white plate and mixed with the garlic mashed potatoes.

"The fucking legislation is almost a hundred years old, and no one told me about it," Nick interjected.

"Yet Stefan, who we both know is incompetent, was able to find the legislation."

"Paul, listen—"

"No. It doesn't matter, Nick. I'm not working another day on that fucking death fund."

"Believe me, Mihkel is not going to like this—"

"I don't care what that bastard says. He can go fuck himself," Paul said, putting down his knife and fork.

"I didn't come here to fight, Paul. Please, eat your steak," Nick implored. He worried that Paul might bolt.

"Man, aren't you tired of being Ivanov's sock puppet?" Paul asked loudly. He pushed his plate away.

"Come on, you can't just walk away from the file," Nick said in a low voice, hoping Paul would lower his. "Mihkel won't—"

Paul stood up and said, "I can and I will," his words taking on an acid tone.

"Paul, don't…come on—"

Paul grabbed his coat. "Sorry, man. I'm outta here."

Nick lunged across the booth and grabbed Paul's arm. "Please be reasonable!"

Paul shook loose of Nick's grasp. "Let me give you some advice, Nick. Save your soul *and* your career and stop working with Mihkel. Get out while you can." And he strode off toward the front door.

"Paul, wait, goddammit!"

Nick threw a couple of bills on the table and hurried out of the restaurant into the pouring rain. He scanned the sea of umbrellas on the street and spotted Paul on the curb a few yards away, waving down a cab.

Nick called out Paul's name, but his voice was lost in the noise of the busy street. Nick was making his way to Paul when he spotted a man in a hooded sweatshirt, jeans, and a black baseball hat approach Paul.

Nick heard the man asked, "Spare any cash?"

Paul went through the motions, patting his pockets with his hands. "Sorry, buddy, I don't have any money on me."

Paul turned away, but the man asked again, more aggressively this time, "How about it? A few bills?"

"Get lost!" Paul scowled just as Nick reached his side.

Nick put a hand on Paul's arm and said, "I'm sorry about what happened in there."

Paul glanced derisively in Nick's direction and said, "Leave me alone."

"I will. I will," Nick said. "I just wanted to—"

"Hey, man," a loud voice interrupted. "Spare a buck?"

Nick caught a flash of the stranger's hand grabbing at Paul.

Paul turned back to the stranger, and then—as if in slow motion—he fell forward into the street.

Nick heard the brakes of the city transit bus before he saw it. He yelled out Paul's name, instinctively grabbing for the back of Paul's overcoat, but it was too late. The bus swept Paul out of Nick's grip and into the air.

Nick staggered back and watched in horror as Paul landed on the windshield of an oncoming car and then bounced onto the street beside a line of cabbies. Traffic screamed to a stop all around Paul's crumpled body.

Nick ran across the street, with the sound of screeching brakes—and the thud of the bus hitting Paul—echoing in his ears. He knelt beside his friend in the pouring rain and screamed for someone to call an ambulance.

Paul, his bloodied face contorted with pain, looked up wildly at Nick. Small bubbles of blood popped out of Paul's mouth and ran down the sides of his chin as he tried to speak. Then his eyes fluttered and went blank.

Nick fumbled for a pulse, but there was none. He sat on the street beside Paul's mangled body, put his face in his hands, and sobbed.

Chapter Twelve
Boston, Massachusetts
October 2019

Soaking wet and shaking from shock, Nick was sitting on the slick pavement beside Paul's body when the ambulance arrived. A medic wrapped a metallic blanket around his shoulders and helped Nick to his feet.

"Are you okay, sir?" the medic asked.

"I'm fine. Just take care of Paul," Nick said.

"We'll do what we can for your friend, sir. Let's get you out of the rain," the medic said, guiding Nick to one of the emergency vehicles blocking the street in front of Morton's.

The medic sat him down on the back bumper of the vehicle and said, "Wait here. I'll be back in a few minutes."

Nick watched in disbelief as the medics checked Paul for vitals and, finding none, placed his body into a body bag on a stretcher. None of it made any sense.

When the medic returned, Nick choked out, "He's dead, isn't he? Paul's dead." Tears streamed down his face.

The medic looked grim. "I'm sorry, sir—he didn't make it."

"I just want to go home," Nick said flatly.

"The police would like to speak to you about the accident. Can you handle that?"

Nick gave a cursory nod.

A few minutes later, a female voice broke through Nick's thoughts. "What's your name, sir?"

Nick looked up at a police officer standing in front of him and blinked.

"Name, sir?" the police officer asked again.

Nick hesitated. "Erm, my name is Nick Martin."

"Mr. Martin, we need you to come to the police station and answer a few questions about what you saw this evening."

Nick squinted at the officer as if through a haze, trying to understand what was being asked of him. "You want me to go with you?"

"Yes, we need a dry place to take your statement," the officer said.

Nick nodded absentmindedly, and the officer helped Nick out of the back of the ambulance and guided him to a police cruiser.

They arrived at the State Street Station thirty minutes later, and Nick was escorted into an interview room with no windows and a one-way mirror. He tried to text Laura, but there was no reception. He swore to himself; he should have texted her on the way over. He got up and checked the door. It was locked.

Nick pounded on the solid metal door and called for someone to let him out. Moments later, a uniformed cop opened the door and explained that all the interview rooms were the same: they locked automatically. He assured Nick that he was not under arrest and was free to leave, and that a detective would be by shortly.

It was almost midnight before a fiftysomething, overweight detective in a bad suit walked into the interview room, introduced himself as Detective Cece, and sat across from Nick.

Cece flicked his hair over his balding head and said, "Thank you for coming in, Mr. Martin. I'm sorry for the loss of your friend."

"Thank you," Nick said quietly. He still couldn't believe Paul was dead.

"We'll record the interview," Detective Cece said.

"Do you do this with all witnesses?"

"No, we don't record all witnesses, but we will record you," Cece said matter-of-factly. He turned on the recording device and gave everyone's name as well as the time and location of the interview. "Now, Mr. Martin, I'm going to read you your Miranda rights. You have the right—"

Nick jumped up. "Hold it. Why do you need to read my Miranda rights? I came here voluntarily to help you with the investigation."

"Relax, Mr. Martin. Please sit," Cece said. "You're here as a witness and not as a person of interest, though that could change."

"Do I need an attorney?" Nick pressed. Despite his exhaustion, his heart was racing. *Fucking cops.*

"If you want to call an attorney, just say so, and we'll wait for your attorney to get here."

Nick looked at his watch; it was after midnight. If he called an attorney now, he could be here all night. If things got sticky, he'd pull the plug on the combed-over fucker sitting in front of him.

"No, let's do this," Nick said. "But I reserve my right to call an attorney."

"Of course," Cece said, and he read Nick his Miranda rights.

Cece asked Nick several questions about his relationship with Paul before giving Nick an opportunity to describe in his own words what had happened that evening.

When Nick was done, Cece said, "Thank you, that was very helpful. I'd like to ask a few more questions. Is that okay?"

Nick nodded.

"Is that a yes, Mr. Martin?"

"That is a yes."

"I understand that you had an argument with Mr. Field before he and you left Morton's. You didn't mention that."

Nick looked at him. "Paul and I worked at the same law firm. Solicitor-client privilege covers our conversations."

"We both know that privilege only extends to discussions about your clients. Are you saying you were arguing with Mr. Field about a client, Mr. Martin?" Cece pressed.

"I'm not answering that question," Nick said.

"One patron in the restaurant overheard Mr. Field saying he did not want to work on a 'death fund' anymore," Cece said. "What did he mean by a 'death fund'?"

"I am not discussing my conversations with Paul."

"The witness said that you threatened Mr. Field and claimed there'd be trouble if he 'dropped the file.'

What is this in reference to, Mr. Martin?" Cece continued in a monotone voice.

"If you want to pursue this line of questioning, I'll need to call an attorney," Nick said, repeating his earlier position.

Cece nodded. "Okay, fair enough, let me reframe my question. Our witness stated that Mr. Field got up abruptly, and you followed him outside. Is that correct?"

"Yes, that is correct."

"Once outside the restaurant, you followed Mr. Field to the curb—where you continued to argue with him. Is that correct?"

"You're not listening to me," Nick said brusquely. "I'm not answering questions that could violate solicitor-client privilege."

"Okay. What else can you remember about Mr. Field's death?" Cece asked.

"Nothing really; it all happened so fast," Nick said, shaking his head. "I was standing on the curb beside Paul when this guy walked up to Paul and asked for money. I think the guy grabbed Paul's arm because Paul yanked his arm back before he fell forward. I tried to hold on to the back of Paul's coat, but I couldn't save him. The bus caught Paul, and he was gone."

Nick paused, trying to control his emotions. "Paul was one of my best friends."

"What else can you tell me about this guy who asked you and Mr. Field for money?" Cece asked. "The guy you *allege* grabbed Mr. Field's arm?"

Nick glared at Cece. What was he trying to insinuate?

"The guy was wearing a dark hoodie and jeans…and a black baseball hat."

"Any markings on the hat—a logo, perhaps?" Cece asked.

"Nothing I can remember. You might have more luck if you check the security cameras in the area."

"Thanks for the tip on how to do my job," Cece said. "What can you tell me about the interloper's face?"

"Not much. His hat was pulled down."

"Funny thing, Mr. Martin. None of the other witnesses mentioned your mystery attacker. But they all remembered you," Cece said.

Nick stood up. "Enough. I'm not answering any more questions."

"And I'm not finished interviewing you," Cece replied, touching his comb-over for the tenth time that evening.

"Am I under arrest?" Nick asked defiantly.

Cece shook his head. "No, you are not under arrest *at this time.*"

"Then I'm going home," Nick said.

Cece stood up and, taking a more conciliatory tone, said, "I get it. You're stressed, and your friend just died. Go home and rest. Come back tomorrow with an attorney. Can you do that for me?"

Nick sighed heavily. "Do I have any choice?"

Cece, with a thin smile, handed Nick his card. "Here's my direct number. See you tomorrow."

***

Nick took a cab back to the office, picked up his car, and was still shaky as he drove home along I-90. It was a slow drive because of the weather, and by the time

Nick parked next to Laura's Audi SUV in the garage, it was past 4:00 a.m.

Laura was standing in the mudroom waiting for him.

"Where were you?" she demanded.

Nick took off his sodden overcoat and attempted to hang it on a hook, but it fell to the floor. Nick left it there.

"Paul's dead."

"What?" Laura said. "Paul's dead? How?"

"He was hit by a bus outside Morton's. I just left the police station."

"Dear God," Laura said, tears streaming down her face. She gave Nick a tight hug.

Laura hadn't done that in a while, and the warmth of her body was familiar and reassuring.

Nick held onto her until she pulled back and took his hand, leading him to the couch in the family room. She turned on the gas fireplace. "I will get you a drink."

Nick sank into the sofa, kicked off his shoes, and put his feet up on the ottoman. The heat from the fireplace quickly warmed him.

Laura returned with a glass of amber liquid. "Here, take this," she said and sat on the arm of the sofa, next to Nick.

Nick looked at her and smiled weakly. He took a sip of the cognac. "Thanks, babe," he said as Laura put her arm around his shoulder and pulled him in close.

Chapter Thirteen
Boston, Massachusetts
October 2019

Jennifer Rose lay in her bed, listening to the rain softly hitting the windows of her Back Bay condo. Her sleep app wasn't working for her tonight. She couldn't stop thinking about her meeting with Nick. *He still loves me.*

She thought she was over Nick, but hearing him say those words again had devastated her. All her hard work over the last few months—reading self-help books, talking to her friends, visiting her psychotherapist—went out the window. She was back where she'd started, pining for a relationship that would never be. *But what did I expect?* Nick was married with two kids, and he'd never leave his wife. Jennifer couldn't blame him. Laura had always been there for him, and had given up her own law career to take care of the girls. Nick said that he owed her. *And he did.*

But that didn't make it easier.

Jennifer had broken all the rules when she told Nick about the Viatical Act. She hoped that she would not live to regret that.

She had put off taking a sleeping pill in case she missed Paul's call. Paul had promised to update her on his dinner with Nick at Morton's, but she had not heard from him. She had, however, gotten a call from Mihkel.

The bastard had asked to come over to talk to her about burying the Viatical Act. When Jennifer said no, he threatened her, saying that she'd be on the street if she didn't keep her mouth shut.

Who the hell does Mihkel think he is? That arrogant bastard is messing with the wrong attorney.

Just thinking about Mihkel made Jennifer's heart race. She tried to calm herself. She took several deep breaths: breathing in—one, two, three—holding, and breathing out—one, two, three. Memories of Nick flooded her mind, especially the times they'd made love in her bed. Tears trickled down her face as she remembered how he gently rocked in and out of her, his face so close to hers, until she climaxed. She touched herself and thought of their lovemaking: he had always been so tender. Jennifer masturbated until an orgasmic warmth spread over her body.

Yawning, she reached to turn off her sleep app, but a knock on her front door startled her.

She checked the alarm clock on her nightstand. It was 11:23 p.m. Access to her building was key-fob protected, and visitors could not get in without the permission of the unit owner. The concierge had called earlier, but she had not picked up, thinking that it might be Mihkel.

It would be just like him to show up at her place even though she told him no. Mihkel didn't like it when he didn't get his own way, especially with women. Jennifer had always been a little afraid of him. There were too many stories floating around the firm about what happened when someone said no to Mihkel.

Then there was another knock.

Jennifer opened the drawer of the night table and took out her gun—a small, nickel-plated Beretta M9 semi-automatic. She'd bought it in a fit of paranoia after a burglary in the building a couple of years before, but she'd never used it.

Heart pounding in her chest, Jennifer got out of bed, put on her bathrobe, and slipped the gun in her pocket. She walked down the hall and through her living room to her front door.

"Who is it?" she asked.

"It's security. I have a package for you," a muffled male voice said.

"It's too late for a delivery," Jennifer said. "Can you leave it downstairs?"

"Harry at the front desk said to bring it up," came back the muted reply. It sounded like the guy had a scarf over his mouth.

Jennifer debated whether to open the door, but before she could respond, a faint voice said, "I'll leave it outside the door."

Embarrassed at her overreaction, Jennifer released her grip on the gun in her pocket. "Yes, please. Thank you."

Jennifer heard rustling outside her door, followed by receding footsteps and the elevator opening and closing. She waited another minute before she opened the door and reached down to pick up the manila envelope. Then her head exploded with pain.

Chapter Fourteen
Boston, Massachusetts
October 2019

Despite her late night with Hugo, Alex managed to get some work done on the seven-hour flight from Paris to Boston. Once they'd reached cruising altitude, Alex, who was co-piloting the plane, retired to the cabin to review the material that Max had uploaded for her the night before. Judging from the size of the file, she suspected Max hadn't slept much either.

Max, at Alex's request, had hacked into the SEC internal database and accessed Prosperity's confidential correspondence between Houghton's attorneys and the SEC. Alex frowned as she reviewed the documents. The SEC had raised concerns about Ponzi-like attributes of the life settlement fund. The preliminary prospectus stated that Prosperity would make monthly distributions of cash to investors during the first year of operation. But the revenue projections told a different story. According to the mortality tables, the insureds would not die fast enough to pay distributions for at least five years.

Where would the fund get the cash to pay distributions in the first four years? Alex wondered. The SEC had asked for proof that the fund was not operating a Ponzi scheme, and that's when the prospectus filing had gone stale.

Alex shook her head in disbelief.

The SEC was more concerned that investors might be paid distributions out of their own money than about the fact that the fund monetized death. *Go figure.*

Alex finished her review of the material that Max had gathered for her and was about to take a short nap when a text from Daniel Berger, her contact at Interpol, popped up, asking her to call him.

Alex went up to the cockpit. "Max, can you patch me through to Daniel's private cell?"

"With the communications setup we have on this plane, I could get you Melania Trump on the shitter."

Alex smirked. "I bet you could, but Daniel will be fine. Thanks."

Max dialed the number and handed Alex the phone. Daniel answered after two rings.

"What have you got for me?" Alex asked.

"Your Prosperity Fund has Russian mafia written all over it," Daniel said. "Bulgarin has close ties with a number of ex-KGB oligarchs who are well known to Interpol."

"Tell me something I don't already know, Daniel. I need specifics," Alex replied.

"I'll give you a specific. The Russians have hired a contractor to assist them with, uh, improving their mortality rates, you might say."

"Who's the hired heat?"

Without answering Alex's question, Daniel said, "Yes, I do. I'll send you all the information by secure email."

Then the phone clicked, and Daniel was gone.

Alex returned to the cabin and opened Daniel's email. Daniel had attached a dossier on Bulgarin as well as one on Workman.

Alex read the dossier and (surprise, surprise) Bulgarin, part bad boy, part financing wizard, had ties with a cabal of ex-KGB and current members of the Federal Security Service, the KGB's successor, who—along with the military—had their hands on the gears of the Russian economy.

The dossier on Workman, the Russians' hired assassin, was more interesting. Workman, known as "Wolfman," was an Israeli national and former Mossad agent who had resigned from the Mossad after botching an assignment in a rural compound near the Iranian port city of Bandar Abbas. The target, an anti-Israel fanatic, along with his wife and seven children, died in a blast intended to kill only him. Rather than risk being court-martialed for his misstep, Workman retired.

There was only one picture of Workman in the file, and it dated back to his days in the Israeli army. Judging from his pimply skin and wispy mustache, he could not have been older than twenty.

Russian mafia, hired assassins…Alex's investigation had just become more complicated.

Chapter Fifteen
Northern Michigan
October 2019

Rob Parrish loved to hunt moose in the wilds of northern Michigan. It was his chance to commune with nature and then kill a small part of it. He liked that.

Parrish had made a name for himself on Wall Street with a hedge fund bearing his own name. He had famously stayed calm while others panicked during the Great Recession of 2008. During the post-2008 sell-off, Rob had bought up companies for pennies on the dollar, and when the markets rebounded, he was a very rich man.

The woods of Michigan were as far away from Wall Street as Parrish could be. He had been hunting in these woods for decades, first coming up with his dad and later coming on his own after his dad died.

Now, Rob took a week off work every autumn to stay in his favorite lodge outside of Cheboygan, a small town on the shores of Lake Huron. Calling it a "lodge" was a bit of a stretch; one of the local yokels rented him a shack that had a bed, an old stove, fridge, a fifties-style chrome kitchen table, and no indoor plumbing.

Rob brought his own sleeping bag and groceries. The crisp air gave Rob a voracious appetite, and he had stocked up with wieners and beans, Wonder bread, and peanut butter. It was the food of his youth.

As a kid, Rob spent hours in the bush with his dad, stalking moose and deer. Rob's job was to chase the wildlife out of the trees to make it easier for his dad to bag them. Those days were long gone, and Rob, sporting a growing gut and working on his third chin, now found that just walking through the loose brush with a backpack and rifle made him pant and sweat. Long workdays and constant drinking had taken their toll on his forty-seven-year-old body. His once good-looking face was reddened with alcohol-induced rosacea, and he was slowly but surely losing the battle against male pattern baldness.

Rob had enough money to buy the entire county, but he still stayed in the shack that he and his dad had visited. *Dad would have liked that.* His dad had died in his early fifties of diabetes when Rob was still in college. Parrish knew that no one in America should die of diabetes at that age, but his dad, who worked in a bakery, didn't have health insurance.

God bless America. It was a great fucking country if you had money. If you didn't, you lived like shit.

Now that Rob was divorced from his third wife, Marta, he had more time to do the things that he loved, like hunting, and for the first time in a long time, he was at peace. The divorce had been brutal, and despite an ironclad prenup, Marta had walked away with a sizable portion of his net worth and a court order that required Rob to take out a ten-million-dollar life insurance policy with Marta as the beneficiary.

At least he'd been able to sell the life insurance policy to a life settlement fund out of Boston. Bunch of ghouls, if you asked him, but their money was the right color; if his father had taught him one thing—besides how to shoot a high-power rifle—it was to not look a gift horse in the mouth.

The fund took over the payments on the ten-million-dollar policy and paid him cash upfront to boot. It was only a few cents on the dollar, but it was enough to pay off the divorce attorneys and make a respectable donation to his father's favorite charity, the National Rifle Association Foundation.

It was Rob's second day in the bush and near dusk when he spotted a big bull moose, a twelve-pointer judging by its antlers, standing idly in a stream about a hundred feet away. After tramping through the woods all afternoon, he had been close to giving up when he heard the rustling and the cracking of the underbrush. He unslung his .303 Lee-Enfield, pulled the rifle butt under his shoulder, and adjusted its telescopic sight. He curled his finger around the trigger and focused on his target. The moose had no idea what was about to happen. Rob took a deep breath, and a shot rang out, echoing through the woods. The shot came from behind and sent the moose plunging back into cover.

Rob was momentarily puzzled. He had not pulled the trigger. A high-powered round slammed through Rob's back and burst out of his chest, spewing blood, flesh, and bone. Blood welling in his mouth, Rob fell to the ground, landing on his rifle.

He never knew what hit him.

Sheriff Layla of the Cheboygan Sheriff's Department "investigated" Rob Parrish's death, but she never found out who fired the fatal shot. She chalked it up to an unfortunate hunting accident, even though it happened in broad daylight while Rob was wearing a fluorescent orange safety vest.

In the course of her investigation, Sheriff Layla had interviewed several local hunters who were in the area that day who had reported that there were a dozen hunters out there, all after the same moose. Many shots had been fired, but no one had bagged the moose.

One local, a veteran who had served two tours of duty in Afghanistan as a sniper, reported that one hunter caught his attention. The vet said the stranger, who wore a black baseball hat and dark clothes, carried a rifle that stood out. The gun's barrel was longer than a standard hunting rifle, and it had a specialized scope—like on a military-issued gun.

To him, it looked like an M24 sniper rifle.

Chapter Sixteen

Boston, Massachusetts and Steubenville, Ohio
October 2019

Max and Alex arrived midday at Logan International Airport and, after parking the Gulfstream in a private hangar, drove in their leased Mercedes sedan to a luxury townhouse in Beacon Hill. The townhouse was owned by Basel Re and had all the amenities of home, including three bedrooms, four bathrooms, a full office setup, and a state-of-the-art security system. They were just settling in when Alex's cell rang.

Guttmann's familiar voice came on the line. "How's the townhouse?"

"So far, so good," Alex replied. "What's up?"

"You're taking a side trip to Steubenville, Ohio."

"What's in Steubenville?" Alex asked.

"One of the Prosperity Fund's insureds, a young man named Charles Yusky, recently died in a car crash. The coroner ruled it undetermined even though the other driver fled the scene in a vehicle with stolen plates. But my understanding is that the Steubenville police have not concluded their investigation yet."

"Another suspicious death," Alex said, her voice trailing off. *The Wolfman at work?*

Alex hung up and turned to Max. "We're going to Ohio."

"I'm on it," Max said, typing on his laptop. "The closest airport to Steubenville is Pittsburgh. I've booked a runway time at Logan, and the jet is being refueled as we speak."

"Before we take off, Max, I need you to hack into the Steubenville Police Department internal filing system and see what you can find on Yusky's death."

***

After they took off from Logan, Alex went back into the cabin of the Gulfstream and got herself a drink from the jet's well-stocked bar. Drink in hand, she reviewed the material on Yusky's death that Karl had sent by secure email. There wasn't much. The coroner's report, ruling Yusky's cause of death as undetermined, detailed Yusky's injuries, including internal bleeding and head trauma caused by the collision.

Max had hacked into the Steubenville Police Department's internal database and downloaded the notes on the system on the police investigation. Again, there was not much there; either the investigating officers had not entered their notes into the database or the investigation had stalled.

Max had more success conducting his own online investigation in the few hours prior to their flight. He had downloaded the stream from the webcams on the highway where the crash had occurred. The footage showed a gray Hummer entering the interstate a few minutes before Yusky died and then leaving at the next exit. The accident itself had not been captured, and it was difficult to see the Hummer's driver.

But Max had picked up the Hummer's model type, a series that General Motors started making in the

United States in 2016. He had also checked the Hummer's plates; the stolen plates belonged to an SUV in long-term parking at the O'Hare International Airport outside of Chicago. Then he ran out of time.

Ghost Hummer. Ghost assassin.

***

They arrived at Pittsburgh International Airport at 6:00 p.m. and drove the twenty-three miles to Steubenville along the same interstate Yusky had died on. At the site of the crash, the skid marks on the asphalt and the black scrape mark along the concrete barrier were still visible.

After a few minutes of searching around the site, Max returned with a grille, holding it out for Alex to see. "I found this on the other side of the crash barrier. It could be from the Hummer," he said. He rotated the bumper so Alex could see the serial number.

"Can you trace it?" Alex asked.

"I should be able to," Max replied.

"Nice work. All I found were used condoms. Funny place to get laid," Alex said, and they both laughed.

Back in the SUV, Max checked online for the bumper's serial number on the database of GM parts. The grille was from a Hummer sold by a Boston dealer. Max hacked into the dealer's sales records. The Hummer had been sold to a Delaware numbered company two years earlier. The Delaware company was owned by a numbered company out of Cyprus, and there the trail ended. But it was enough for Alex. Cyprus was a popular money-laundering destination for the Russian mafia, and Wolfman's footprints were all over Yusky's death. If

Wolfman was responsible for the deaths, he was good. The hits looked like they were caused by criminal acts, accidents, or misadventures and certainly not the work of a hired killer.

"All roads lead back to the Russian mafia," Alex said. She knew she should update Karl about the Russian mafia connection and the hired hitman, but she wasn't ready to tell him. All in good time. Karl was by nature risk-averse, and his response would be to bring in the police. Alex preferred to work on her own and wasn't prepared to give up control of the investigation; not yet, anyway.

Their first stop in Steubenville was the police station on Third Street. The chief of police, John McNamara, kept Alex waiting, even though Max had called ahead. McNamara was entirely disinterested in Yusky's case and not forthcoming with any new information. But he made it clear that the investigation into Charlie's death was on hold. The out-of-state stolen plates had made the investigation more complicated. Any further investigation would require FBI involvement, and he didn't see the need to bring in the FBI just yet.

It was late in the day by the time they reached Julie Yusky's home. Alex rang the doorbell and stepped back. Moments later, she heard footsteps and the sound of a security chain being engaged, and a fair-haired woman peered out suspiciously at the stranger dressed in Italian black slacks, black Gucci boots, and a black Max Mara midi coat.

"What do you want?"

"Mrs. Julie Yusky?"

"Yes, that's me. Who are you?"

"My name is Alex Greene. I'm an insurance investigator with Basel Re, and I'd like to ask you a few questions about your husband's life insurance policy," Alex said, holding up her business card for Julie to see through the partially opened door.

"My husband sold his insurance policy."

"Yes, I know, Mrs. Yusky. The Prosperity Fund has made a claim on your husband's life insurance policy. I'd like to talk to you about your husband's decision to sell the policy."

"Those vultures stole my girls' inheritance. Can you get that money back for us?" Julie blurted out, swinging open the door.

"Possibly," Alex said, trying to keep eye contact with Julie. "May I come in?"

Julie nodded and led Alex to her kitchen. Alex took off her coat and placed it on a chair at the end of the table, and sat down without being asked. She took a folder out of her bag and placed it on the table still cluttered with dishes from their evening meal, and turned her attention to Julie, who sat down on a chair across from her.

"Do you know why your husband sold his insurance policy to the Prosperity Fund?"

"Charlie did it all without telling me," Julie said, her voice rising. "He met with that guy from Boston and was fed a pack of lies."

"What do you mean? What lies?" Alex asked.

"The guy told Charlie he could get another policy." Julie shook her head. "But that was a lie to get my Charlie to sell his life insurance." She sounded close to tears.

"Did your husband try to get more insurance?"

Julie's face contorted. "Yes, Charlie tried, but he was denied coverage. He had a heart problem that we didn't even know about."

"Do you know the name of the insurance broker that Charlie met with?"

Julie asked, "You mean the guy from Boston?"

"Yes, that's who I mean," Alex said.

"I have his card," Julie said, and got up and left the room. She came back carrying a folder and a business card, which she placed on the table in front of Alex.

Alex stared at it. *Nick Martin.* Was Martin acting as both attorney and insurance broker for Prosperity?

"Did you ever meet with Mr. Martin?" Alex asked.

"No, I didn't. Charlie didn't tell me till it was a done deal," Julie said. "Here's all the paperwork."

Alex opened the folder and thumbed through the documents. She slid a piece of paper across the table and pointed to the signature at the bottom of the page. "Do you know who witnessed Charlie's signature?"

Julie glanced over. "That's Mildred Hanson's signature. She works at the FedEx in town."

"So you didn't sign any of the documents?"

Julie shook her head. "Nope."

Alex knew from her limited research that this would be a problem. Alex placed another form in front of Julie. "I'm showing you Charlie's acknowledgment that he may never get another life insurance policy."

Alex paused to give Julie a chance to review the document. "Are those your husband's initials, Mrs. Yusky?"

"I don't care whose initials are there. Charlie told me that the attorney said that he was young and could get another insurance policy."

"Can I make a copy of the documents?" Alex asked.

Julie nodded, so Alex pulled her iPhone out of her purse and took a snap of each document.

When she had finished, Alex said, "One more question. Is there anyone who might have wanted to hurt Charlie?"

Julie's head jerked up, and she look confused. "Do you think someone—?"

"Mrs. Yusky," Alex interrupted, "I don't know if someone deliberately killed your husband, but he did die in very suspicious circumstances."

All color drained out of Julie's face. "Did the guy from Boston have anything to do with Charlie's death?"

"I don't know if he did, but we're investigating his role in your husband's death," Alex answered.

"An investigation won't bring my Charlie back." Julie began to cry.

Alex stood up, grabbing her coat. "No, it won't, but it may invalidate the fund's claim to the payout on your husband's policy. Thank you very much for speaking to me, Mrs. Yusky. I'm very sorry for your loss." Alex picked up her tote and walked out the front door.

Back in the SUV, Alex briefed Max on the visit. "That was painful. Let's get out of here."

"Yes, boss," Max said and headed for the interstate.

She hadn't told Julie that her lack of consent would likely result in the sale of the policy being unenforceable. If that happened, Charlie's death benefit would be paid to Julie as the original beneficiary under the policy. Alex wasn't going to jump the gun and raise Julie's hopes. Alex's job was to save Basel Re money, and a payment to Julie was no different than a payment to the Prosperity Fund. Basel Re would be out of pocket, and Alex would not get her big commission.

Alex sat back and looked out the window at the blur of small, boxy houses flying by until her cell buzzed in her pocket. She pulled it out. It was Karl again, and she answered on speakerphone.

"Alex, glad I caught you," Karl said, his voice flooding the interior of the car. "We have two more claims on deaths linked to the Prosperity Fund—both were partners at Houghton & Willis. One was an attorney named Paul Field, who was hit by a bus. And later the same night, a second attorney, Jennifer Rose, was raped and beaten to death in a home invasion."

The deaths sounded too messy to be Wolfman's work, but it was a hell of a coincidence. *Maybe he's getting sloppy in his old age.*

"Send me anything you have on the deaths," Alex said.

"I will. And feel free to consult with the Boston Police and the FBI if necessary. This is getting out of hand. I'll text you with the name of the investigating officer."

"Thanks for the heads-up," Alex said.

"Keep me apprised of developments," Karl said, signing off.

Max looked at Alex in the rearview mirror after she hung up. She could see it in his eyes.

Time to bring in the FBI.

But she wasn't ready to do that yet.

Chapter Seventeen
Weston, Massachusetts
October 2019

Carolyn Burke was forty something and nobody special, except to her husband, her two teenage sons, and her students at the Northwoods Academy, an all-girls' school outside of Boston. Before Carolyn landed her position at Northwoods, she had worked in the public school system for fifteen years, where she had become disillusioned about her ability to motivate young women to pursue the sciences. She jumped at the chance to work in a private school where, with the additional teaching resources, she believed she could make a difference.

Carolyn also loved golf. She'd gone to Boston College on a golf scholarship and won several state championships. That's where she met her husband, Jeff, also a competitive golfer. But she ended up teaching chemistry, and her husband had landed a plum job as a golf pro at the exclusive country club where they were now members. *Go figure.*

Carolyn purchased a family membership at the golf course where her husband worked with the proceeds of the sale of her life insurance policy. She had thought long and hard about cashing in her policy, but the insurance broker from Boston had convinced her. *She could spend the money now on her family.*

The boys were thrilled with the golf club membership with its unlimited access to the greens and the clubhouse. Carolyn used the rest of the money to book a dream vacation for her family—a four-week, first-class tour of Scotland's golf courses. She was saving that surprise for Christmas.

It was Monday morning, and Carolyn was rushing to get ready for school. Seeing her reflection in the bathroom mirror, she admonished herself for not keeping the appointment with her hairstylist on the weekend. She shuffled through one of the drawers for a spray bottle of dye to touch up her roots. Instead of getting her hair colored on Saturday, she had played golf with her husband and sons.

Carolyn greeted her chemistry class that morning with the same cheery hello she had every other day. After quickly reviewing the main difference between exothermic and endothermic reactions, Carolyn moved on to the day's experiment. Satisfied that all her students were in their assigned groups and wearing their safety gear, Carolyn commenced the lesson.

"First, we'll pour about fifty milliliters of the thirty percent hydrogen peroxide solution into our graduated cylinders." She stopped. "Please raise your hand if you have a question." Carolyn surveyed the classroom for raised hands and, seeing none, continued. "Next, add a squirt of the dishwashing fluid. Now you can turn on your Bunsen burners."

One student raised her hand.

"Yes, Yasmine?"

"I smell something funny," Yasmine said, wrinkling her nose. "Like rotten eggs."

Carolyn took a deep breath. The distinct odor of hydrogen sulfide was flooding into the classroom. Her mind racing, Carolyn considered what could be causing the smell. Hydrogen sulfide was not a byproduct of the experiment and was highly combustible. What the hell was going on? Then it hit Carolyn. They had all ignited their Bunsen burners!

"Everyone, get out now! This is not a drill!" Carolyn screamed as she ran to the back of the classroom and threw the classroom door open.

"Let's go, let's go!" she shouted as the girls rushed past her. "Get out of the school as quickly as you can!"

When the last of her students was out, Carolyn's heart sank. In her rush to get the girls out, she had not pulled the fire alarm inside the classroom door. She knew the room could blow at any minute, but she needed to warn the other staff and students. She opened the door and reached over and pulled down the alarm. As she turned to leave, the air convulsed, and the room filled with broiling gas and razor-sharp debris. The entire school shook from the blast.

Carolyn's body took the full force of the explosion. Her severed torso hit the back of the classroom, and her other body parts blasted into the parking lot, along with a series of rapidly dissipating fireballs. A storm of shard-like pieces of glass and metal rose into the air over the parking lot and then fell like stones, hitting windshields and setting off car alarms. The door to the classroom skidded down the hallway, blown off its hinges.

Panicking students and teachers, coughing from the black, toxic smoke billowing throughout the school, surged toward the emergency exits.

By the time the rescue workers arrived, the school had been evacuated, and Carolyn Burke was being heralded as a hero.

Chapter Eighteen
Boston, Massachusetts
October 2019

Joshua Workman had an hour to kill before his midnight flight out of Boston's Logan Airport to Heathrow and then on to Mauritius. He had a home on the island, which he escaped to whenever he could. His recent assignments in America had been grueling, and he needed a break. On the way to the airport, he stopped in at a late night bookstore on Commonwealth to buy a book by an Icelandic mystery writer whom he was fond of reading for the trip. The book was easy to find, and after paying for it, he bought a double espresso on the main floor, relishing both its warmth and the attendant caffeine rush as he leaned up against the coffee bar.

Despite the late hour the bookstore was still full, mostly students from Boston College chatting aimlessly about their studies and lives. A street cop stood in the lineup ahead of him, oblivious to the fact that a killer stood inches away.

Americans. They don't have a care in the world. How unlike his childhood in Tel Aviv. That had been a war zone.

A few minutes later, Joshua walked out of the bookstore and flagged down a cab. He was settling into the back seat when his cell rang.

"Yes," Joshua said.

A familiar voice came on the line and said, "I have a new contract for you. We need you to stay in Boston."

"I'm listening."

"High value, high difficulty."

"It'll be twice my usual rate," Joshua replied.

"Agreed," responded the other without missing a beat. "The first installment will be in your account within fifteen minutes. I will forward the details to your phone."

"You're lucky I'm still working for you."

"Excuse me?"

"That last assignment was a total fuckup. Never do that to me again."

There was a silence at the other end of the phone.

"I'm a professional, not a psychopath for hire. You didn't tell me that there would be students there," Joshua said. "One more like that and you'll have to find yourself a new contractor."

"Understood," the voice answered and hung up.

This last assignment, outside of Boston, had bothered Joshua. He was given only twenty-four hours to prepare and had few details on the target. All he knew was to go into a girls' school and take the target, a teacher, out. He did that but was not happy with the outcome. It could have been catastrophic with a classroom of young women killed along with the target. With this assignment he had had even less time. According to his contact, he had an hour to terminate the target. If he couldn't make that deadline, the contract was off, and he would not get his final payment. The double comp was amazing, given that he was already in town and the private plane that he had negotiated with his contact would be waiting for him at Logan to fly him directly to Mauritius. It was an assignment that he could not afford to pass up.

***

It took Joshua about twenty minutes to travel across town to the location of his new assignment. His instructions were to go in and finish off a young woman who had been badly beaten by one of his clients. According to his contact, the local buffoon had tried to make it look like break-in gone bad but had been unable to finish the job.

When he arrived the young woman was scarcely alive. He found her lying face down on the bloodied carpet of her living room, her nightgown twisted over her hips, the evidence of a rape obvious. Workman quickly averted his eyes.

He knelt beside her and rolled her onto her back. Her splayed legs twitched involuntarily, and her face contorted in pain as she moaned. Blood swelled out of her nose and mouth, and her long, blood-matted blonde hair framed her blackened, half-closed eyes.

She looked up at Joshua and, with a trembling hand, touched his cheek. It was then he noticed the bloodied gun lying on the carpet beside her. The weapon explained the blunt force trauma to her head and face. A raging monster had done this.

The woman's swollen eyes flickered open and closed again. She wheezed, "H-Help me, p-please," as blood-flecked spittle foamed on her lips. A single tear trickled down her bloodstained cheek.

Joshua took a deep breath. He had to act fast.

"Rest easy. It will soon be over. Close your eyes," Joshua whispered.

The woman closed her eyes and exhaled raggedly.

Joshua put his gloved hand over her mouth and her nose and held it there until she stopped struggling, which didn't take long. It had been a brutal assignment, but he'd made the best of it.

Chapter Nineteen
Boston, Massachusetts
November 2019

Nick lay in the predawn light with Laura, naked and warm, curled up against him. There had been a tenderness in their lovemaking the night before that hadn't been there for a while. But Nick had slept fitfully; he couldn't stop thinking about Paul's death. If he hadn't followed Paul out onto the street, maybe Paul would still be alive.

Damn it, Paul. Why couldn't you bend for once?

Nick had just dozed off when his cell rang. Startled, he sat up and looked at the clock; it was 6:17 a.m. He checked his cell—a blocked number.

"Ah—who's that?" Laura said as she stirred against him.

"Probably work," Nick said, and he answered the call.

"You're awake," Mihkel growled. He sounded rough.

"Hey, Mihkel. I guess you heard about Paul."

"Yeah," Mihkel said.

"It's been a bad night," Nick said.

"Well, it just got worse," Mihkel said.

"What do you mean?" Nick asked, holding his breath.

"Jennifer's dead."

Nick was stunned. His brain went blank; Mihkel wasn't making any sense. Paul was dead, not Jennifer.

"She's dead, Nick. We'll talk when you get into the office," Mihkel said and hung up.

Nick redialed, but Mihkel did not pick up. "Damn it, Mihkel, answer!"

Laura looked up at him, her eyes bleary from sleep.

"What's going on?"

"Jennifer's dead," Nick said as tears streamed down his face. He looked to Laura for comfort, but when he saw the anguish on her face, he quickly turned away.

Laura slipped out of bed and disappeared into the bathroom. Nick could hear her muffled sobs from behind the closed door. Nick knew he should go to his wife and say something. *But what?* He still loved Jennifer, and now his wife knew it.

Minutes later, the bathroom door opened, and Laura walked out, eyes red and swollen. Without looking at Nick, she said, "I'll get the girls up," and left the bedroom.

When Nick entered the kitchen thirty minutes later, showered and dressed for work, Laura did not look at him.

Nicole, the younger of his daughters, jumped up and ran to Nick, giving him an enormous hug. They were beautiful like their mother.

"Daddy, you're home! You missed Halloween. It was so much fun."

Nicole turned to Laura and asked, "Mom, can we show Daddy all our candy?"

"No, sweetheart, not now. Please finish your breakfast," Laura said, her voice nearly breaking.

"Listen to your mom, Nicole. You can show me later," Nick said, trying to make eye contact with Laura from across the table.

Laura got up and poured Nick a cup of coffee. Touched by her gesture, he reached out and put his arm around her waist. Laura's body stiffened at his embrace, and he let her go. He had assumed too much. Laura's show of normalcy was for the girls, not him.

Laura returned the carafe to the counter and sat down. She picked up the cereal box, shook cornflakes into a bowl, poured some milk, and handed the bowl to Nick.

He took the bowl, but he could not stop the tears from rolling down his cheeks.

"Are you okay, Daddy?" Nicole asked, playing with her cereal.

"Sure am, sugar," Nick replied, and wiped his tears with a napkin.

"Your dad has been working hard. He misses you," Laura said and shot Nick a cautioning look.

Smiling, Neena said, "Daddy, Daddy—"

"What, munchkin?" Nick asked as he spooned cornflakes into his mouth.

"Are you coming to my birthday party next week?"

"I'll be there with bells on, munchkin." It was always a doubleheader with Neena: Halloween, then her birthday.

Nick finished his cereal as his two daughters filled the silence between himself and Laura with their cheerful chattering. Then he got up and gave both girls a kiss on the tops of their heads.

He bent down to kiss Laura, but she turned her head so quickly that he kissed her ear. Neena and Nicole saw the awkward interaction and giggled nervously.

"Bye, girls," Nick said. "Be good for your mom today."

"Yes, Daddy!" the girls promised in unison.

***

By the time Nick got to the office, Kristen was already at her desk. She looked up at him and said, "I'm so sorry, Nick."

"Thanks," Nick said and walked into his office. He wasn't ready to talk to Kristen or anyone else about what had happened.

He pulled the door shut and collapsed into his chair. Nick couldn't make sense of the last twenty-four hours. *How could Paul and Jennifer both be dead?* It was incomprehensible to him.

And now he had Cece breathing down his neck. Nick had called a criminal attorney, Tim Horner, on the drive into the office. Nick knew Horner only by reputation. By all accounts, Horner was the toughest son of a bitch on the street. He had been a cop for fifteen years before he quit the force and went to law school. After a quick conversation, Horner agreed to represent Nick and said he would give Cece a heads-up about the retainer. Horner said that he knew Cece well; they had been in the same class at the Boston Police Academy. Nick arranged to meet at Horner's office at six that evening and had just hung up when there was a knock on his door.

Kristen stuck her head in and said, "Stefan wants to talk to you. I said you were busy, but—"

Stefan stood grim-faced behind Kristen. If there was one person in the world Nick didn't want to see right then, it was Stefan.

After Kristen ducked out, Stefan said, "I'm sorry about Paul and Jennifer. Must've been awful watching Paul die like that. I mean—"

"Really, Stefan?" Nick interrupted. "You're here to gossip about how Paul died? Give me a fucking break."

Stefan's face fell. "Sorry, I just meant it must have been bad."

"What do you want?" Nick asked.

"Did you read my update yet?" Stefan said.

"What fucking update?"

"The update on the Prosperity Fund," Stefan said.

Isn't that special. Paul and Jennifer are dead, but it's business as usual in this shit shop.

Stefan hesitated after pushing the door wider.

Nick glared at him. "Get the fuck out of my office."

Stefan left without saying another word.

Nick turned in his chair and stared out the window at the gray skies over the choppy Atlantic. *What am I even doing in the office?*

Kristen knocked on the door again. "Sorry, Nick—Mihkel wants to see you right away."

Nick exhaled. "Can you tell Vivian I'll be up in a minute?"

"Will do," Kristen said.

Nick needed to collect his thoughts. He was not entirely sure how to play this with Mihkel. Mihkel said that he would deal with Jennifer, and now Jennifer was dead. Nick told Mihkel about Paul wanting off the Prosperity team, and now Paul was dead. How could their deaths, both occurring on the same day, be a coincidence?

An involuntary shudder ran through Nick's body as he forced himself to get up and go to Mihkel's office.

Mihkel shook his head as Nick sat down across from him.

"Hell of thing, Nick. Losing both is a huge hit for the firm. Hell of a thing."

"Do you know what happened to Jennifer?" Nick asked.

"The police told me that someone broke into her apartment. It was pretty bad; she was beaten and, uh, raped."

Beaten and raped? Nick felt sick.

"Yeah, the cops showed up at my house just after two in the morning and took me downtown. A real mess. I spent most of the night answering questions. I couldn't fucking believe it," Mihkel said, chewing his cigar.

"Wait, why were *you* talking to the police?" Nick asked.

"Because my name was on the fucking visitors' log at Jennifer's condo, that's why."

"Why would your name be on the visitors' log?"

"Because *she* invited me over," Mihkel said.

"She invited you over?" Nick asked incredulously.

"I thought I might talk some sense into her, but I didn't get to see her. She didn't pick up to let me in."

"Jennifer would never invite you over," Nick said.

Mihkel looked at Nick from the corner of his eye and said, "How can you be so sure of that? I told her I was trying to save your bacon, asshole."

"What the fuck did you say to her?" Nick asked.

"What fucking difference does it make? She invited me over. I stopped by her condo, but I didn't see her—end of fucking story."

"Why wouldn't you just talk to her at work?" Nick asked. Mihkel's story wasn't hanging together.

"Enough with the fucking questions. I didn't fucking kill her," Mihkel said.

Nick was speechless for a moment. "Who said anything about you killing her?"

Mihkel slammed his fist on his desk. "I said enough!" His jaw was taut with anger, and veins were popping out of his forehead.

Mihkel is a fucking psychopath, Nick thought and shifted in his seat.

"Now what the fuck happened with Paul?" Mihkel asked, quickly regaining his composure. He took a sip from his morning coffee.

Fucking Dr. Jekyll, Mr. Hyde.

"Paul got pissed and walked out of Morton's. I went after him. Paul didn't see the bus because he was trying to get away from me," Nick choked out.

"Jesus, man, get a grip—it's not like you pushed him."

"Yeah, tell that to the Boston Police. They kept me at the State Street Station for three hours, and it's not over—I have to go back today."

Mihkel gave Nick a sympathetic glance. "Well, get a good fucking attorney. These detectives are like hyenas. Once you're in their sights, watch out. They'll do anything to get a fast conviction," Mihkel said, and he pivoted in his chair to stare out the window.

After a few moments, he turned back to Nick. "You know, maybe these deaths are a blessing in disguise."

Nick's mouth dropped open.

"Now, no one knows about the Prosperity file fuckup except you, me, and Stefan, and he's not talking. The Insurance Council will be none the wiser, and we can go back to the SEC to ask for more time. We'll tell them we're mourning Paul's death, blah, blah. You know the drill. We'll use that time to get the consents."

Nick was horrified, but he suspected Mihkel was right. The two deaths had occurred at a very opportune time for them. Jennifer's research would never see the light of day, and the SEC would give them the time they needed—no questions asked—out of respect for Paul.

"I'll stall the SEC," Nick offered.

But Mihkel just shook his head and replied, "Stefan is calling the SEC. I've already spoken to him."

Nick did a double take. "I'm supposed to be managing the transaction," Nick replied.

"Yeah, look how well that's gone," Mihkel snorted. "I'm taking over the file."

Nick panicked. "I have no other billable work, Mihkel."

"That's the only fucking thing that you have to say?" Mihkel shot back. "Two people are dead and you're worried about your fucking hours. Get the fuck out of my office."

Head whirling, Nick leaned back against the elevator rail on the way down to his office. Mihkel was being remarkably calm, too calm. Clearly, Mihkel had a plan.

A shudder ran through Nick's body. Mihkel was about to throw him under the bus, along with the firm, the Russian clients, and maybe even the SEC.

Nick knew what he had to do.

When he got off the elevator, Nick went directly to Jennifer's office, pulling the door closed behind him.

The viatical settlements file was still sitting in a black metal tray on the corner of Jennifer's desk. He grabbed it and stuffed it inside his jacket.

The fully illuminated screen of Jennifer's desktop caught his eye as he turned to leave. He sat at her desk and moved her mouse. She was still logged into the Insurance Council intranet. *Finally, a lucky break*, Nick thought.

Nick quickly typed "viatical" into the search box, and a nanosecond later, dozens of documents popped up on the screen. Without opening them, Nick right-clicked on the rows of documents and deleted them. The monitor blinked, and the files disappeared. Nick opened Jennifer's emails and conducted a similar search. Hundreds of emails came up. He put his cursor on one of them, toggled down on the "edit" tab, and selected "delete all." It took a few seconds for the deletions to go through. Then Nick went into the trash and deleted everything again.

His heart raced as he stepped out into the corridor and came face-to-face with Stefan.

"What were you doing in there?" Stefan demanded.

Fucking Stefan.

"Jennifer and I were close. I wanted to spend some time in her office before it got cleared out," Nick said and brushed past Stefan.

He stopped at Kristen's desk. "No calls, and don't let anyone in. Got it?"

"Absolutely," Kristen said.

Nick entered his office and shut the door. He pulled the folder out of his jacket. And there it was: Jennifer's letter to the Insurance Council, which outlined the issues related to consent and the Viatical Act.

The letter was thorough and damning; it would have been the end of the fund. *And Nick's career.*

Nick carefully scanned all the documents and saved them onto an external drive. He ejected the drive and put it in his briefcase. Reaching down beside his desk, Nick turned on his shredder. After setting it to "extra fine," he fed the pages into the machine.

So much for the Viatical Settlements Act of 1935.

Chapter Twenty
Boston, Massachusetts
November 2019

Alex scanned the crowd outside the Basilica on Tremont Avenue for Nick Martin. The memorial service for Paul Field had ended, and mourners were filing out of the big stone church into the rain, filling the sidewalk with umbrellas. Alex spotted Nick walking down the street with a petite blonde woman.

She jumped out of the car and walked up to Nick and said, "I need a few moments of your time."

Startled, both Nick and the woman looked up, and the woman pulled herself closer to Martin.

"Do I know you?" Nick said.

"My name is Alex Greene," Alex said, handing Nick a card. "We need to speak in private."

Nick glanced at the card and, his face clouding over, said, "It's not a good time."

"When *is* a good time?" Alex persisted.

"I'll call you, when I get back to my office, Ms. Greene," Nick said, sliding the card into the pocket of his jacket. "Now, if you'll excuse us," Nick said and took his wife's arm.

But Laura was having none of it and shook off his grasp. When they reached her car, Laura turned to Nick and said, "It's always something with you, Nick, isn't it? You just can't keep your dick in your pants."

"I have never seen that woman before, and I have no idea why she wants to talk to me. Anyway, it's business. Can't you see that?"

"Sure, business. Just like it was business when you were with Jennifer."

"Can we talk about this in the car?" Nick asked, looking around nervously. The area was crawling with attorneys from his firm.

"No, we can't talk about it in the car because you're not getting into my car," Laura said, and she got in and locked the doors, leaving Nick standing awkwardly on the street.

Laura started the car, but before pulling away from the curb, she opened her window and called out, "It's Neena's birthday dinner tonight. Be there or don't bother coming home."

She drove off before Nick could answer.

Nick watched as Laura sped away and shook his head. Laura had just started speaking to him again after Nick agreed not to go to Jennifer's funeral. But the truth was he hadn't been invited. Through back channels, Jennifer's family had let Nick know he was not welcome. Jennifer had been very close with her parents, and he guessed they knew about the affair.

Now Nick was in Laura's bad books again because of Greene. It hadn't taken much. Alex, attractive and exceptionally well-dressed, was the type of woman who always made Laura feel insecure: the type Laura had been before she gave up her career to take care of their girls.

Nick grabbed a cab back to the office. He stopped at Kristen's desk and said that, unless Mihkel called, he was not to be disturbed. But instead of doing any work, he sat in his office and stared out the window, tracking the jumbo jets taking off from Logan Airport as his mind tried to process the recent events.

Mihkel had a Plan B, but what was his? Nick didn't think for a moment that Mihkel had his back. Mihkel would throw him under the bus in a nanosecond. *But who was Nick going to throw under the bus?*

Stefan was the obvious choice. Nick considered confronting Stefan about not showing him the Viatical Act memo, but there was no point. Stefan would say that Mihkel buried the memo, and he was probably telling the truth. Mihkel was a pathological liar. But Nick didn't care what Stefan's story was; Stefan was going to dangle for this one.

That fucking cockroach Mihkel would survive, but so would he.

Nick frowned as he saw the message light on his landline light up. He punched the voice mail button.

"Hello, Mr. Martin. It's Alex Greene…" Her voice echoed throughout his office.

Fuck! He slammed the phone down. She wasn't cutting him any slack.

He Googled "Alex Greene." Nothing appeared on the first page or the second page or the third page. He scrolled to the tenth page. Nick had never scrolled that far down before. *Alex Greene was a ghost.*

Nick dialed Mihkel's cell.

Mihkel picked up after a few rings. "Can't talk right now—I'm expecting a call."

"I'll keep it short," Nick said. "I've got someone from Basel Re snooping around, asking questions about the Prosperity Fund. Any idea why?"

"No. Who is he?"

"He's a she," Nick said. "Her name is Alex Greene."

"Alex Greene!" Mihkel shouted. "Get your ass up here!"

Within minutes, Nick was in Mihkel's office. "What's the big deal about Greene?" he asked.

"If she's investigating the Russians, we have a problem." Fear distorted Mihkel's voice. "I've heard things about her. She's a fucking pit bull. She sinks her teeth into you, and you're up shit creek without a paddle."

Nick asked, "Why would we have a problem?"

"Trust me on this one. You don't want to talk to her."

"Not sure how I'm going to avoid speaking to her, Mihkel; she's very persistent."

"Just keep your fucking mouth shut. *Comprende?*" Mihkel's voice rose. "Steer clear of her."

"Okay, okay, take it easy. I get the message," Nick said, trying to lower the temperature in the room.

Mihkel glared at him. "Remember, if that Greene bitch contacts you, clam the fuck up. Got that?"

Nick nodded. Mihkel was right: Greene was to be avoided at all costs.

Nick called Kristen's line as soon as he returned to his office. "Can you find out what's going on with the Prosperity file?" Things had been unusually quiet. Normally, as team leader, Nick would be copied on all correspondence regarding the file. Those emails—billed in six-minute increments—were his bread and butter. They had a team of attorneys and clerks working on the Prosperity files. That meant dozens, sometimes hundreds, of emails a day, but where were they?

"Yeah, I wondered about that. Your email flow on Prosperity is down, and you're not making your daily billing targets," Kristen said, almost in a whisper.

"Fuck me. What the hell is going on?" Nick hung up and quickly sent out a group email to the Prosperity team as a reminder to copy him on all emails. *And I mean ALL*, Nick typed. When the response was radio silence, Nick knew that Mihkel had already put the word out that he was off the Prosperity file.

Nick had to get out of the office or else he was going to blow. He went to the Starbucks at street level to grab a coffee. He had just finished giving his order when he heard, "Penny for your thoughts?"

Nick turned at the sound of the familiar voice. *Fucking Greene. Where'd she come from?*

"Look, um…" Nick hemmed. He scanned the coffee shop. "I can't talk to you right now."

"Can't or won't?" Alex asked.

"Both. Now, please excuse me," Nick said.

Alex leaned in close and said, "Death seems to follow you wherever you go, Mr. Martin."

"What kind of bullshit is that?" Nick sputtered.

"You tell me, Mr. Martin. Is it the kind of bullshit that got your friends killed?"

"Can you lower your voice?" Nick said, looking around.

"Come with me," Alex said.

Nick hesitated for a moment. Greene was right; Paul and Jennifer's deaths had to be connected to the Prosperity file. He grabbed his coffee and followed Alex to a table at the back of the coffee shop.

"Why are you investigating the Russians?" Nick asked as they sat down.

Alex stared at him. "Who said that I was investigating the Russians?"

"Answer my question, or I'm not talking to you," Nick said, his voice strained.

"You don't have a choice, Mr. Martin. Talk to me, or I'll have a little chat with your buddy, Detective Cece."

"No need to bring in the police," Nick said, moistening his lips. *How does Greene know about Cece?*

"What's the connection between the death of your colleagues and the Prosperity Fund?" Alex asked.

"There is no connection," Nick said.

"Is that right? I understand that you were arguing with Mr. Field about the fund just before he died. That sounds like a connection to me."

"Paul wanted off the Prosperity file, and I was trying to convince him to stay on. That's it," Nick said, and he immediately regretted it.

"Why? Did Paul have a problem with the fund?"

Nick did not answer.

"And what about Jennifer Rose?" Alex pushed. "Did she have a problem with the fund too?"

Nick's head was spinning. Mihkel was right; it was a mistake to talk to Greene, a huge mistake.

"And what about the insureds who you personally signed up for the fund? Are you and your KGB clients killing them off?"

Nick's mouth fell open, but he said nothing. Drops of sweat formed on his forehead.

"How long before the police figure it out?" Alex pushed.

"I have no idea what you are talking about," Nick said, finally finding his voice. "And I had nothing to do with Jennifer's or Paul's death."

"You may not have killed them, but your hands are dirty. Jennifer Rose was investigating the life settlement industry, and now she's dead."

"You're nuts if you think I killed Jennifer. I loved her," Nick said defensively.

"I'm nuts?" Alex sneered. "If you loved her, why did you wipe her work computer?"

"Where are you getting this?" Nick asked. *How the fuck does Greene know all this? Had she talked to Stefan?*

"And what about Paul Field?" Alex persisted.

"Paul's death was a terrible, terrible accident. I was there. You don't know what you're talking about."

"I don't? Eyewitnesses in the restaurant said that you and Field were arguing. Don't insult me."

"How did you know that?" Nick asked as another paralyzing wave of anxiety crashed over him. Greene must have been talking to Cece. Nick and Horner had met with Cece, and the word back was that Cece was leaning toward Paul's death being accidental. *Now fucking Greene was fucking him up.* The idea that he had anything to do with Paul's death was preposterous. *He didn't need this shit.*

"I'm done talking to you," Nick shot back at Alex. "I did not kill Paul or Jennifer. They were my friends. And I know nothing about those insureds dying, nothing!"

To Nick's amazement, Alex suddenly checked her watch and stood up. She extended her hand to Nick and said, "Oh, look at the time. I have to run, but it's been a pleasure chatting with you."

What the fuck? One minute he was dealing with a psycho bitch, and the next minute, Queen Elizabeth.

As Nick shook Alex's hand, he felt a sharp jab. Nick winced and pulled his hand back. "You scratched me," Nick said, looking at the side of his hand.

Alex smiled demurely. "Sometimes my ring will do that." She flashed a glittering, two-carat-plus solitaire on her right hand before turning and walking out of the coffee shop.

Chapter Twenty-One
Boston, Massachusetts
November 2019

Nick's heart was pounding as he watched Greene walk away. *How did she know so much?* He was having a hard time catching his breath, and he needed fresh air. He got up and walked unsteadily out the emergency exit door into an adjacent back lane.

With his hands on his knees, Nick took deep breaths until his heart rate returned to something close to normal. Luckily, the alley was deserted except for one of the building custodians clearing recyclables off a platform.

Nick stood, straightened his tie, and walked around to the underground path that connected all the high-rise buildings in the area; by the time he got back to his office, the worst of his panic attack was gone.

Nick had to admit that Greene was right about one thing: death did seem to follow him. What were the chances of Paul and Jennifer dying on the same day? And what about Yusky, the last guy he signed up? Mihkel said Yusky wasn't the only accidental death, and the mortality rates were going in the "right direction." Was that actually true, or was it just more of Mihkel's bullshit? Nick needed to find out.

Nick went back to his office and logged into the Prosperity intranet, where the mortality data, including the cause of death, were all tracked.

ENTRY DENIED popped up on his screen.

Nick frowned and entered the password again, his fingers rattling on the keyboard.

ENTRY DENIED.

Fuck.

Nick dialed Houghton's IT help desk. The phone rang and rang before someone finally picked up.

"Help desk, Mistry speaking."

"Hi, this is Nick Martin. I can't get into the Prosperity Fund intranet system."

"Let me check." After a few moments of background keyboard clicking, Mistry said, "I'm sorry, Mr. Martin, your password privileges on the Prosperity intranet have been revoked."

"Revoked? By whom?" Nick asked.

There was a silence, and then, "Mr. Ivanov."

Nick hung up and a fresh wave of panic passed over him. Mihkel had taken him off the file, and the fucker didn't even have the decency to tell him to his face. Now Nick wouldn't get another billable minute from the Prosperity file. He had fuck-all to do, and his head felt like it might explode. He needed to get out of the office. He looked at his watch; it was nearly 4:00 p.m., and Neena's birthday party started in an hour. For once, he would be there for his kid.

He shut down his computer and said to Kristen as he passed, "I'm leaving early. It's Neena's birthday."

Kristen looked up and winked at him. "Your secret is safe with me. Say happy birthday to Neena for me."

Nick had just merged onto the I-90 out of Boston when his cell rang on his car's Bluetooth and Mihkel's voice thundered out of the speakers: "You're on the red-eye to London tonight to meet with Vladim Bulgarin and his partner. Kristen has your reservations."

"You want me where?" Nick asked.

"You need a fucking written invitation or something?"

"I'm not going anywhere tonight. It's my daughter's birthday," Nick said indignantly.

"Cool your jets, little buddy. Your flight leaves at midnight. You have lots of time to party."

"Hey, what's this bullshit about locking me out of the Prosperity Fund intranet?" Nick countered.

"We'll talk about that later. Just make that flight," Mihkel said and hung up.

Nick shook his head. He couldn't figure out what Mihkel was playing at, but given his lack of work, Nick had little choice but to join him in London. Nick needed the hours, and he could bill his travel time at full freight.

He voice-dialed Kristen.

"Hi, boss," she answered cheerfully. "I guess you heard from Mihkel. Do you want me to arrange for a limo pickup tonight?"

"Yeah, that would be great," Nick replied.

"I've checked you in electronically. Your boarding pass should be in your email. If it's not, call me."

"Okay, thanks. By the way, I've been cut out of the Prosperity Fund intranet. Can you still access it?"

"Give me a second," Kristen said, and Nick could hear her typing on her keyboard. "No, I'm locked out as well."

Nick frowned. "I have no idea what's going on. I asked Mihkel about it, but he put me off. Now it's up to Stefan to close that deal. God help us."

"Mihkel must have a plan," Kristen said, trying to sound helpful.

"Yeah, right," Nick said sarcastically. "Monitor my email while I am away. Who knows? Maybe some new work will come in."

"Will do. Have a safe trip and enjoy Neena's birthday."

When Nick arrived home and told Laura about his trip to London, she lost it.

"That's why you're home early," Laura said, shaking her head in disgust. "I should have known it wasn't for your daughter."

"Honey, it's not as if I have a choice," Nick said.

"You *always* have a choice. You just never choose your family," Laura said.

"I can't say no to Mihkel. As long as he controls my workflow, he owns me."

"You always say that—I'm sick and tired of hearing it. For once, can you put the interests of this family before your job?" Laura asked.

"Look, once this deal is done, I'll get my own files. I promise," Nick said. That was not much of a concession. Mihkel was already giving his new files to

Karla Murphy. "I'm sorry—you and the girls are everything to me. Please trust me on this one."

When she didn't answer, he took Laura's hand and said, "Can we please have a nice evening? It's Neena's birthday."

For a moment, the only sounds were the music on the *Little Mermaid* CD mixing with the delighted hoots and whoops of the children in the next room.

"What time's your flight?" Laura said.

"Around midnight. I don't leave here till ten."

Laura looked at her watch. "Great, you have six hours for your family. You think that makes it all better?"

Nick pulled his cell out of his pocket and waved it at Laura. "Look, I'm turning my cell off. I'm one hundred percent here for you and the girls tonight." He pulled Laura toward him, but she just stood with her arms hanging limply by her sides.

After a few moments, Nick let her go and went to the family room to join Neena's party.

Chapter Twenty-Two
Weston, Massachusetts
November 2019

Alex walked out of the Starbucks after her meeting with Nick and looked around for Max. She spotted him ten feet from the entrance, leaning up against the car with his Boston Red Sox hat on. She pushed her way through the pedestrian traffic to where the car was parked, and Max opened the back door for her.

"Guttmann's been trying to get a hold of you, boss," Max said after he pulled out into traffic.

Alex dialed Guttmann's cell, and he answered on the second ring.

"Alex, thanks for getting back to me so quickly."

"No problem. What's up?" Alex replied.

"Another of the Prosperity Fund's insureds died today under suspicious circumstances."

"What happened?"

"An explosion at a school outside Boston. I need you to take a look before the school starts the cleanup. I understand that local police have already been over the scene. Can you get there right away?"

Alex, her cell still in her ear, said to Max, "Google Northwoods Academy. There has been another death."

"We'll email what we have, it's not much," Karl said.

An hour later, Alex stood outside the waterlogged remains of Northwoods' science classroom with the school principal, James Fishburn. Alex lifted the yellow police tape and entered the classroom, gingerly stepping over the twisted and soot-streaked metal strewn across the floor. The smell of smoke and chemicals was overwhelming.

The blast had been strong enough to blow most of the ceiling panels out of their metal frame. Pieces of the demonstration counter were embedded in the shattered blackboards. The windows were broken and the desks were a mangled mess; papers and lab equipment were strewn throughout the room. Water still dripped from what was left of the fire extinguisher system in the ceiling.

When Alex reached the front of the room, she turned to Fishburn and said, "May I ask you some questions?"

Fishburn reluctantly nodded and, keeping his gaze on the floor, joined Alex.

"Was the damage contained to this classroom?"

"Yes," Fishburn said before clearing his throat.

"And Mrs. Burke was the only death?"

"Yes, thank God. She got all her girls out, but…" Fishburn's voice dropped to a whisper, "she couldn't save herself."

"I'm sorry, but I can't hear you," Alex said.

"Carolyn was the only fatality," Fishburn said, his voice louder but strained.

"I understand that one of Mrs. Burke's students reported smelling rotten eggs before the blast. Is that correct?"

"Yes, ma'am, that's what she told us," Fishburn said.

Alex thought for a second. "Did you have any maintenance done recently to your heating or air conditioning systems?"

Principal Fishburn blinked several times and said, "Why, yes, the day before yesterday. My assistant, Mrs. Munroe, told me about it this morning after the police were here." He looked at her, alarmed. "Could that be related to the blast?"

Alex glanced around the room. "Did the service technician come in here?"

Fishburn looked away before answering. "Yes, he did."

Alex's eyes focused on an air vent at the front of the classroom. She pulled a pair of rubber gloves and a small screwdriver out of her backpack. She walked through the wreckage to reach the vent in the far wall, carefully unscrewed the grille, and took it off. Then she picked up her Maglite and peered into the vent. She couldn't see much even with the light of her flashlight. She shone it up and down the long metal duct, looking for any trace of the source of the explosion.

Then she spotted it, barely visible near the turn in the duct. A narrow clear hose caught on a metal shard.

Alex reached in, struggling to reach the hose. She grabbed it and pulled it and the attached detonator toward her.

She sniffed the bronze tip of the hose and wrinkled her nose. *Rotten eggs.* Hydrogen sulfide, all right. That solved one mystery. The remote detonator was small and sophisticated. Likely set off from some distance.

Fishburn looked at the hose, and his eyes widened. "How come the police didn't find that?"

"I don't know, but you better get them back," Alex said. She put the cylinder back in the vent. "They're going to want to see this. I'm finished here, but I'd like to speak to your assistant before I go."

"Of course," Fishburn said, waving for Alex to follow.

Alex obliged, wondering on the way why Workman had chosen this method of assassination. Blowing up an entire classroom for a single target was sloppy. Maybe he was losing his touch.

Alex followed Fishburn to the front office, where a middle-aged woman was sitting behind a reception desk.

Addressing the woman, Fishburn said, "Pat, Ms. Greene is here from the insurance company, and she has some questions for you."

"Mrs. Munroe, may we chat in private?" Alex asked.

"You can use my office," Fishburn said, nodding toward the open door to his inner office.

Without looking at Fishburn or Alex, Mrs. Munroe got up and walked into the principal's office. She sat down at a round table in the corner of the room, hands tightly clasped in her lap.

Alex closed the door behind them and sat across from Mrs. Munroe. "I'd like to ask you some questions about the repair person who came in the day before the blast."

Mrs. Munroe nodded, and after a painful back and forth, she confirmed that a tall, handsome, middle-aged man wearing a black baseball hat and navy-blue overalls had signed in at the front office under a local company's name and asked to be escorted to Mrs. Burke's classroom. When the janitor did not respond to Mrs. Munroe's request over the intercom system, the repairman said he'd find the classroom himself. That was the last she saw of him. Mrs. Munroe followed up with the janitor after the blast. No one had called for service. That's when Mrs. Munroe told the principal about the security breach.

Tears streamed down Mrs. Munroe's face as she answered Alex's questions.

Although Mrs. Munroe had screwed up in a major way, Alex already knew that there was nothing Mrs. Munroe could have done to stop the man who planted the explosive device in the classroom. She would have gotten herself killed had she tried.

Alex returned to the outer office and found Fishburn talking to a middle-aged man with a comb-over who stepped forward and extended his hand.

"Nice to meet you, Ms. Greene. I'm Detective Cece."

She shook his hand and took his card.

"You found the cause of the explosion, Ms. Greene," Cece continued sarcastically. "I guess I should thank you."

"You're welcome. I'm surprised you didn't find it yourselves," Alex shot back.

"Why don't you tell me what you're doing at my crime scene?" Cece said.

"I'm an insurance investigator," Alex replied. She offered him her card. "My employer underwrote Mrs. Burke's life insurance policy."

Cece peered at her card. "You work out of Paris. Long way from home, no?"

"I was in Boston when the explosion occurred."

Cece looked at her dubiously. "So, what do you know about the explosion?"

"I can walk you through what I found in Mrs. Burke's classroom, but the Boston Police Department will have to form its own conclusions about the cause of Mrs. Burke's death," Alex said bluntly.

Alex's policy was to cooperate with local police to the extent that it helped her, but she would not do their work for them.

"No problem, my dear. Don't worry about us doing our job. You just make sure you do yours," Cece said, flashing a crooked smile in Alex's direction. Dribble formed in the corners of his mouth, and Alex couldn't tell if he was flirting with her or having a stroke.

"I'm not your fucking *dear*. And I always do my job. Now, if you'll excuse me, my driver is waiting," Alex said and left the office.

Cece was clearly unaware of the tsunami of deaths related to the Prosperity Fund, and at least for now, Alex would leave it that way.

Chapter Twenty-Three
Boston, MA, and somewhere over Greenland
November 2019

Neena's birthday was a great success. Neena was delighted that her dad came home for her afternoon party, and Laura was civil to Nick, at least in front of her parents.

It felt odd, but liberating, for Nick to be at home for a family celebration. But the evening headed downhill fast after the partygoers departed. The girls went to bed, and Laura locked herself in the spare bedroom. Nick and Laura hadn't slept in the same bed since the night that Jennifer and Paul died.

Nick went upstairs and packed his carry-on. He still had over an hour to kill. With nothing else to do and no one to talk to, he retreated to the family room to watch TV and wait for his ride.

By the time the airport limo arrived, Nick was anxious to get back to work, even though "work" was sitting on a plane for seven hours. He left the house without saying goodbye to his family: the girls were sleeping, and when he knocked on Laura's locked door, there was no response.

When it appeared he might miss the flight to London because of an accident on the I-90, Nick's stress level soared.

Luckily, he motored through security and arrived at the departure gate just as his name was booming over the intercom: "This is the last call for British Airways flight 7279 to London, England. Would Nick Martin and Mihkel Ivanov please proceed to gate D31?"

Nick surveyed the airport terminal's waiting area as the steward scanned his boarding pass and passport. *Where the fuck is Mihkel?*

Nick pulled out his cell to call him, but the steward interrupted him, saying, "I'm sorry, sir, you need to board the plane right now."

Nick settled into his business-class seat and looked around the cabin. Mihkel had not made the flight. He checked his emails and found none from Mihkel explaining his absence.

But there was an email from Nick's attorney.

Nick's heart raced as he read the update. The coroner's report had concluded that the bruising on Paul's right arm showed someone had pushed him with force. Cece—suspecting foul play—wanted to talk to Nick.

Nick texted Horner that he was on his way to London and would call him on his return.

Horner responded to remind Nick that he was not supposed to leave Boston without Cece's permission.

It had totally slipped Nick's mind, and he swore quietly to himself as he texted: *Tell Cece I'll be back in Boston the day after tomorrow.*

Horner's response was swift: *If Cece finds out you left the country without telling him, he could get a warrant for your arrest and register that with Interpol.*

Nick typed: *I need you to handle this for me.*

He was waiting for Horner's return text when a flight steward asked him to put his cell away.

The message came in just before Nick switched his screen to airplane mode: *Don't worry. I'll take care of it.*

"Yeah, you'd better fucking take care of it," Nick muttered under his breath.

Nick picked up the very generous Glenfiddich scotch the steward had brought him and drank it in one gulp. By the time the jumbo jet hit cruising altitude, Nick was ready for a nap. He extended his lounge-style reclining seat to a flatbed, put on the complimentary sleeping mask, and drifted off to the low droning of the 747's engines.

***

Nick woke with a start, trying to shake off a nightmare. Laura and the girls had been in trouble, and he couldn't get back to Boston to help them.

He tried to go back to sleep, but he couldn't stop thinking about what Alex Greene had said. Mihkel would do anything for his clients, especially his Russian ones. But killing insureds to raise the ROI on the Prosperity Fund? Not even Mihkel would go that far.

Nick motioned for the flight attendant. "Can I have a cup of tea, please?" he asked. The scotch had knocked him out, but it also left him with a splitting headache.

He checked out the featured movies and found, to his delight, that the latest *John Wick* flick was available. Nick loved Keanu Reeves, and he fell asleep again just after Wick's death count hit thirty-two.

Chapter Twenty-Four
London, England
November 2019

By the time Nick's flight landed at Heathrow Airport, his anxiety level had risen to a breaking point. An hour before landing, Nick's inbox blew up, revealing a train wreck in the making. The email chain—shared among Stefan, Mihkel, Nick, Vladim Bulgarin, and his not-so-silent partner, Igor Dimitrov—started with Stefan sending out a lawyerly notice to inform the Russians that the firm had missed the Viatical Act and, as a result, the sales of the life insurance policies to the fund were invalid.

Stefan then described, in some detail, what the SEC would do if they found out about the omission. He ended the email with an assurance that the firm was making every effort to correct that mistake.

"Fuck, fuck, fuck," Nick swore as he read the emails. *Did Mihkel see the email before it went out?*

Nick winced as he read Igor's demand of a guarantee from the firm that the Viatical Act would not be a problem for the fund. And he wanted that assurance in person.

Now Nick knew what was waiting for him in London.

Mihkel was setting him up.

After a short train ride from the airport, Nick stepped out of Paddington Station and blinked in the bright sunlight. He dug his Ray-Bans out of the inside pocket of his overcoat and caught a cab to his hotel.

The driver pulled out into midafternoon traffic and took Oxford Street through Piccadilly Circus—with its neon signage, famous shops, and crowded sidewalks—to the Park Lane Hilton, towering over Hyde Park. The hotel sported a Michelin-starred restaurant and was the go-to business hotel in downtown London, especially among Russian oligarchs.

Nick was greeted at the door of the hotel by a porter who took his carry-on and escorted him through the sleek, art nouveau–style lobby. The clerk at the check-in counter relayed a message from Bulgarin: they were meeting in the Sky Bar at 4:00 p.m.

The porter, who had remained at Nick's side during the check-in, escorted Nick to his fifteenth-floor suite and made a grand gesture of pulling back the drapes to point out the postcard views of central London, Piccadilly Circus, and Buckingham Palace.

After the porter departed with a generous tip, Nick stepped into the bathroom and took off his clothes. He was beat; he hadn't slept much on the way over, and the time change had caught up with him. After a quick shower, he caught the reflection of his naked body in the mirror and took a full-on look. *Not bad.* He turned sideways and gave his gut a hearty slap. He still had a six-pack even though he rarely went to the gym. Without thinking, Nick grabbed his dangling penis and gave it a tug. It was his habit since childhood. He always gave his penis a short tug when he was naked.

Seeing himself naked had made him hard. Truthfully, it took little to get him going these days. Laura had not exactly been putting out since she found out about Jennifer, not that she did before. Ten years of marriage will do that to a relationship. Sure, the sex with Laura on the night that Paul died had been special, but like most guys on the planet, he would happily substitute quantity for quality.

Nick stepped into the shower, boner in hand. His penis knew the drill, and so did his right hand.

***

The alarm jerked Nick out of a dead man's sleep at 3:30 p.m. He grabbed his phone to check for messages—*still* nothing from Mihkel.

"That fucker," Nick swore and got dressed.

He arrived at the Sky Bar a few minutes early and asked for a booth near the windows. Nick liked to be early for appointments. Mihkel, on the other hand, was always late.

Nick ordered a bottle of sparkling water from the white-jacketed waiter and dialed Mihkel's cell for the tenth time that day.

Still no answer.

The waiter came back with Nick's water and asked, "Would you like to order something from the bar?"

"No. I'll wait till the other parties arrive," Nick said, rechecking his watch. It was 4:00 p.m. with no Mihkel in sight. *Was the fucker even in London?*

Nick looked around the room. There was no one else in the bar except him; it felt like a setup.

At just after four, the maître d' escorted a well-dressed man to the booth.

Two enormous, muscular men in dark suits with close-cropped hair stood back at a not-so-discreet distance. *Who the fuck needs two bodyguards in downtown London?*

The man extended his hand across the table and, with a barely discernible accent, said, "You must be Nick Martin. I'm Vladim Bulgarin."

"Mr. Bulgarin, it's a pleasure to finally meet you," Nick said, shaking Vladim's hand.

"The pleasure is all mine, Mr. Martin," Vladim said, sitting across from Nick.

Nick pulled a business card from the inside pocket of his suit jacket and handed it to Vladim. "Mr. Ivanov should be here any minute."

"It is I who should apologize, Mr. Martin," Vladim said. "My colleague Mr. Dimitrov has been unavoidably detained and cannot meet with you today."

Vladim cyed the sparkling water bottle on the table. "It's still early in America, yes?" He turned to the waiter and asked, "Can you bring my friend a drink?"

He turned back to Nick. "What will you have?"

"A scotch with water, please," Nick said.

"And I'll have Beluga vodka on ice," said Vladim.

The waiter nodded and retreated toward the bar.

"So, Mr. Martin, I trust your daughter's birthday party went well?"

"It, uh, did, thank you," Nick said. *How the fuck did he know about Neena's birthday?*

After the waiter delivered their order, Vladim raised his glass and said, "*Nostrovia.*" He took a long draw on his vodka and set the glass on the white tablecloth.

Nick took a sip of his scotch. "What am I doing here?"

This was bullshit. Only Mihkel would ask Nick to travel thousands of miles to attend a meeting where neither he nor the client showed up.

"Mihkel said that you would give us an update on the SEC filing," Vladim replied.

I bet he did, that useless sonofabitch, Nick thought.

Nick decided to say his piece and get the hell out of there. "I'll make this simple: the Viatical Act requires Prosperity to obtain the consents of beneficiaries to the sale of the policies. We are now getting those releases."

Vladim sipped his vodka. "So, you're saying that the legislation is a problem, but the problem is basically correctible."

"Yes," Nick nodded. "It can be solved."

"And what about the SEC? How do they view all this?" Vladim asked.

"There is a potential issue," Nick continued, "but only if the SEC finds out before corrective measures are taken."

"Potential issue?" Vladim chuckled. "You have a way with words, my young friend." He steepled his fingers and said, "But please continue."

"Our strategy is to buy time with the SEC by pleading that the death of Paul Field is causing critical delays. Paul was our point person on the file until he died last week. The SEC has agreed to an extension, which gives us the time we need to get the consents. They should be none the wiser."

Nick shuddered. Using Paul's death to cover up the firm's fuckup was a new low.

Vladim nodded and took another draft of his vodka.

"The prospectus," Nick continued, "states that Prosperity has complied with all applicable state and federal laws. That statement will be true once we've obtained those consents."

"Excellent. And the presales?"

"Sold out, with a waiting list."

"Good, good," Vladim said. "Now, I must ask you about another thing that disquiets me, my young friend. I understand you've been speaking to Alex Greene."

"I've said nothing to her about your file," Nick said, trying not to sound defensive.

Vladim narrowed his eyes. "Nothing?"

"I've told Greene nothing," Nick repeated. *Were the Russians watching him?*

Vladim started to say something but was interrupted by a booming voice.

"Hey, guys!" Mihkel called out as he teetered toward their booth with two heavily made-up women hanging on his arms. The blonde wore a long-sleeved, lacy black dress, which barely covered her ass, and black stilettos. The brunette was decked out with a black silk camisole, short black leather skirt, and thigh-high black boots. Both women appeared to be beneficiaries of recent advancements within the silicone industry.

Oh God. Nick felt himself redden as Mihkel, reeking of vodka and musky body odor, plopped himself down beside him. The blonde slid in beside Mihkel, and the brunette sidled up to Nick and clumsily pawed at his tie. Nick tried to push her away, but she pressed in closer.

"Hey, mister, what's wrong? You don't like me?" she asked in a strong Russian accent, rubbing her fake tits against him.

Mihkel smiled drunkenly and planted a deep kiss on the mouth of the blonde.

That was enough for Vladim. He slammed his vodka down and snarled at his goons in guttural Russian.

The men dragged the hookers out from behind the table. "You owe us money!" the blonde yelled at Mihkel.

"Anastasia! Svetlana!" Mihkel called out at the top of his drunken lungs. "Come back, my beauties!" He tried to get up but only succeeded in knocking the drinks over.

Vladim stood up quickly and his chair crashed to the floor behind him.

Nick was not so lucky; the onslaught of vodka and scotch soaked his pants. He was mortified. *How could this get any worse?*

"Idiot!" Vladim shouted, and he slapped Mihkel across the face with the back of his hand.

The sound of the slap and Mihkel's groan echoed throughout the bar. Mihkel's head snapped back and then dropped forward. When he looked up, his nose was bleeding and saliva was dripping from the sides of his mouth.

"Get control of yourself, you fucking idiot! I gave you those whores to play with, not to make fools of us!" Vladim shouted and walked briskly out of the bar with the two Ivans on his six.

Mihkel grinned crookedly at Nick and slurred, "I fucked up, didn't I, little buddy? Don't be mad at me." Then he belched.

"Let's get the hell outta here," Nick said. "Give me your fucking room card."

Mihkel sheepishly pulled the card out of his breast pocket and thrust it in Nick's direction.

Nick grabbed it out of Mihkel's hand and waved the waiter over. "Can you bill this to my room?"

Nick half carried and dragged Mihkel back to his room. When he dropped Mihkel on the king-size bed, Mihkel looked up at Nick in that stupid way that all drunks do.

Within seconds, Mihkel was snoring.

Nick threw the card at Mihkel and shouted, "You're a fucking idiot, and I'm done!"

Mihkel's only response was a loud, soft fart as he repositioned himself on the bed.

"I'm the fucking idiot, huh?" Nick muttered as he stomped out of the suite. He wanted to go home.

Nick went back to his own suite and was checking for flights to the States on his laptop when his cell rang; he recognized it as a Russian number and ignored it. The fucker could leave a message. He was done with Mihkel and his fucking Russian clients. A few minutes later the hotel landline rang. Against his better judgment, Nick picked up. Before Nick even had a chance to say hello, Vladim bellowed in his ear, "Igor wants you in Moscow tomorrow to explain your firm's fuckup on the Prosperity Fund."

Nick held the phone away from his head and looked at it with shocked disbelief. He wished he had let it ring.

"I'm not going to Moscow. Mihkel can talk to Igor."

"That *nekulturny* is an idiot. We both know that. So, *you* will meet with Igor in Moscow tomorrow."

"You're not listening to me. I'm not going to Moscow," Nick said in a strained tone. "I'll Zoom with Igor as soon as I am back in the office."

There was a brief silence before Vladim said, "What if the meeting is at Houghton's offices in Moscow?"

Nick was quiet. Not an unreasonable request, but still, he did not want to go to Moscow. He'd been there a few times on business, and he hated the place. The air pollution, the dreariness, the blankness in the faces of the Russian people, and the monolithic Soviet architecture gave Nick the creeps.

Vladim took advantage of Nick's pause and said, "Given your firm's fuckup with the viatical legislation, I think you owe Igor a meeting."

Nick said nothing. Sadly, Vladim was right. There was a lot on the line, especially after Stefan sent that fucking email to the Russians, which admitted the firm had made a mistake on the file. He needed to placate the Russians, and if that meant going to Moscow, he had no choice but to go.

"You don't even have to stay twenty-four hours," Vladim said. "Aeroflot has four or five flights a day from Moscow to the US. You can leave Moscow right after the meeting. Think about it, but don't take too long."

Then Nick heard a click. *The fucker had hung up.*

Nick accepted that he wasn't going home. *He was going to fucking Moscow.*

Chapter Twenty-Five
Steubenville, Ohio
November 2019

Julie Yusky sat across from Blaine Bennett, the mortgage officer at the Steubenville National Bank, and sobbed. Bennett, who had been dealing with Julie and her family for decades, had seen a lot of misery in Steubenville over his career. Too many people were still hurting from the closing of the steel plant.

Bennett shook his head and said, "I'm truly sorry, but I can't extend you any more credit. You need to come up with the cash to pay the balloon interest payment, or the developers are going to foreclose."

"But Charlie paid down on the mortgage," Julie pleaded.

"I'm sorry to say this, Julie, but that was a mistake; he should have put the money aside for the interest payment."

Julie sat back on the plastic chair and cried softly.

Bennett shifted uncomfortably in his seat and said, "I hate to see this happen, Julie, after what you went through with Charlie, but there's nothing I can do."

"I don't have money for the payment," Julie choked out.

"I'm sorry," Blaine said.

"What will I do?" Julie asked.

"Sell the house. Your mom still has her condo, right?"

***

Julie didn't take long to sell their house, and a month later, she and her daughters were living in her mother's two-bedroom condo. After taxes, the sale of the house had only netted $10,000. The agent had warned her that Christmas was a bad time to sell, but Julie had no choice. She put the small profit from the sale aside for the girls' college. *Charlie would have wanted that.*

Things were tight at her mother's condo. Her mother had given up her bedroom with an ensuite and walk-in closet to her granddaughters and Julie. There was just enough room for a double bed for Julie and bunk beds for the girls. Thank God for the walk-in closet. It was filled with the girls' toys, clothing, and a few personal items. Julie had sold everything else in a yard sale, and the proceeds came to less than $1,500—a pathetic amount for the contents of the home that she had shared with Charlie.

Julie was determined to keep her spirits up. She owed her girls and her mom that much. But hard as she tried to be positive, the strains of life without Charlie were taking a toll. She missed Charlie, and so did the girls. Julie came home exhausted every night and had little energy to take care of the girls, let alone her mother, who was showing early symptoms of Alzheimer's. At first, her mom simply forgot things, like where she had put her keys or what day of the week it was, but her memory loss was becoming increasingly concerning.

One evening, after working ten solid hours, Julie came home to find Creedence Clearwater Revival playing on her mother's old-school stereo. Hearing "Fortunate Son" always brought back memories of her dad: he used to play the album over and over.

"Hello, Mom, I'm home," Julie called out as she took off her coat.

"In here, Jules," her mom called from the kitchen.

Jules? Her mom had not called Julie that in years.

Julie found her mother seated at the circular wooden table in the dining nook. On the table, in its green web belt, was an automatic pistol, along with a military medal.

Julie sucked in her breath when she saw the gun.

"Mom? Is everything okay?"

Julie's mother looked up at her, smiling. "Oh, I know you think I'm losing it. Maybe I am, but I'm not crazy." She put her hand on the pistol. "It's your dad's gun. I found it today in an old suitcase in the locker. It's been there since your dad died."

Julie let out a long breath and sat beside her mother.

"He fought in the Vietnam War," Julie's mother continued, with a distant look in her eyes. "I forgot all about this revolver. And this medal." She picked up the military decoration and showed it to Julie. "Did you know your dad got a Purple Heart?"

Julie smiled. "I remember, Mom. Why don't you give me the gun for safekeeping?"

Her mother slid the belt across the table.

Julie picked up the gun. "I'll look after it. Promise."

Chapter Twenty-Six
London, England
November 2019

Alex and Max arrived in London on the Gulfstream jet just six hours after Nick's British Airways flight. Thanks to the microchip transponder Alex had injected into Nick's hand with her ring, they had tracked him to the Park Lane Hilton in London. Alex was counting on Nick to lead her to the Russian backers of the Prosperity Fund, and—judging from what the porter in the hotel lobby told her—he would not disappoint.

After Alex slipped him a £50 note, the hotel porter happily recounted the commotion earlier that day. In hushed tones, he described the Sky Bar dustup between the Americans and the Russians. The story had quickly spread among hotel staff.

After slipping the porter another crisp bill, Alex followed him to the Sky Bar and the tuxedo-wearing maître d'hôtel.

But before Alex could get a word out, the maître d' said, "I'm sorry, madam, but we are about to close. We open again at nine tonight."

"I'm not here for a drink." Alex discreetly pressed a £100 note into the man's hand. "I have questions about a party of Americans and Russians who were in the bar earlier today."

The maître d' palmed the note. "I'm not sure what I can tell you, madam. They didn't stay long, thankfully."

Alex showed him two pictures on her iPhone of Mihkel and Nick. "Are these the two men?"

"Yes, those are the Americans. They were here with Mr. Bulgarin this afternoon."

"Vladim Bulgarin? Are you sure?" Alex asked.

"Yes, of course I'm sure. Mr. Bulgarin often stays at our hotel, and he frequently entertains business clients in our bar," the maître d' said. He looked at his watch. "If there is nothing else—"

"I understand from your colleague that there was a bit of a situation. Do you know what that was about?" Alex asked.

"I do not. But I wouldn't tell you even if I did; our customers expect discretion," the maître d' said haughtily. "Now, if you don't mind." He indicated with a sway of his arm that Alex should leave the restaurant.

Alex had not gotten much for her money, but it *was* London, after all. She had been tempted to point out that—despite his privacy concerns—the maître d' had given her Bulgarin's name, but she decided against delivering that parting shot.

She was waiting for the elevator when one of the bar's staff surreptitiously approached her. "Excuse me, miss, but I couldn't help overhearing your conversation. I may be able to help you."

"Is that right?" Alex asked, eyeballing her newest snitch.

"How much is it worth to you, miss?" the waiter asked, nervously glancing at the entrance to the Sky Bar.

The waiter snatched the money out of Alex's hand and stuffed it into his pocket. "I served the Americans and Mr. Bulgarin. The older American was drunk and caused quite a scene. The younger guy's name is Nick Martin. He charged the drinks to his room," the waiter reported, showing it to Alex.

Alex said with a forced politeness, "I am aware of the commotion. Can you tell me what they were discussing?"

"Before the drunk American arrived, Mr. Bulgarin and Mr. Martin were discussing the SCE or something like that."

"Do you mean the SEC?" Alex said.

"That could have been it. Anyway, Mr. Martin said that they were working on correcting the problem. But this was the interesting part: someone had died— someone called Paul—and the American said that his death would give them more time with the SEC."

"What did the death have to do with the SEC?" Alex asked. "Did they say?" *Could there be a direct link between the Russians and Field's death?*

"Ma'am, the conversation was very technical, and I'm not sure I got it right," the waiter said.

Alex slipped him another note. "Anything else?"

"Yeah, Mr. Bulgarin came back later looking for the two Americans, but they were gone."

The waiter leaned in closer. "Mr. Bulgarin wanted Mr. Martin's room number, but I didn't want to give it to him. You never know with the Russians." He looked knowingly at Alex.

"That was probably wise," Alex said.

"I gave him a phone number for the room."

"And?" Alex said, losing her patience.

The waiter nodded in the direction of the lobby. "Mr. Bulgarin called Mr. Martin from that phone over there."

"Did you hear any of the conversation?" Alex asked.

"Yeah," the waiter said, lowering his voice. "Mr. Bulgarin told Mr. Martin that he had to go to Moscow to meet someone called Igor, but it sounded like Mr. Martin didn't want to go."

"Did you catch Igor's last name?"

"I think Mr. Bulgarin meant Igor Dimitrov. The two of them often come in here together. They drink the same vodka—Beluga Noble," the waiter said, looking around again. He was getting antsy.

"Anything else?" Alex asked.

"Not really. Mr. Bulgarin said that Mr. Martin had to be there. That's about it." The waiter glanced toward the restaurant door. "Look, I have to go," he said and scurried down the hallway.

The waiter's info had been well worth the £200. Igor Dimitrov was a former KGB officer turned billionaire with direct links to the Voiny, the largest organized crime syndicate in the world. As Alex had hoped, Nick Martin was leading her to the Russian criminals behind the Prosperity Fund. *Just like a baited cockroach carrying poison to the nest.*

She wondered if Nick realized who he was dealing with; Dimitrov was a very dangerous man.

Alex exited the lobby of the hotel and walked down Park Lane toward Green Park, where Max was waiting for her. While making her way through the crush of people moving in and out of the upscale restaurants and bars along the street, she heard someone call out her name.

Alex's jaw dropped when she looked up at the man walking beside her. "Joshua?"

Joshua nodded. "Been a long time, Alex."

Alex mumbled under her breath, "What are you doing here?" She had met Joshua in Barcelona over a decade before. She was out on her own for dinner and ran into him in a tapas bar in the old city. They shared several small plates, and then Joshua showed her around the nightclub scene. After having rambunctious sex in a toilet cubicle in one of the all-night bars, they ended up on the beach, where they sat, huddled under his jacket, till dawn. That was the last time she'd seen him. Then it hit her: Barcelona Joshua was one and the same of Joshua Workman. How did she miss that?

"This is awkward," Joshua said, forcing her to focus.

"Why awkward? Are you going to kill me?" Alex asked, half joking.

Joshua answered, "I'm trying to not do that." His face was expressionless: his wide mouth and fair eyebrows and lashes gave nothing away.

Alex felt her chest tighten as she recalled the Interpol dossier. Finally, she knew Joshua's last name—Workman. She hadn't recognized his photo on file with Interpol, but seeing him now, she had no doubt. Her Barcelona fling and the Mossad assassin known as "Wolfman" were the same person. *What were the odds?*

Alex glanced at him again as they walked. Joshua was even more attractive than she'd remembered. His silver-blonde hair fell forward into his hazel eyes. His tanned face needed a shave, but the two-day growth only enhanced his rugged good looks. She could see why she'd fucked him all those years before.

"If you knew it was me, why did you take the contract?"

"It was too late to say no by the time I figured out that it was you. Either way, you are compromised."

"What do you want from me, Joshua?"

"I'm here to warn you. You need to abandon your present line of inquiry."

"What line of inquiry?" Alex said.

"Don't be coy, Alex—it doesn't suit you. I'm giving you a way out." Joshua leaned over and whispered in her ear, "It's me or someone else, Alex. You're a dead woman unless you drop this file."

Alex jerked away from him. "That goes both ways, Joshua," she said, spotting Max rushing toward them. His hand was tucked inside his jacket, clutching his automatic pistol.

"Is that your driver?" Joshua asked.

"You know it is," Alex answered. "Next time, call first."

Joshua gave her a curt nod and turned on his heel in the opposite direction.

Max reached Alex's side a few seconds later, but he kept his eyes on the retreating figure. "Who was that?"

Alex looked back, but Joshua had already disappeared into the crowd. "Wolfman."

"What the hell did he want?" Max growled.

"He warned me off the Prosperity investigation. There's a hit out on me."

Max gave her a quizzical look. "He *warned* you?"

Alex was not going to tell Max about Barcelona. "We have to be more careful from now on."

Joshua Workman had given her a second chance, and she would not waste it.

Chapter Twenty-Seven
Moscow, Russia
November 2019

Nick looked over at Mihkel snoring beside him on the early morning Aeroflot flight to Moscow. They had hardly spoken two words during the flight. Mihkel, hungover and cranky, had kept to himself. *Just as well,* thought Nick. He had nothing to say to him. His plan to get the hell out of Moscow within twenty-four hours was already going to shit. The two-hour time difference and the five-hour flight meant Nick would have to stay in Moscow for at least one night.

Nick looked over at Mihkel, snoring beside him.

Mihkel mumbled, stirring. His eyes flickered open. He sat up and looked around. "Where are we?"

Nick was silent.

"I need a piss and a drink," Mihkel said, running his hand over his face.

"Can you stay off the fucking booze till we meet with the Russians?" Nick blurted out.

"Fuck you," muttered Mihkel. "Order me a scotch. Make it a double."

"No. Fuck you," Nick hissed and looked out the window. He didn't give a shit anymore. He'd attend this one meeting, and then he was done—done with the Russians, done with Mihkel.

Mihkel grunted noncommittally, pulled himself up, and stumbled to the toilet. When he came back, a coffee waited for him. Mihkel swore loudly and sat down—nearly knocking the coffee over.

"Why did you order me a fucking coffee? I said a double scotch." Mihkel's face twisted into a sneer.

"Why did you lock me out of fucking Prosperity?"

"I did you a fucking favor. So shut the fuck up about the fucking Prosperity intranet," snapped Mihkel.

"You did me a fucking favor? Give me break. You've taken over the file and cut me out of the intranet account and yet here, I am Mihkel, on my way to Moscow to meet your fucking Russian clients."

Mihkel snickered and shook his head. "You're a real piece of work. A real piece of work. This is one mess that you are going to have to clean up yourself."

They lapsed back into a bitter silence.

A few hours later, the pilot came on the intercom system announcing that they had begun their final approach into Moscow's Domodedovo Airport. Once they landed, one of the flight attendants extracted their carry-on luggage from the overhead while another enthusiastically thanked them for traveling Aeroflot.

But that's where the pleasantries ended. The usual painful interaction with the uniformed Russian immigration officer at the passport control booth was made even more difficult by the fact that they had not obtained the requisite business visas before departing from London.

The immigration officer alerted the Russian military, and Nick and Mihkel were escorted to a windowless room lit by flickering fluorescent lights. They were relieved of their passports, carry-on bags, and cell phones, and directed to sit on the hard metal chairs. Mihkel and Nick complied without protesting.

Nick looked up at the ubiquitous security camera hanging from the ceiling and, through gritted teeth, said, "Well, this gets better and better, doesn't it, Mihkel?"

Mihkel said nothing and stared blankly at the grease-stained wall in front of him.

When a military officer walked into the room an hour later, Mihkel did the talking, speaking in Russian while giving him a card with Igor's name on it.

"Why don't you give Mr. Dimitrov a call?" Mihkel suggested in English.

"Uh, of course, sir," the officer said in English, his face visibly pale. Obviously, Igor was a known entity to the Russian military.

The officer politely excused himself and returned twenty minutes later with Nick's and Mihkel's passports and other belongings.

"You are free to leave," he said, motioning toward the door. "Please enjoy your stay."

Nick and Mihkel grabbed their belongings and hurried out of the secure area. On the other side of the sliding one-way door was a uniformed driver holding up a card with Mihkel's name written on it. They followed the driver through the terminal into the brisk afternoon air.

The gray haze covering Moscow was as Nick remembered it. The city was shrouded in toxic smog caused by cars with substandard emission control systems. They rode in silence past Stalinesque architecture broken up by bursts of bright neon signs and flashy window displays of high-priced Western goods and modern, towering condos.

The traffic was, as always, horrendous, and it took nearly two hours to reach the Hotel Metropol, a pre-revolutionary hotel favored by Russian billionaire oligarchs and affluent Western business travelers alike.

On the way, they passed the broad expanse of Red Square, with the onion-domed fortress of the Kremlin and the spires of St. Basil's Cathedral. Nick watched smartly dressed Muscovites streaming in and out of the redeveloped GUM department store—once a model of Bolshevik retail enterprise, now transformed into an upscale shopping mall featuring Chanel, Cartier, Tiffany's, Prada, and Rolex stores.

When they finally pulled up to the hotel, situated across the street from a tree-lined park where Karl Marx's brooding face was covered in early snow, Nick felt relieved. They had made it to the hotel without an international incident. For the time being, Mihkel was behaving himself.

The check-in process went smoothly. The smiling desk clerk tapped her computer keyboard a couple of times and handed them their room cards.

"Mr. Martin and Mr. Ivanov, your porters will take you up to your suites. Please enjoy your stay with us," she said in perfect English.

Two obsequious porters picked up their bags and whisked them to separate elevators. Nick and Mihkel had not exchanged more than a few words since they landed, and they remained silent as they parted.

The porter escorted Nick to his three-room suite and offered to unpack his carry-on. Nick politely declined and slipped two twenty-dollar American bills into the porter's hand. He couldn't read the look on the porter's face; however, after hearing the door slam, Nick realized forty bucks was probably not enough.

Nick took off his overcoat, threw it on a chair, and collapsed onto an uber-plush couch. He was beat.

Fighting his fatigue, Nick pulled out his laptop to search for flights back to the US. There were several promising options the next day, and he booked himself on a 4:00 p.m. British Airways flight to Boston via New York.

Next, he tapped out a text to Vladim: *Mihkel and I have checked into the Hotel Metropol. When can we meet with you and Mr. Dimitrov?*

Vladim replied immediately: *Igor will be available tomorrow at 2:00 p.m.*

"Fuck," Nick blurted out. That meant that there was no way that he could make his 4:00 flight the next day.

Nick had ignored repeated emails from Horton, his attorney, requesting a meeting. Horton had been vague about the reason for the meeting, which made Nick nervous. Horton didn't know that Nick had left the London, and Nick's plan had been to respond once he was back in the US. Nick couldn't wait any longer.

Nick emailed Horton, his attorney: *I'm in Moscow for meetings with clients of the firm. Long story. I won't be back in Boston till Friday.*

Horton texted back instantly: *Cece is not going to be happy. He has not eliminated you as a person of interest in Paul's death and he wants to interview you again. When he finds out you're in Moscow, guaranteed he'll escalate his investigation and charge you. He'll get Interpol to issue a Red Notice.*

Nick replied: *Don't tell Cece that I'm gone. If Interpol issues a Red Notice, I'll get arrested when I try to leave Moscow. Please help me out here. Tell Cece I got sick, food poisoning, anything. Just buy me some more time.*

Horton responded: *We both know that I can't do that.*

Fuck him, Nick thought. He'd fire Horton's sorry ass as soon as he got back to Boston. Then it hit him: in all the commotion, he had forgotten to call Laura.

The phone rang and rang before Laura picked up. "Hello?" she answered.

"Hi. It's me," Nick said, and when there was no response, he added, "It's Nick."

"Where are you?"

"In Moscow. I'm sorry. Things got crazy in London."

"What?"

"It's a long story—"

"It's always a long story with you, Nick," Laura interrupted, sounding pissed. "When will you be home?"

"I have a meeting with the client in our Moscow office tomorrow afternoon, and then I'll be on the next plane home. I promise."

The line went silent. "Laura, are you still there?"

"Yes," Laura said.

Nick took a deep breath and said, "Once I wrap up this file, it's going to be different."

"Okay, whatever you say, I guess." Laura paused. "We'll see you when we see you."

No smart reply, no angry diatribe lobbed his way. It sounded as if she had given up.

"Things will be different. Trust me. Please tell the girls I love them."

Without answering, Laura hung up.

Why was she like that? He was doing this for her and the girls. *Doesn't she get that?*

Overcome with exhaustion, Nick rested his head on the back of the couch and closed his eyes.

***

Nick's cell rang, dragging him out of a deep sleep. "Hello?"

"Hello, motherfucker," Mihkel said, his speech slightly slurred. "Come down and join me in the sauna for a vodka."

"Mihkel, I thought we agreed—no drinking till after the meeting tomorrow," Nick said, now wide awake.

Mihkel's voice turned hard-edged. "Get your ass down here," he said and hung up.

Twenty minutes later, Nick stood at the entrance to the hotel's spa on the concourse floor. He was escorted to a change room and given a complimentary bathrobe and flip-flops.

Nick showered, put on the bathrobe, and went to find the steam room and Mihkel.

A naked older couple enjoying the hydromassage benches gave him a hearty *zdravstuyte* as he walked by. Their voluptuous bodies flopped on the bench, and their splayed legs revealed hairless crotches. The man's breasts lolled on his extended gut, just like his wife's.

When he reached the steam room, Nick hung his robe on a door hook and wrapped a towel around his waist. He walked into the sauna and hit a wall of steam. He could almost make out Mihkel on an upper wooden bench in front of him.

Mihkel was not alone. Two very naked and very young women, each with a set of fake triple-E tits and hairless crotches, sat beside Mihkel. *Professionals.*

They waved their hands and smiled vacantly at Nick.

"Hey, Nicky boy, over here!" Mihkel called out. He was drunk but in a good mood. "Get yourself some vodka!" he said, pointing toward a bottle of Starka in an ice bucket by the door.

"No vodka, thank you," Nick said, trying not to look at Mihkel's sloppy man-tits resting on a gut that rolled over his fat crotch. The visuals were disturbing. Nick stepped up to the upper bench and sat down on his towel, his cock and balls dangling in front of him. Nick silently cursed himself for agreeing to meet Mihkel in the steam room.

"Darlings, can you leave us for a few minutes?" Mihkel asked the women. "Try out the whirlpool or something."

Both women stood up, and Mihkel delivered a well-aimed swat to the ass of the closest one. He grinned and mopped his forehead with his hand.

"What the fuck is going on?" Nick asked.

"Relax for once. Let's have a little fun. I got two girls."

"We've been in Moscow for six hours, and you're already drinking vodka and whoring around. What's wrong with you?"

Mihkel stepped down unsteadily from the upper bench and refilled his glass of vodka. Nick looked away, but not before he saw three pinkish protuberances sticking out between Mihkel's legs: a small, flaccid penis and two shiny, small balls. *That explains it.*

Nick cleared his throat. "Why am I even in Moscow, Mihkel? Stefan's taken over the file."

"Nick, I can't exactly introduce Stefan to Igor, can I? The guy is a *durak*. You're here to assure Igor everything's under control. Then I don't give a fuck what you do."

"Who the fuck is Igor anyway?" Nick asked. He had a sinking feeling that Paul had been right—Igor was ex-KGB.

"All you need to know is he's the money guy. Otherwise, it's none of your fucking business," Mihkel said.

"None of my fucking business? You've got to do better than that," Nick shot back. "And what's on the fucking Prosperity intranet that I can't see?"

Mihkel pointed a finger at him. "If I told you once, I told you a thousand fucking times, just drop it." He took another snog of vodka and said, "Trust me."
***

Nick and Mihkel were late for their 2:00 p.m. meeting with Vladim and Igor. They had underestimated the drive time in midday traffic, and it was just after 3:30 p.m. when they stepped off the elevator on the forty-fourth floor of the glass-and-steel tower in Moscow.

Mihkel approached the smiling receptionist with his eyes fixed on her creamy white breasts bubbling out of her tight, low-necked sweater, and he asked for Vladim in Russian.

"Mr. Bulgarin is waiting for you in the Crimea boardroom," the receptionist answered back with a husky Russian accent. She waved in the direction of a boardroom off the reception area.

"You're late," Vladim said before Nick and Mihkel were even through the door.

"Sorry—bad traffic," Nick said. "Where's Igor?"

"Sit," Vladim said, gesturing to the black leather chairs surrounding the rectangular cherry wood table. "Igor waited for an hour and then he left. No one keeps Igor waiting."

"It couldn't be helped," Nick said defensively.

"We're meeting Igor at his *dacha* outside Moscow later this afternoon," Vladim said.

"At his what?" Nick sat forward. "Look, I agreed to meet here at the Houghton offices—not some fucking *dacha*."

"I don't think you heard Vladim. We were late. Now we're going to Igor's *dacha*," Mihkel said flatly.

Vladim and Mihkel exchanged looks, and then Vladim said, "Mr. Martin, you disappoint me. You're happy to take our legal fees, but you won't visit one of our homes?"

Nick glared at Mihkel. He couldn't win this one. *He was going to Igor's fucking dacha.*

Chapter Twenty-Eight
Outside of Moscow, Russia
November 2019

Nick watched the decorative, domed buildings that marked the center of Moscow recede into crumbling Soviet-era apartment blocks and then into the countryside, with snow-covered fields and thick stands of pine. He tried to block out Mihkel's endless chattering with Karla Murphy about yet another life settlement fund he had referred to her. This one was out of Prague.

Nick was furious. He was on his way to Igor's fucking *dacha* so that Mihkel could keep his Russian clients happy, and the fucker was shamelessly pushing work to Karla right in front of his face. Nick didn't even want to think about the Interpol Red Notice out there waiting for him when he tried to leave this shithole.

"You're sending another file to Karla?" Nick said as soon as Mihkel hung up.

"Look, it's a loser file. Some two-bit client out of the Prague office. Why do you give a shit?" Mihkel answered.

Nick mouthed "fuck you" in Mihkel's direction.

Silent after that, they exchanged looks when their driver made several sharp turns, only to return to the main road later.

After one such detour, Nick leaned over to Mihkel and whispered, "Are we being followed?"

"Who the fuck cares?" muttered Mihkel, and they both turned back to the frozen countryside.

By the time they got to Igor Dimitrov's onion-turreted *dacha*, it was late in the afternoon and near dark. Two ski-jacketed guards with folding-stock AK-47s slung casually over their shoulders stopped them at the front gate. Their driver nodded to the guard, and the electronic gate opened slowly, revealing the estate; framed by tall, leafless poplars, a medieval castle, complete with towers and stone battlements, appeared in the gloom.

The Bentley pulled up in front of two massive wood doors, and a security guard rushed forward, opened the sedan's doors, and ushered the men into a room off the foyer. A wood-burning fireplace dominated the dimly lit room. Exposed wooden beams crisscrossed the ceiling, and beneath the oversized furniture, Turkish carpets crisscrossed the stone floors. The dark, wood-paneled walls featured the heads and carcasses of dead animals—some local but many African. *Great. Igor's an equal-opportunity slaughterer.*

Igor stepped forward and shook Mihkel's and Nick's hands. "Please sit," he said in his guttural English, gesturing to a seating area near one of the massive bay windows overlooking the lit courtyard.

The contrast between Igor and Vladim was striking. Igor was a big, bald, muscular man with coarse facial features. Dressed in a black turtleneck, blue jeans, and pointy-toed, snakeskin cowboy boots, Igor was a cross between a Cold War–era Politburo thug and a Russian ad for the Gap.

Vladim, on the other hand, looked elegant—and wealthy—dressed from head to toe in Bruno Cucinelli, an iconic brand of Italian sophistication.

Nick noticed a young, thin girl with stringy blonde hair standing in the corner of the room wearing skintight jeans, a tight sweater, and heels. Her right eye was puffy and covered with too much makeup. She was barely a teenager.

Igor flashed her a dirty look, and she left the room, her high heels clicking on the hard stone floor.

When the heavy wood door banged shut behind her, Igor said, "I apologize for Valeria's rude behavior. She is a *tyolka* and still needs to be trained."

Then he turned to Mihkel and, flashing his white-capped teeth and purplish gums, said, "Mr. Ivanov, I must congratulate you for the admirable level of presales you've provided for the Prosperity Fund."

"Thank you, Igor," said Mihkel. "We've worked hard, and in a few days, we'll close the offering. The proceeds of the presale are in the dealers' accounts."

"Vladim has briefed me on the steps your firm is taking to deal with, what do you call it, the Viatical Act? All is under control, I understand," Igor said, focusing on Nick.

"That's right. It's all under control," Nick added brightly.

"Good," Igor said. "I would have expected nothing less from your firm."

He motioned for the security guard, whispering something in his ear. The guard left, and Igor continued. "I congratulate you for going on the road and sourcing those low-cost life insurance policies. You have laid the groundwork for our future success."

"Thank you, Mr. Dimitrov," replied Nick, visibly relieved that Igor was happy with him.

"But now we have a problem," Igor said, his black eyes narrowing. "Basel Re is blocking payout on the life insurance policies, and they've put their best investigator, Alex Greene, on the file. You're a very naughty boy, my friend. You've been helping her."

As Nick looked to Mihkel for support, Mihkel blurted, "I told him not to speak to Greene. I said she was trouble."

That was not the response that Nick wanted. Mihkel was throwing him under the bus.

Igor's voice took on a threatening tone. "What did you tell Greene?"

"Believe me, I told her nothing."

"You told her nothing?" Igor shouted. "She followed you here, you *durak*. Don't lie to me."

"I—" Nick started to say, but he was cut off by Vladim, who had sat quietly till now.

"Igor," Vladim began, "you know that we've hired the best to take care of Greene. He'll neutralize her."

Nick looked at Mihkel. *Neutralize her? What was Vladim talking about?*

Then, without warning, Igor was on his feet. He strode across the room, grabbed Nick by his jacket lapels, and lifted him out of his chair.

"What did you say to that bitch?" He heaved Nick back down with such force that the chair—and Nick—toppled over.

Nick tried to get up, but Igor stomped down hard on his chest. "I ask you again: What did you say to her?"

Nick coughed, stammering, "N-Nothing!"

"Then why did she follow you here?" Igor brought his boot back and kicked Nick hard in his ribs.

Nick heard his ribs crack, and he convulsed with pain. He rolled over on his side, moaning.

"What did you say to Greene?" Igor roared, and then he kicked Nick in the face.

Nick's head flew back, and blood poured from his mouth and nose. Writhing in pain, Nick groaned. "Nothing. I said nothing!"

Nick didn't see Igor raise his boot and slam it down hard on the side of his head. He felt only exploding pain, and then darkness consumed him.
***

Alex and Max huddled outside the *dacha*'s six-foot stone fence. Using the overcast November evening to their advantage, they had set up their surveillance along the estate's sheltered perimeter. Max, wearing thermal imaging night goggles, kept watch, tracking the security guards patrolling the fence's inner perimeter. Alex aimed the dish-shaped parabolic laser microphone at the windows and listened to the conversation inside.

Alex turned to Max. "Dimitrov knows we're here."

"Then we need to get out," Max whispered back. "We don't stand a chance against these guys. Dimitrov has a small army guarding the place."

Alex and Max had followed Nick and Mihkel earlier that afternoon to the Houghton offices, and when

Nick, Mihkel, and Vladim emerged thirty minutes later and got into a black Bentley, Alex and Max tailed them in their Mercedes.

Tracking Nick to Houghton's Moscow office had been a combination of luck and careful surveillance. They had been several hours behind Nick and Mihkel after arriving in Moscow late in the evening in Basel Re's private jet.

They had followed Nick to the Hotel Metropol with the transponder, and then to Igor's *dacha*, and waited for Nick to resurface.

Alex hiked herself to the top of the stone perimeter wall and trained her night-vision binoculars on the front door of the fortress-like home. Finally the huge front doors swung open and Mihkel walked out, followed by two of Igor's security guards carrying an unconscious Nick. Mihkel got in the Bentley's back seat, and the two thugs dumped Nick's limp body into the trunk of the car. Vladim and Igor were nowhere in sight.

Alex turned to Max and whispered, "Martin's in trouble."

"There's nothing we can do for him. We need to leave," Max urged as a guard with a German shepherd on a leash rounded the corner, walking across the frozen ground less than fifty feet from them.

"Let's go," Max insisted as the dog picked up their scent and, straining in their direction, started barking hysterically. The guard called out in Russian and let the dog go.

Alex and Max grabbed their gear and ran. They could hear the dog's snarling barks on the other side of the fence as they tore through the dense foliage.

Bursts of bullets sprayed the surrounding trees, and they both dove into the underbrush. Max rolled over on his stomach and, leaning on his elbows, fired at the Russians. The first shot caught the guard in the shoulder, and the second in the head. There would be others right behind him.

Max yelled, "Let's go, boss!" but Alex was already up and running. They reached their Mercedes as two of Igor's goons in an open jeep came barreling down the road.

"We have company," Alex said.

Max looked in the rearview mirror. "We're outta here." He slapped the Mercedes into overdrive, and the car surged forward as bullets from the Russians' AK-47s flew around them.

Chapter Twenty-Nine
Moscow, Russia
November 2019

Nick lay naked in a dimly lit, dingy hotel room, swimming in a sea of pain. He lifted his head and sheltered his eyes from a blinding spotlight that shone at him from the end of the bed. He could barely make out the shadowy figures shouting in Russian—not at him, but at someone lying beside him.

Nick turned his head and saw the profile of a young woman; greasy tendrils of bleached-blonde hair obscured her face. She tried to say something, but before she could finish, one man stepped forward and slapped her hard across the side of the head. She groaned in pain.

Another man shouted, grabbed her by the hair, and shoved her face into Nick's groin. She tried to suck Nick's flaccid penis, but she kept gagging. There was more shouting, and the sobbing young woman straddled Nick.

He struggled to sit up, but a punch to his skull sent him flying back on the dirty mattress. Stunned, Nick tried to focus on the surrounding melee, but the room was spinning out of control. The ringing in his ears was so loud he could hardly hear the shuddering cries of the woman on top of him. One of the men grabbed the young woman, and in one swift motion, he put her into a chokehold and slit her throat with a switchblade.

She fell forward on Nick, blood gurgling from her neck. Nick, slick with her blood, struggled to pull himself out from under her. Then he felt a sharp prick on the side of his neck, and darkness found him.

***

Nick's eyes flickered open. The morning light flooded the silent hotel room. His naked body shivered in the cold. *How long have I been out?*

He turned his head and came face-to-face with the cloudy blue eyes of a corpse. *Oh God.* It was Valeria, the girl from Igor's *dacha*.

Nick sat up so quickly he saws stars. He grabbed one of Valeria's arms and cried out, "Come on, wake up. You gotta wake up." But Valeria's head flopped over on the filthy, bloodstained mattress.

He heard a series of low, guttural moans that he did not recognize as his own till they stopped.

Heart pounding in his ears, Nick tried to stand up, but the room started spinning. He sat down hard on the side of the bed and put his head between his knees. When the spinning stopped, he looked around. There was nothing in the room except the bed. *Where were his belongings—his clothes, wallet, and phone?*

Nausea overwhelmed him. Clutching his cramping stomach, Nick staggered to the bathroom, only getting as far as the doorway before dropping to his knees and spewing dark-green vomit on the grimy tiled floor. Nick crawled to the filthy toilet, but his stomach was empty; the dry heaves produced nothing more than a slimy, yellow fluid. He collapsed by the toilet and tried to catch his breath.

The taste in his mouth of bile and stale blood was sickening. Gripping the sink, he got up and looked at himself in the cracked mirror. His face was bruised and swollen and covered in dried blood. He turned on the rust-stained tap and rinsed his mouth, spitting bile-streaked water down the dirty drain.

Nick was scrubbing the blood from his face and hands when he heard a sharp knock at his hotel door. He froze.

A stern voice called out, *"Politsiya!"*

Then he heard more banging and choruses of *"Politsiya. Otkryt'! Otkryt'!"*

Christ. The police. Stall, stall. "Just—just a minute," Nick called out in desperation as he frantically searched the room for something, anything, to cover himself.

There was a crashing noise, and the door flew open, knocked off its hinges by a battering ram. Four broad-shouldered police officers in long coats and jackboots rushed into the room, pistols drawn.

"Ruki vverkh! Ruki vverkh!" one officer screamed.

Nick raised his bloodstained hands over his head. In that instant, Nick knew he was fucked. "I'm an American," he pleaded. "I, erm, I didn't do this."

"Americanski?" That made the cops even angrier, and two burly officers dragged Nick from the room.

Nick screamed in pain as the cops threw him up against the wall and twisted his arms behind his back. They handcuffed him before shoving him down the hotel hallway to the waiting police van.

Nick cursed Mihkel. *That fucker had set him up.*

Chapter Thirty
Outside of Moscow, Russia
December 2019

Nick sat silently on his paper-thin mattress in his cell and stared at the concrete wall. A thin, polyester blanket draped over his shoulders made the dampness and cold tolerable—but barely. At least he wasn't naked anymore. His prison-issued sweat suit was worn and full of holes, and the elastic on the pants was so stretched that he had to hold on to his pants when he stood up.

Graffiti decorated the cell's dark-green-painted walls, and the place reeked of shit, piss, and puke. The only heat in his stone-walled cell came from a barred grille in the metal door, and the only light came from a single bulb hanging from the ceiling. The light flicked on at 6:00 a.m. and sputtered out at midnight, marking the days of his incarceration. There was no running water, only a shit bucket.

It had been nearly two weeks since the Russian police had dragged Nick out of the hotel room and deposited him naked at the Lefortovskaya Prison just outside Moscow.

After a rocky admission process and a cursory medical examination, Nick had been taken to a cell in an isolation wing of the jail, where he'd remained on a twenty-four-hour basis, only leaving his cell for the daily dumping of his shit pail.

Despite it all, Nick was feeling better: His ribs hurt less. His blinding headaches had subsided. And the vertigo was mostly gone. But the cell remained cold and poorly ventilated, and after hearing the hacking coughs of the other inmates reverberating down the corridors at night, Nick feared that an extended stay in a facility like this could be a death sentence in itself.

On the second day of his captivity, Nick was visited by a young Russian attorney dressed in a cheap, factory-made suit, who informed Nick in broken English that he was on remand for murder and would be sentenced in a few weeks.

"No trial?" Nick had asked, shocked.

"*Nyet,*" the lawyer said before relaying that the evidence against Nick was overwhelming, and it was best to waive a trial for a reduced sentence. If Nick agreed to confess, the Russian attorney promised he'd be taken to a more comfortable facility with a gym and a library, a place where—for a couple hundred American dollars a month—he could live like a king.

When Nick balked at making a deal and begged to speak to someone from Houghton's Moscow office or the American Embassy, the attorney said, "*Nyet.*"

Nick hadn't seen the attorney again, despite his repeated requests, and his last demand for assistance had earned him a sharp crack across the arm from the guard's truncheon.

The rattling of keys in the cell door's lock startled Nick late one afternoon during his third week of captivity, and he anxiously watched as the door swung open. It wasn't mealtime, and Nick had declined any activity that would take him outside the cell. *The best chance of staying alive.*

A prison guard escorted a thin man wearing a black, tailored overcoat into his cell.

The man stepped forward and extended his hand. "Mr. Martin, my name is Gary Getz. I'm from the US Embassy."

Nick jumped up and grabbed Getz's hand with two of his. "Thank God! Finally."

Getz looked around the cell and grimaced. "I've arranged for your return to the United States."

"I was framed. I didn't do anything wrong," Nick said.

"I'm not here to judge, but it's not been easy to get you out of the country. You were found in a hotel room with a dead girl, and your fingerprints are all over the crime scene, including on a knife that the police say was used to kill the girl. You've been given a twenty-four-hour window to leave Russia. After that, I can't help you."

"What about Mihkel? Where is Mihkel Ivanov?"

"Mr. Ivanov left Russia weeks ago."

Nick gritted his teeth. *That self-serving piece of shit.*

Getz had brought clothes for Nick: a ratty white shirt, a frayed black suit, and a pair of fake leather shoes. They were secondhand goods, but at least they looked clean.

Nick undressed, gingerly pulling the prison sweatshirt over his head. He tried not to cringe, but his ribs still hurt like hell. He let his sweatpants drop to the floor and, standing naked in front of Getz, slipped on the new pants.

Getz winced when he saw the full extent of the bruises and cuts on Nick's body and, looking away, said, "That's quite a beating you took. Sorry I couldn't get to you earlier."

Not as fucking sorry as I am. Nick put on the oversized shirt and picked up a shoe. They were two sizes too big, but he slipped them over his sockless feet without complaint.

The worn polyester suit jacket completed the outfit, and Nick ran his hand up and down the front in search of a button to do up—but there were none.

"Got a belt?" Nick asked, hiking his pants. He felt like a circus clown.

"This is a prison. They don't hand out belts," Getz said. He passed Nick a folded document. "Here's your temporary passport."

Nick slipped the paper into the inside pocket of his suit without looking at it and said, "Let's get out of here."

They arrived at the Vnukovo International Airport west of Moscow an hour later. Their SUV, which had diplomatic plates, was waved through the front gate and, after crossing a concrete apron, came to a stop in front of a huge hangar.

As they walked to the hangar, Getz said, "You wait here," and he left Nick standing awkwardly by the door in his cheap, ill-fitting suit.

Nick shivered against the cold, but he dared not complain. Nick watched Getz stride across the expansive hangar and speak to a group of grim-faced Americans.

Then he saw her: Alex fucking Greene.

Her smug, impassive gaze angered him. *That bitch—it was because of her that Igor turned on him. What was she doing here?*

Nick started off toward her when he felt a restraining hand on his shoulder. He turned to see a uniformed soldier who barked out, "*Stoy!*"

Nick yanked his shoulder away, and the guard threw Nick on the ground, pinning him with a knee on his neck.

Getz hurried over, waving the guard off.

"I told you not to move," Getz said, helping Nick up.

"Why is Greene here? I want to talk to her," Nick said.

"Not now. It's time for you to board the plane."

"I need to talk to her!" Nick shouted.

"No. Board the plane," Getz repeated, and he took Nick's arm and duck-marched him toward a Bombardier Challenger business jet parked several hundred yards from the hangar. "You still don't appreciate the trouble you're in. The plane *must* take off now."

Nick looked back over his shoulder, but Greene was gone. He shook off Getz's grip and followed him across the icy tarmac. Nick was only ten yards from the plane when he slipped and fell backward onto the slick pavement. The fall knocked the wind out of him and reignited the pain in his rib cage. Dazed, he rolled over and got up on his hands and knees.

Nick saw a military officer running toward him, shouting in Russian.

Getz yelled, "Get up! Get up! Get on the plane!"

The whine of the jet's engines spooling up added urgency as Getz ran back toward Nick, hauled him to his feet, and rushed him to the plane.

"Do not come back to Russia, ever!" Getz shouted, pushing Nick up the stairs. "Do you understand? I won't be able to help you if you do!"

A steward hurried Nick into the plane, and within minutes, the jet was taxiing down the airstrip. The Russian soldier reached Getz just as the plane was taking off, and Nick watched as Getz turned and walked briskly to the terminal, leaving the Russian officer alone on the windy runway screaming into his cell phone.

Once they were at cruising altitude, Nick unbuckled his seat belt and surveyed the luxurious interior of the jet. He sat at the back of the plane in a row of beige leather seats with marble-topped side tables. At the front was a seating area with leather couches, coffee tables, and an entertainment center. The off-white carpeting and paneling gave the interior of the plane an ethereal effect. Nick was not sure who Getz had to blow to get him on a plane like this, but it had to be someone high up in the US Embassy food chain. When the co-pilot came back and asked Nick, in a thick Russian accent, if he could get him anything, Nick asked for a brandy and a blanket. He was still chilled from the wintery Moscow weather. He really wanted a pair of socks, but he kept that to himself.

The co-pilot brought him a Dujardin VSOP brandy, and Nick downed it in one gulp and asked for another. He also asked for a phone.

"I need to call my wife," Nick explained.

He downed the second brandy and dialed his home number. It rang and rang and then went to voicemail. He dialed Laura's cell, but she didn't pick up. He figured it must be early evening in Boston. Why wasn't she picking up?

He called the home line again and left a brief message: "It's me. I'm on my way home. I'll explain everything when I get there."

Nick hung up, and suddenly he felt very tired.

The booze had warmed him, and he could barely keep his eyes open.

Nick pushed the seat back into a reclining position, pulled the blanket over his shoulders, and fell into a deep, dark sleep as the jet winged its way over continental Europe.

Chapter Thirty-One
Curaçao, Caribbean
December 2019

Nick opened his eyes and watched steamy, hot sunlight stream into the cabin through the open door of the landed jet. He rubbed his eyes. *Where the fuck was he?* The last thing that he remembered was downing a brandy, pulling a blanket over his shivering body, and falling into a dead sleep.

He called out, "Anyone there?" But his voice echoed in the empty cabin.

He unbuckled his seat belt and slowly stood, unpeeling his sweaty jacket and pants from the leather seat.

The oppressively hot and humid air in the cabin made it hard to breathe, and Nick walked over and stuck his head out the open door. Squinting in the bright sunlight, Nick spotted a sign in the distance: *Welcome to Curaçao.*

Curaçao? What the hell am I doing in Curaçao? He had traveled to Curaçao with Laura when they were first married. No wonder it was so fucking hot: Curaçao was nearly on the equator.

He took off his jacket and checked for his temporary passport. *Still there, thank God.* He stuffed it into his back pocket and went into the galley kitchen to find some water. The fridge was empty.

He opened the other cupboards below the counter—lots of booze, but no water. When he opened one of the overhead cupboards, an aluminum briefcase slid out and nearly hit him in the head. He caught the heavy briefcase midair and placed it on the floor.

When he finally found several small bottles of water in a drawer, Nick drained two in succession, grabbed a third, and headed for the exit—only to trip over the briefcase. He fell against the galley wall, igniting fireworks of pain around his broken ribs.

After catching his breath, Nick put the briefcase on the counter and popped open the latches.

Shit.

There had to be at least a couple million bucks in large-denomination American bills in there. Nick checked the bulging zipped flap inside the briefcase's lid. His eyebrows rose as he pulled a gun out of the side pocket. It was a 9mm Browning Hi-Power. *Nice shooting gun.*

He'd practiced with one before, back in Boston at his gun club. He shook his head. *It seemed like a lifetime ago.* He ran the slide back and cocked it. *Loaded, too.*

After checking that the safety was on, he stuck the Browning into his right-side pants pocket. There was a spare thirteen-round clip of ammo in the briefcase, which he shoved into the other pocket. *Just in case.*

Nick thought he heard a vehicle approaching. He grabbed the briefcase and stuck his head out the door. A yellow jeep was racing across the tarmac toward the jet. Nick stepped out and waved at the jeep just as a hefty man stood up with an AK-47 in his hands.

Balancing himself against the windshield, the man fired at Nick, and a spray of bullets kicked up bits of pavement in front of the plane.

Nick ducked under the plane's wing and dropped the briefcase. He whipped out the Browning, thumbed off the safety, and taking a two-handed grip, squeezed off four shots at the approaching jeep.

Tires squealed as the jeep swerved out of the line of fire. Nick snatched the briefcase off the tarmac and, with bullets pinging around him, sprinted for the six-foot chain-link fence. He could hear the jeep's engine revving behind him. When he was close to the perimeter, he swung his arm back and tossed the briefcase up and over the fence into the dense bush of bamboo trees. With newfound strength, Nick scaled the fence and ran for cover, just as the jeep rolled to a stop a few yards from where he crouched in the thick bamboo underbrush.

Heart thumping in his ears, Nick held his breath as the shooter, gripping his assault rifle, got out of the vehicle and walked up to the fence.

The driver shouted something in Russian, and the shooter let off a round of bullets into the fence.

Fucking Russians.

The rapid fire ricocheted off the chain-link fence back toward the jeep, narrowly missing the driver, who ducked as the windshield exploded. Another argument ensued between the driver and the shooter before they drove off back toward the abandoned jet.

Exhaling, Nick stood and pushed his way out of the underbrush, only to discover that he was now on another and even wider runway, with a long line of planes waiting to take off. Beyond the next fence, Nick could see a four-lane highway busy with cars and buses; a Marriott hotel blotted the landscape.

After a quick check for the shooters, Nick sprinted across the runway, reaching the other side as a jumbo jet screamed over him. Nick scaled a second fence, ripping his shirt, and ran along the highway shoulder before traversing the four-lane gauntlet of vehicles; drivers braked and blasted their horns at him as he weaved through traffic. When he reached the front door of the Marriott, Nick was dripping in sweat.

A bemused doorman, who had watched Nick traverse the busy highway, greeted him as he opened the door. "Welcome to the Marriott, sir. Glad to see you made it in one piece."

Nick, keeping his head high and shoulders squared, calmly tucked his torn shirt into his oversized trousers. With his sockless feet squelching in his plastic shoes, he crossed the threshold and was immediately met with a blast of icy air and a uniquely American decorating style: gilt mirrors, huge canvases, hanging chandeliers, faux Persian carpets, and plastic flower arrangements. He would have once ridiculed the style, but now he found it oddly comforting.

Nick weaved through the crowded lobby to the hotel's front desk. He put the briefcase on the counter, opened the lid, and pulled out a bundle of hundred-dollar bills.

Nick peered at the name tag of the clerk behind the desk as he stuffed the wad of money in his pocket. "Hi, Lorna," he said to the large middle-aged woman in a cheap navy suit. "I need to make a call to Boston. Can you help me with that?"

"Are you a guest of the hotel, sir?" Lorna asked, eyes riveted on the briefcase.

Flashing his best grin, Nick handed her a hundred-dollar bill and said, "I'm not."

"I'm sorry, sir. You need to be a hotel guest."

Nick pulled another bill from the wad and put it on the counter. "Please."

Lorna took the two one-hundred-dollar bills and put them into her jacket pocket. "I'll allow you one short call, but I'll have to dial the number for you."

Lorna picked up the receiver and waited for Nick to give her the number.

Nick thought for a second; if he could make only one call, it better be to Mihkel. The time on his temporary passport was running out. *Fucking Mihkel had left him for dead. Mihkel owed him, and Mihkel would get him home.*

As Nick gave Lorna the last two digits of Mihkel's phone number, he glimpsed two casually dressed, broad-shouldered men enter the lobby. Nick recognized them immediately as the airport welcome committee. *The two Ivans.*

"I'll be back," Nick said, and flashing a big smile at Lorna, he grabbed the briefcase and headed across the crowded lobby to the lounge at the back of the hotel.

It took Nick a few seconds for his eyes to adjust to the lounge's dim lighting. The room was crowded with hotel guests, and in the corner, a man played the piano, crooning softly. Nick made his way to the dark mahogany bar that ran the length of the room and sat beside a tourist dressed in a fluorescent pink T-shirt. Nick set his briefcase by his bar stool and shoved his protruding pistol deeper into his pocket.

The tourist, who was contentedly nursing a rum punch, extended his hand. "Hi, I'm Hans. From Dusseldorf."

Nick ignored the extended hand and gave Hans his best fuck-off look.

The bartender, a bald man with his extended gut bulging out of his white shirt, asked, "What can I get you?"

Nick pulled out the wad of hundred-dollar bills, peeled one off, and plunked it down on the bar. "A glass of lager, please." When the bartender reached for the bill, Nick said, "Keep the change, but just tell me if you see two big Russian goons come into the bar."

The bartender took the money, replacing it with a tall glass of cold beer. He wiped the counter with a cloth. "Friends of yours?"

"Not exactly," Nick said.

The German tourist pulled his stool closer to Nick and said in a lowered voice, "Are you an American gangster?"

Nick held an index finger to his lips and said in an exaggerated whisper, "Shhh and I won't kill you."

The German's eyes widened. He picked up his drink, slid off the stool, and deferentially bowed his head.

"*Auf Wiedersehen*," he said and waddled off in search of another drinking perch.

Nick finished his beer. "Is there another way out of here?" he asked the bartender.

The bartender nodded at an exit door to his right. "Yeah, take that door. It opens to a hallway, and at the end, there's a fire exit that leads to the loading docks at the back of the hotel. The alarm hasn't worked in years."

Nick looked toward the door. "I'll need transport."

"There's a taxi stand across the street. Can't miss it," the bartender said. This obviously wasn't the first time he'd given these directions.

Nick slid another hundred-dollar bill to the bartender.

"Thanks. I'll have another round."

The bartender set another cold beer in front of Nick and, glancing at the bar's entrance, said, "You've got company."

Nick looked over his shoulder; sure enough, the two Russians from the airstrip had arrived, and they were scanning the room like a pair of hunting dogs. Nodding his thanks to the bartender, Nick picked up his briefcase and walked briskly toward the exit.

Blinking in the bright sunlight, he hurried across the street and climbed into a battered orange Fiat at the front of the taxi line.

"Where to, man?" asked the cabbie, flashing a toothy smile and tipping the frayed brim of his Dodgers baseball hat.

"Anywhere but here," Nick said, gripping the briefcase with both hands.

"You got it!" The driver turned the key in the ignition, but the car stalled.

Nick looked out the rear window and saw the two men running across the street. *Shit.* Nick sat forward and yelled, "We have to leave now!"

The driver pumped the gas and turned the key again; the engine turned over with a rasp.

"Gun it!" Nick shouted, watching the two goons dodge traffic to get to him.

The cabbie slapped the manual transmission into first gear, and the car squealed away from the stand just as the Ivans crossed the street.

"Let's go! Let's go!"

"I'm on it, brother. I'm on it," the cabbie called back as he raced the little Fiat through an amber light and then up a side road into the hills running along the coast.

As the car rose and fell on the winding road, the driver kept a lookout, but the Russians did not follow them.

Finally, the cabbie slowed down. "I think we lost 'em."

"Hope so," said Nick. He sat forward and handed the driver two hundred-dollar bills. "Can you take me someplace where I can make a phone call? Somewhere those guys won't find me?"

The driver grinned and took the money. "No problem, man."

Fifteen minutes later, the cabbie dropped Nick off on the side of a dirt road. He pointed to a dusty laneway and assured Nick he would find a phone in the café at the end of the lane.

"It's my cousin's café," he explained. "Ask for Markus. He'll be waiting for you."

Yeah, he'll be waiting for my greenbacks, Nick thought.

Chapter Thirty-Two
Curaçao, Caribbean
December 2019

The cabbie honked and waved as he drove off in his little Fiat and left Nick standing on a mountain road, flanked on both sides by a canopy of small shrub-like trees. Nick waved back and watched the car disappear around a curve. *What had he gotten himself into?* He was in the middle of nowhere under a relentless midday sun. The cabbie said to follow the dirt lane through the dense brush to his cousin's snack bar, so Nick, briefcase in hand, trudged up the steep hill.

After a few minutes, Nick reached an opening in the bush and spied a large painted sign advertising the Curaçao Hato Caves and Interpretation Center. Behind the sign stood a grove of palm trees and a small kiosk with a corrugated tin roof.

Nick walked up to the counter and picked up a pamphlet: "The Arawak people first used the Hato Caves over two millennia ago… They left behind many cave drawings… Later, the caves were used as a refuge for runaway slaves… Today, they are one of the world's most popular caves."

As interesting as the brochure was, it didn't tell Nick how to find a phone. Then he noticed a young boy dozing on a lawn chair near the kiosk.

"Hey, kid! Do you have a phone I can use? I was told to ask for Markus."

The young teenager looked up, bleary-eyed. "Markus is gone, man. But there's a phone at the café."

Nick pulled out a hundred-dollar bill and held it in front of the kid, who sat up quickly. "Now, do you have a phone I can use?"

"I can take you to it." The kid jerked a thumb toward a rundown shack on the edge of the parking lot and snatched the bill with his other hand. Nick followed him across the clearing.

"The phone's in here," the kid said, opening the rickety screen door. The white walls and floors of the café were clean, but other than a small bar and a few metal tables and chairs, there was nothing to suggest that food or booze was served on the premises.

Nick took a double step back when he saw a four-foot iguana sitting on the windowsill behind the bar, happily sunning itself. The kid stepped forward and tried to shoo the lizard out the window. Having none of it, the reptile landed on the floor with a thud and stalked past them through the open door.

Nick spotted an old rotary phone at the end of the bar and picked up the receiver. To his surprise, there was a dial tone. He dialed Mihkel's cell, every number taking an eternity to roll back.

Just as Mihkel's phone started to ring, Nick heard the sound of a vehicle. He rushed to the door and spotted a yellow jeep kicking up a cloud of dust as it charged across the parking lot. *Fucking Russians.*

The two Russians jumped out of the jeep with AK-47s.

"Who are those guys?" the young man asked in disbelief.

Nick pulled the Browning out of his pocket and thumbed the safety off. The boy's eyes bulged when he saw the gun.

"Kid, what's your name?" Nick asked.

The gangly teenager nervously licked his lips. "Luis."

"Luis, we need a place to hide. These Russians want to kill me. I'm afraid they'll kill you too."

"Shit." Luis winced. "Come on, the caves are this way, man. We can hide in there."

Nick followed Luis out of the café to a narrow trail up the side of the mountain. They had only gone a few steps before shots started whizzing over their heads.

"Get down!" Nick shouted, and he shoved the boy to the ground before returning fire. When the two gunmen dove for cover, Nick grabbed Luis by the arm, and they both ran toward the caves.

The two Ivans recovered quickly, and Nick could hear them lumbering up the path. Just before reaching the cave entrance, Nick turned and squeezed off two more shots at the Ivans.

Nick rushed into the cave and followed Luis's flickering cell phone light into a tunnel. When Nick caught up, he asked Luis in a lowered voice, "Where are we going?"

"Just keep up!" Luis said over his shoulder, and he broke into a slow jog, leading them deeper into the caves. After a few minutes, Luis slowed down and turned to Nick. "Why do those guys want to kill you?"

Nick grimaced. "It's complicated. We need to keep moving."

"My phone's nearly dead," Luis said, waving his cell in Nick's direction. "Give me yours."

"I don't have one to give. Let's go."

Luis sighed as the cell light flickered in front of him. "Don't worry, I know these caves like the back of my hand. Just stay close," Luis said, "and don't shoot me."

"Roger that," Nick said with a chuckle. He clicked the safety and put the gun into the front pocket of his pants, then followed the progressively weakening light of Luis's cell.

Suddenly, a motion detector light illuminated a huge cavern. Nick blinked at the blinding light, and it took a few moments before he could make out the jagged stalactites hanging from the cave's ceiling and the faded, prehistoric paintings of warriors that decorated the walls. It was quiet now, except for the noise of dripping water. Nick wondered at the etchings. *Nothing ever changes. Hunters and their prey.*

"How far till the exit?" Nick asked.

Luis was silent for a moment, and then he turned to Nick. "Listen up. We need a plan. The motion detector lights will go out as soon as we leave the cave. We'll wait over there," Luis said, pointing to a passage near a pile of rocks on the cave's other side.

"As soon as they get here, the lights will come back on, and you can kill them," Luis said matter-of-factly. Then, pointing to the ceiling light, he continued, "If you miss, shoot out the light, and we're outta here."

Nick looked at Luis with renewed respect.

Within minutes of Nick and Luis getting into position, the lights went off. They didn't have to wait long before the two Ivans arrived, and the lights flashed on.

Nick was able to get off three shots before both Russians dropped to the ground, one of them yelping in pain. Then Nick took careful aim and knocked out the light with one shot.

Luis grabbed Nick's arm to run, but before they could get away, the Russians opened fire, the flash from their guns temporarily illuminating the cave. Nick pushed Luis to the ground as bullets ricocheted off the surrounding rocks.

When the shooting stopped, Nick pulled himself up and squeezed off two shots into the darkness in the direction of the Russians. *That'll keep their heads down.* Then his gun clicked. *Empty.* Nick quickly ejected the spent clip from the Browning's butt and inserted the spare clip from his pocket. He cocked the automatic, pulling the slide back and forth, and listened. He could hear whispers—then footsteps.

Luis grabbed Nick's arm and hissed. "What are you waiting for, man?"

"Just trying to keep us alive," Nick said, and he followed Luis into a dark, narrow side passage. Nick could feel the uneven ground rising under his feet, and he called out to Luis to wait up.

Luis called back, "We're almost out!"

And then Nick felt a cool, fresh breeze blow across his face and saw a sliver of light ahead of them. *The exit.*

He picked up the pace, and within minutes, he was standing on a stone outcrop overlooking the island's coast and the blue-green water of the Caribbean.

Nick inhaled the fresh air and, squinting in the blazing sun, scanned the rocky outcrop. He spotted Luis by the edge. Luis pointed to a steep path going down the mountain. "We need to keep moving."

But before Nick could cross the rocky surface, the two Russians rushed out of the cave. One of the Russians had been hit, and his bleeding right arm dangled at his side. *At least he got one of the fuckers.*

The other Ivan leveled his weapon at them and shouted in a thick Russian accent, "Where is money!"

"Okay, okay," Nick said. He couldn't take a chance in getting the kid killed. *They could have their fucking dirty money.*

He set the briefcase down on the ground in front of him and said, "There's the money. Now let the kid go."

The wounded Russian, still clutching his gun in his right hand, shouted, "I kill you both, and I take the money."

Chapter Thirty-Three
Curaçao, Caribbean
December 2019

Nick felt the weight of the gun in his pocket and went for it. But before he could flip the safety latch and shoot, the wounded Russian raised his rifle and fired wildly at Nick. The rifle punched back against the Russian's injured arm, and he screamed in pain. Bullets flew in all directions, ricocheting against the stony outcrop and mountainside. Nick pushed Luis to the ground and threw himself on top of him. The Russian couldn't hold on to the rifle, and it skidded across the rocks into the foliage below.

Then, without warning, a distant crack sounded, and the Russian's scalp disintegrated into a reddish-gray pulp before he dropped to the ground. The other Russian scanned the horizon for the source of the sniper fire and then ran toward the opening of the cave.

Nick jumped out and, raising his Browning with both hands, squeezed off two shots.

The injured Russian toppled forward onto the ground, a pool of blood welling under him.

"Shit, man, you got him," Luis whispered. Luis seemed a lot older than when Nick first met him.

Nick pulled out a wad of hundred-dollar bills and shoved it at Luis. "Get the hell outta here."

Luis grabbed the cash and rushed to the entrance to the cave. Before disappearing into the cavernous black opening, Luis turned and called out, "Ten minutes down that path and you'll be on the highway."

Nick shoved his gun back into his pocket and considered his options. The sniper shot had come from the top of the stone outcrop that he was now sheltering against, and it was only a matter of time till the shooter spotted him. He had to make a dash to the path, but by running into the open, he risked a bullet in the back.

Nick had just decided to take his chances on the mountainside when a voice called out from above him, "Stay where you are, Mr. Martin. Don't move."

Nick looked up as a lanky man in a black baseball hat scrambled down the side of the mountain, holding tight to a high-powered sniper rifle.

"Nice shot," the sniper said.

Nick froze and stared stupidly at the man as he approached. There was something oddly familiar about the guy, but Nick couldn't place him.

The guy was not going to kill him. Nick knew that much. Otherwise, he would be dead.

Nick took a deep breath and said evenly, "I suppose I should thank you for saving my life."

"Don't thank me. You can thank my client. He's waiting for you."

Nick followed the sniper across the mountainside to an opening where a small, four-seat Robinson R44 helicopter sat waiting for them. The sniper got into the chopper, and Nick, still holding his briefcase, clambered in beside him.

The sniper gave a thumbs-up to the pilot, and the chopper spooled the engine and lifted off the ground.

"Where are we going?" Nick asked as the chopper continued to rise.

The stranger pointed at a white yacht in the distance, floating in the blue-green water of the Caribbean Sea. Minutes later, they were hovering over the small landing pad on the yacht's stern. The pilot set the chopper down with a slight bump, and Nick climbed out, briefcase in hand. He followed his new acquaintance down a set of stairs to the upper deck.

To Nick's amazement, Vladim Bulgarin was waiting for him.

"Welcome to Curaçao, Mr. Martin," he said, extending his hand.

Nick ignored Vladim's extended hand and said, "What the fuck is going on?"

Vladim motioned for Nick's escort to leave them. "Relax, Nick, relax. I saved your ass from Igor's goons. A little gratitude might be in order, yes?"

"No, I will not fucking relax," Nick spit out. "I almost died because of you and your Russian partners. Now you're telling me I should thank you?"

Vladim held up his hand and said, "Let me show you something." He undid his shirt, revealing a long red scar slashed across his chest. "A little present from Igor. You and I have something in common, my young friend: we both hate him."

Nick was silent as Vladim did up the buttons on his shirt.

"You look like you could use a drink. Come," Vladim said, and he led Nick down another set of stairs to a deck with a seating area and a well-stocked bar.

Vladim motioned to one of the leather club chairs. "Please sit. What would you like to drink?"

"A cold beer would be great," Nick said. He sat, placing the briefcase between his feet.

Vladim pulled two bottles of beer out of a bar fridge, opened one, and handed it to Nick.

Nick tipped the beer bottle back and, after nearly emptying it, said, "Why is Igor trying to kill me?"

"It's simple. You were supposed to spend the rest of your life in a Russian jail. But your friend Alex Greene intervened and brought in the State Department. Igor couldn't stop you from leaving Russia, so he tried to prevent you from setting foot on US soil again. The two Russians were supposed to kill you."

"You're telling me that Igor had this planned all along, and the US State Department went along with it?" Nick asked incredulously.

"Did you actually think that Russians would let you leave the country against Igor's wishes? You don't get it, my friend. Oligarchs like Igor run Russia. They control Putin and Putin's government. You Americans are so naive."

"Then Igor's not finished with me, is he?"

"No, Igor's not finished with you," Vladim said, chuckling slightly.

"Alex Greene was at the airport. What was her role in all of this?" Nick scratched his head. "She's the one who got me in the shit in the first place."

Vladim sat across from Nick. "You're missing the point. You fucked up by talking to—"

"I told Greene nothing."

"Maybe so, but she followed you to Igor's *dacha*. That is a little too close for comfort, as you Americans would say."

"That bitch. I knew she was trouble," Nick said.

Vladim scoffed. "Greene did her job. Without her, you would be rotting away in the fucking gulag for the rest of your life."

"And why Curaçao?"

"Simple. Russians basically own this island—as well as everyone on it. Customs and immigration checks do not apply to Russian nationals. There is no record of you ever entering Curaçao," Vladim said.

A look of relief crossed Nick's face. He had shot an unarmed man in the back, and if what Vladim said was true, he would get away with it. "So, you're working both sides of this?" he asked.

Vladim drained his bottle before answering. "I work for Igor, but he doesn't own me. I have my own reasons for being here."

"Well, how the hell am I going to get home?" Nick asked, pulling out his temporary visa. "This visa expires in six hours. And I need to call my wife."

"*Nichevo*, I can look after both of your problems," Vladim said. "There is a phone in your cabin. I've taken care of the travel documents." He signaled for a steward.

"William will take you to your cabin. You look like you could use a shower."

Nick stood up and grabbed the briefcase.

Vladim looked at the briefcase and then back at Nick. "That's Igor's money. It was meant for the two guys who tried to kill you. Keep it. You've earned it, my friend."

As soon as William had settled Nick into the spacious mahogany-paneled stateroom, complete with a king-size bed, wet bar, and flat-screen TV, Nick picked up the cabin phone and called Laura.

The phone rang once. Twice. Three times. Laura picked up on the fourth ring.

"Laura, it's me," Nick said. There was silence on the other end of the phone. "It's Nick."

"What do you want, Nick?"

"This is the first chance I've had to call you. When I explain what's happened to me, you won't believe it."

"Oh, I'll believe it," Laura said, her voice dripping with sarcasm. "And you better believe I want a divorce."

"What?"

"I was sent a video of you and that, uh—" Laura choked out a sob. "That little girl in Moscow. She's not much older than your own daughters. God, how could you?"

"What are you talking about? What video?" Nick stammered out.

"Don't bullshit me, Nick. You know what I'm talking about. You were in it."

Nick was too stunned to say anything. Then he remembered and felt instantly sick. "It was a setup—"

"A setup? That's all you can say? You disgust me!" Laura shouted.

"Laura, it's not what you think. I was framed. You've got to believe me," Nick said.

"Believe you?" she snorted. "Why would I believe you? You're a pathological liar."

"Honey, please," Nick pleaded. "Listen—"

"No"—Laura's voice turned very cold—"you need to listen. I sent your clothes to your office. Don't bother coming home. It's over, Nick."

The phone line went dead.

Nick sat on his bed and put his head in his hands. *This can't be happening,* he thought. *I'll talk to Laura when I get home. Once she hears what happened to me, she'll come around. She has to.*

A light tap on his door brought Nick back to reality.

"Come in," Nick called out.

William stepped into the cabin with a garment bag over his arm and said, "Mr. Bulgarin would like you to join him at eight o'clock. He has asked me to give you these clothes in case you wish to change before dinner. May I put them in your wardrobe?"

"Ahh, yes, please, go ahead."

Nick watched the steward hang the clothing in his closet. He marveled at the improbability of it all. Twenty-four hours ago, he was locked up in a stinking Russian jail with no prospect of ever getting out, and now he was being entertained on a hundred-million-dollar yacht.

And according to Vladim, he had Greene to thank for all of it. *Funny world.*

Now he needed to clean himself up and get his sorry ass on deck for dinner. Nick walked into the mirrored bathroom. He truly looked like shit. His greasy hair was matted with sweat, and God only knows what else. He hadn't shaved for weeks, and his teeth had a definite green veneer to them. Nick stripped down and tossed his stinking clothes out on the balcony.

He got into the shower and lathered his entire body over and over, scrubbing off the layers of grime. Then he shaved and brushed his teeth.

When he was finished, Nick surveyed himself in the mirror. The shower hadn't washed away either the black bags under his eyes or the new lines on his face, but he felt better.

Nick quickly sifted through the clothes that Vladim sent for him, settling on beige slacks and a white polo shirt. Vladim had included a suit, shirt, and tie—presumably for his trip back to the United States. He slipped on a pair of light-brown Gucci loafers. The clothing—including the shoes—fit surprisingly well.

He took his Russian castoffs from the balcony and put them outside the stateroom door in a laundry bag. They stank of sweat and death and Russian jails. He considered keeping those floppy, black shoes as a souvenir but decided against it. No one would believe what he had been through. Keeping the shoes would only make him look fucking nuts.

Nick hid Igor's briefcase under the bed and went up to the deck to join Vladim.

Vladim was waiting for Nick on the outer deck with a glass of red wine. The view of the sunset was magnificent: the sky shimmered with hues of burgundy, pink, and gold.

After a toast, Vladim said, "You're booked on a flight home tomorrow morning to Boston." He reached into his jacket's breast pocket and took out a navy-blue passport. "Have a look at your new identity."

Nick opened his new passport and recognized his picture from Houghton's website, but that was about it. "Who is Michael Halls?" Nick asked.

"He's a Canadian diplomat," Vladim said.

Once upon a time, Nick would have refused to participate in such a crass criminal scheme, but now things were different. He had killed a man and stolen from the Russian mafia.

Nick slid the passport into his back pocket. "Thanks."

Two waiters arrived with baked sea bass and set down the plates with a flourish. They deboned the fish and added generous portions of crispy fries and coleslaw to Nick's and Vladim's side plates.

Vladim raised his glass and said, "Nick, I have a proposition for you: come work for me."

Nick could not hide his irritation. "There is *no fucking way* that I am working with Igor."

"Obviously, you cannot work directly with Igor. However, I work for other oligarchs with businesses in the US. I could use someone with your experience on my team."

The job offer was unexpected and had caught Nick off guard.

Nick shook his head and said, "Igor wants me dead and you're offering me a job…"

Vladim cut him off. "Igor does not own me. I'll deal with Igor, do not worry about that."

"I'll think about it but right now all I want to do is go home," Nick responded.

"*Nichevo*," Vladim said, raising his glass again. "Take your time."

By the time Nick went to bed, it was nearly 3:00 a.m., and his mind was reeling with the events of the day.

In truth, the job offer was tempting, but Nick suspected that the majority of Vladim's contacts would be like Igor: oligarchs who had the regime's blessing to make their dirty money off the backs of average Russians. But he might not have a choice. Vladim's offer might be his only option.

Nick was just dropping off to sleep when he heard a soft knock at the door.

He got up and pulled the briefcase out from under the bed. He took out his gun and, releasing the safety, walked to the door. With the gun raised, he called out, "Who is it?"

"Vladim sent me," a soft feminine voice replied.

"Just a minute," Nick said. He shoved the gun into a drawer and opened the door.

A woman with long, curly dark hair stood in a white silk bathrobe, which was loosely draped around her naked body. "My name is Pia. Vladim thought you might be lonely. May I join you?"

Nick smiled and ushered the young woman into the room. "Please, come in."

The woman took Nick's hand and padded slowly across the carpeting of the stateroom. She pushed Nick down on the bed and pulled off his boxer shorts. Then she undid her bathrobe and let it drop to the floor. Nick marveled at her firm breasts and stomach, her fully shaved pubis, and pierced labia minora.

She lay down beside him and took his face in her hands before giving him a long, soft kiss. She smelled faintly of coconut oil.

Nick crawled on top of her. *Vladim really had thought of everything.*

Chapter Thirty-Four
Boston, Massachusetts
December 2019

Michael Halls breezed through US Customs and Border Protection at Logan Airport without a second glance from the armed officials. Briefcase in hand, Nick walked across the busy arrivals concourse and headed straight for the limo stand. He climbed in the back of the first car in the line and gave the driver his office address. He had nowhere else to go. Home was not an option; Laura had been clear about that.

Twenty minutes later, Nick stepped off the elevator and went into his office. He groaned softly when he saw the suitcases sitting in the corner. True to her word, Laura had sent his clothes over.

Within minutes, Kristen was knocking on his door. "You're back! What the hell happened, Nick? Everyone's looking for you. Mihkel said you were staying on in Moscow to work with the client and not to bother you but that made no sense. I covered for you as best I could, but you put me in a very difficult position."

He had put *her* in a difficult position? *That was special.* She had no idea what he had just gone through.

Before Nick could say anything, there was a tentative knock at his door, and Stefan walked in.

"So, you *are* back," Stefan said. "There were some crazy stories going around about you in Moscow, but—"

Nick cut him off. "Is Mihkel in?"

"Yeah, but he's been hunkered down in his office—he's not talking to anyone."

"What do you want, Stefan?" Nick asked.

"We're good with the SEC," Stefan said, taking a seat. "Once they saw the mortality tables, they backed off on their Ponzi concerns. We're filing the final prospectus later today."

"I don't remember asking you to sit down," Nick said, glaring at Stefan.

"I wanted to update you," Stefan said.

"Cut the bullshit. You want the lowdown on Moscow," Nick spat out.

"You don't need to be so rude, Nick," Stefan said defensively. He got up and walked out, slamming the door behind him.

After Stefan left, Kristen asked, "Was that really necessary?" Kristen's tone was unexpected. Over the years, she'd been nothing but loyal to Nick, and now she was taking Stefan's side.

Nick didn't have the energy to take her on. "You're probably right, but I've had a really bad few weeks."

"That's okay," Kristen said, but the look on her face was far from sympathetic.

As she turned to leave, Nick said, "Can you please do me a major favor? I need a suite at the Hyatt Regency for a few nights." He looked over at the suitcases. "And I need that luggage sent over to the hotel."

"I'll make the reservation and send your bags over." She didn't ask any questions, and he was grateful for that.

"And I'll need a new cell and a laptop."

"Will do," Kristen said.

"And tell Vivian I need to see Mihkel."

"Right away," Kristen said and left.

Nick had thought long and hard on the flight home about how to handle Mihkel. He wanted to punch his lights out, but he knew that would end his career at Houghton & Willis. Nick had made major sacrifices for the firm, and he wasn't going to throw it all away because of that fucker. *Mihkel would have to make good or face the consequences.*

Nick looked at the framed photo of Laura and the girls on his desk. He knew he had to call Laura, but he was dreading it. He picked up his landline and dialed the familiar digits of his home phone number.

"Hello?" Laura answered after a few rings.

"Don't hang up," Nick implored.

"What do you want, Nick?" Laura asked. Her voice was flat.

"I wanted to thank you for sending my things," Nick said.

"I said, what do you want?"

"I know I've made mistakes, but I was set up in Moscow. It wasn't my fault."

"Nick, we're done," Laura said.

"Laura, please!" Nick pleaded.

"Don't call again. If you want to see the girls, call my attorney." Laura sighed heavily into the phone. "My attorney has the Moscow tape. I don't want to use it, Nick, but I will," she said and hung up.

Nick set the phone down and stared off into space for a minute before punching in Kristen's line. "Did you tell Vivian I wanted to see Mihkel?" Nick asked.

Kristen's response was icy. "I gave her the message."

"Thank you," Nick said and hung up.

***

Vivian looked up and said, "Hello, Mr. Martin. It's good to have you back."

"Thank you. Is Mihkel in?"

"I gave him your message, Mr. Martin, but Mr. Ivanov does not want to be disturbed. Perhaps I could make an appointment for you?"

Nick strode past her desk.

"Mr. Martin! Please do not go in there!" Vivian said, standing up behind her desk. "Mr. Ivanov will be very upset."

"Don't worry, Vivian, I'll tell him you tried to stop me," Nick said, opening Mihkel's office door.

Mihkel was seated behind his desk, staring out the window, a glass of scotch in his hands. "It's okay, Vivian," he said. "Close the door behind you."

Vivian cast an anxious glance at the two men and left. Mihkel turned to Nick. "So, you finally made it back." Even though it was only midafternoon, Mihkel's eyes were bloodshot, and he was slurring his words.

Without giving Nick a chance to answer, Mihkel nodded at the bottle of scotch on his desk. "Drink?"

Nick's face turned red. "I didn't come here for a drink, you asshole. You set me up with Igor, and then you fucking left me to rot in a Russian prison," he growled.

"Look, sit down and cool your jets, buddy boy."

"Cool my jets? Do you have any fucking idea what I've been through?"

Mihkel glared at Nick. "Lower your fucking voice and sit the fuck down, or I'll call security."

Mihkel waited for Nick to sit before he continued. "I had no fucking choice. I had to come back to Boston to clean up your mess."

"Clean up my mess?" Nick said, his voice strained. "*My* mess? That's bullshit. How did this become my mess?"

"Well, you were supposed to get those fucking consents, weren't you? I had Stefan do a little research, you motherfucker, and we have the consents for our other life settlement funds. You fucked up, little buddy."

Nick took a deep breath. He fought to control the blinding rage building in his chest, but Mihkel was right. Nick had never been responsible for getting the consents directly before on a file; that kind of detail work was below his pay grade. But he'd never gone out before as broker of record and negotiated the purchase of insurance policies. Now his lack of attention to detail was fucking him up. His brain screamed for someone to blame—Stefan, the clerks, others on the file—but he knew the buck stopped with him, and unless Mihkel could save his sorry ass, he was finished.

"But that's all water under the bridge. Stefan has taken care of the consents, and we're waiting on final clearance from the SEC. Done and dusted," Mihkel said, taking another generous gulp of his drink. "You shouldn't have talked to Greene. I warned you."

"You warned me about Greene? That's all you can say, you son of a bitch?" Nick was close to blowing again.

"You got out alive, didn't you?" Mihkel chuckled softly. "Heard from Vladim this morning. He told me about what happened down in Curaçao, you playing James fucking Bond in the caves or something."

"What else did Vladim tell you?" Nick exhaled. "Did you know about the hotel?"

Mihkel smirked and took a second glass out of his desk drawer, poured a drink, and pushed it in Nick's direction.

Despite his earlier protestations, Nick picked up the glass and took a long sip. Hate for Mihkel, the Russians, and the firm welled in his chest, threatening to suffocate him. But Mihkel was his only way out and he needed his support. He took a deep breath and continued, "I've been to hell and back. I need a little sugar here, Mihkel, or…"

Mihkel rolled his eyes. "Or what? If anything comes out about Moscow, it will look bad for only you—no one else."

Nick knew Mihkel was right. *Without Mihkel he was fucked.*

"Look, Nick, you've taken a big hit for the team, and I've made sure the management committee knows it.

I briefed the partners this morning. I told them everything—and I mean *everything*," Mihkel said.

"Everything? I don't believe you."

Mihkel took another drink of his scotch. "The management committee knows you saved the deal. They've agreed to appoint you as an ad hoc member of the management committee as a reward. You'll get an office here on the thirty-third floor with the rest of the management partners. I cut a sweet deal for your future comp, including a major cut of the fees on the Prosperity file. You're going to piss yourself when you see the size of your bonus. Houghton was personally going to tell you the news, but he's on vacation."

Mihkel downed his drink.

Nick was speechless for a moment. This was more than he ever could have hoped for. He stammered out, "Th-thank you." Nick wasn't expecting this. Mihkel had blindsided him. *Again.*

"Now get the fuck out of my office. And you didn't hear it from me," Mihkel said, turning in his chair toward the floor-to-ceiling view of the Atlantic.

Nick left Mihkel's office and nodded at Vivian.

She smiled and said, "Congratulations, Mr. Martin."

Nick gave her a perfunctory "thank you" before taking the elevator down.

That fucking Mihkel. He pulled it off.

Despite the suspicious deaths and the fucking Russian mafia backers, the Prosperity Fund would go public.

Better still, Houghton & Willis would make out like bandits on the legal fees. Mihkel really was a fucking

Houdini. On his way back, Nick stopped by Kristen's desk and asked her to come into his office; he needed to speak to her.

"Give me five," she replied tersely.

Nick gave her a sideways glance. Normally, Kristen would have jumped up and followed him to his office. *Now she was all attitude.*

After a few minutes, Kristen shuffled into his office and put his new iPhone and laptop on his desk. "The passwords are the same."

"Thanks. Do you want to sit down for a minute? I had a very interesting meeting with Mihkel," Nick said, and he told her about his promotion.

"That's great for you, I guess," Kristen said without enthusiasm. "Is that all?"

"Yeah, I guess," Nick said, disappointed at her lackluster response. "That's it."

Kristen got up and asked, "Door open or closed?"

Nick responded without looking up, "Open."

After Kristen left his office, Nick shook his head. Laura wasn't speaking to him, and Kristen was giving him the cold shoulder. He could not seem to please the women in his life.

He allowed himself to think for a moment about Jennifer; she would have been pleased with his promotion. *But she wasn't alive, was she?* Nick shook off her memory.

Nick could feel the familiar tightness in his chest. What if Igor still had a price on his head?

He didn't think that Igor would go after him in the US, but who knew? *The guy was a fucking lunatic.*

Nick unlocked the bottom drawer of his desk and took out a Beretta M9 still in its holster. He had to leave the Browning in Curaçao; not even a Canadian diplomat could get a gun through security. He stuck the gun into the side pocket of the briefcase of cash. He needed to get the money somewhere safe—and fast.

Nick opened his new laptop and clicked on the Outlook icon. The onslaught of emails that he expected to see hadn't materialized. There were, however, several urgent emails from Horner dating back weeks. He opened the most recent one first. There was an international warrant out for Nick's arrest, and Horner had fired him. Attached to the email was a final account from Horner's firm, which conveniently ate up the entire hundred-thousand-dollar advance retainer Nick had given him.

Nice fucking touch.

Chapter Thirty-Five
Boston, Massachusetts
December 2019

Alex had worked hard to get Nick out of that Moscow jail and back to the States, and the detour through Curaçao had been extremely inconvenient. She needed to establish a direct connection between Igor Dimitrov and the Prosperity Fund to void the transfers of the insurance policies to the fund—and only Nick Martin could do that for her. Dimitrov, the backer of the Prosperity Fund, was a known member of the Russian mafia, and that clearly had not been disclosed to Basel Re when they agreed to assume responsibility for the insurance policies owned by the fund. That would be enough to end the fund's entitlement to the death benefits.

She and Max had flown back to Boston and set up shop again at the Basel Re townhouse in Beacon Hill. They were hoping to pick Nick up when his flight from the Vnukovo Airport arrived at Logan. When Nick's plane did not arrive, Max hacked into Nick's home phone account and identified a recent call from an offshore cell. Next, Max tracked down its location, and lo and behold, they found Nick Martin—on a yacht moored outside of Willemstad in Curaçao. Max showed Alex a slightly delayed satellite livestream with Nick standing on the upper deck next to someone who looked like Vladim Bulgarin.

But they had lost Nick again the next morning when the livestream showed no sign of him on the boat.

Max had no good explanation when they discovered the backup had failed, and Alex guessed that Nick would be on a flight to the United States. Max checked the travel manifests for flights out of Curaçao; however, Nick's name did not appear on any of them.

They had no choice but to wait. Alex was sure that sooner or later, Nick would resurface and call home or his office. Alex's hunch paid off when Nick called home from his landline on the thirtieth floor.

Nick didn't notice Alex until she walked up beside him and said, "Leaving early, Mr. Martin?"

Nick instinctively tightened his grip on the metal briefcase. "Leave me alone!" he choked out.

"I need to talk to you," Alex said.

"Talking to you got me into a lot of trouble," Nick said, taking a step back.

Alex nodded at the black Mercedes parked across the street. "My car's right here, so why don't you get in?"

Nick started to walk away, but Alex grabbed him by the arm. "Igor Dimitrov is not going to give up till you're dead. You need me."

Nick shook free of her grasp and looked around. "Okay, okay." He followed Alex, keeping his head down.

They got into the sedan, and Alex asked, "We'll drive you home. You live out in Weston, right?"

"I'm not going home. I'm staying at the Hyatt Regency on Lafayette. But I bet you already knew that."

Alex called out to her driver, "Hear that, Max?"

"Yes, ma'am," Max said, easing the big car into the late afternoon traffic.

"What do you want from me?" Nick said, staring straight ahead.

"It's pretty simple," Alex said. "Igor Dimitrov and his KGB buddies are backing the Prosperity Fund. You know it, and I know it. But I need hard proof."

Nick looked out the window and cursed himself for getting into Alex's car.

"I need an affidavit from you that sets out the relationship between the Prosperity Fund and Dimitrov. Otherwise, I will go to Cece with what I know."

Waves of abject panic formed deep inside Nick and spread throughout his body. He shifted as far away from Alex as he could get. Cece had canceled the warrant for Nick's arrest after an individual who was "known by the police" came forward and admitted to pushing Paul in a drug-addled haze. The weird thing was that Cece hadn't even asked Nick to ID the guy. No doubt Mihkel had worked his back channels and made it all go away.

Alex's voice broke through Nick's thoughts. "I got you out of that stinking Russian jail, and now it's payback time."

"Payback? Talking to you is what got me in that fucking jail in the first place."

"Please. You're working with Russian mafia. Blame them," Alex responded.

"I'm not giving you that affidavit."

"What have you got to lose? Igor already has every hitman on the planet on your tail. And don't tell me you didn't know that the Prosperity Fund's insureds were dropping like flies."

"What are you talking about?" Nick asked. *Is Greene just fishing, or does she actually know something?*

"These are people that you personally signed up, Nick," Alex said.

"Let me out!" Nick demanded, the panic rising in his voice. He reached down for the aluminum briefcase and computer bag at his feet and pulled them up on his lap.

"Relax, Nick, we're at your hotel," Alex said as the car pulled up in front of the Hyatt Regency.

A doorman rushed forward to open the car door, but it was locked.

Nick tried the door. He couldn't open it either.

Alex reached across Nick to unlock the door. Nick could smell her perfume and feel her breasts brush against him as she released the lock.

"Kiddie lock," she said, smiling.

Nick scrambled out of the car, dropping the metal briefcase in the process. The hardback case skidded across the street and ended up at the feet of a porter. Nick grabbed the case and disappeared through the hotel's revolving door.

Nick was waiting in the check-in line when he heard his name being called. He turned and found himself face-to-face with Alex's driver.

"You left your phone in the car."

Nick looked at his returned cell. It had been in the inside pocket of his suit jacket. *How the hell did it fall out?*

When Nick looked up, Max had disappeared in the lobby crowd.

Suddenly, Nick felt very lightheaded and couldn't catch his breath. Did Greene really think he would sign that affidavit? It would be both a violation of solicitor-client privilege and the end of his legal career. It was also a certain death sentence.

Nick tried to focus on the lineup ahead of him, but he couldn't leave his stress behind. It was all too much: first Russia, then Curaçao. And now Greene on his ass.

Nick's legs were trembling as he scanned the hotel lobby for a place to sit down. He spotted a lobby chair near the front door and, clutching his briefcase, walked over. He sat down heavily and willed himself to breathe. *Breathe in, breathe out; breathe in, breathe out.* It took a few minutes, but Nick finally calmed down enough to call over a nearby porter.

Nick glanced at the employee's name tag. "Maddie? My name is Nick Martin. Can you arrange my check-in and get my luggage to my suite? My assistant sent my bags over earlier today." He slipped Maddie a hundred-dollar bill and his business card.

It didn't take long before Maddie returned, pulling his two suitcases. "Follow me, sir," she said and quickly whisked him upstairs to his suite.

After handing Maddie another hundred bucks and sending her on her way, Nick sat on the couch, kicked off Vladim's loafers, and drank three small bottles of scotch from the minibar in rapid succession.

What if Alex Greene was right? What if the Russians were killing off the insureds? The strategy of putting younger, healthy people in the Prosperity pool of insurance policies had never made sense to Nick, but he'd signed them up without asking questions.

There was one way to find out: hack into the Prosperity account. The mortality data would be on the Prosperity intranet, and he could see for himself if Alex was bullshitting him.

Nick opened his new laptop and clicked on the Prosperity login page. He was locked out of it, but he wanted to try logging on with someone else's credentials. He had only two tries per account; the third failure would result in the account being frozen and a password reset notice would be sent by email to the account holder.

After trying everyone on the team with no luck, Nick sat back and drank another small bottle of scotch.

He hadn't tried Paul's username and password. By rights, Paul's access should have been disabled, but Nick had nothing else. He entered Paul's username, and Paul's account came up, asking for a password. Nick tried *grimreaper* and *angelofdeath*, but neither worked.

Then Nick had a sudden jolt of inspiration. His fingers tapped quickly across the laptop's keyboard: *deathfund.*

There was a pause and Paul's welcome page popped up on the screen. Nick could not believe his luck.

After a few minutes, he found the file labeled *Mortality Data*, which contained a spreadsheet with rows of alphabetized names of insureds detailing their ages, preexisting conditions, death benefit, and the date and cause of death.

Shivers ran up and down Nick's backbone as he reviewed the spreadsheets. The Prosperity Fund had made claims on thirty-five life insurance policies within the last four-week period. The thirty-five claims were a small portion of the total policies owned by the fund but still significant, if only because they were all from a younger, healthier cohort. Nick had connected the dots, and now he could see it for himself—someone was killing insureds to increase revenues for the Prosperity Fund.

With a sinking feeling, Nick realized he had signed up all the dead insureds during his three-month-long road trip. Nick scanned the intranet for the Viatical Act consents, but he couldn't find them. Nick shook his head. Slack-ass Stefan probably hadn't gotten around to uploading them.

Nick grabbed an external hard drive from his bag and stuck it into one of the laptop's USB ports. He then copied the entire Prosperity intranet onto the hard drive.

After that, Nick highlighted all the file folders in the Prosperity intranet and deleted them. Now he had the only record of the files.

Nick flipped open the aluminum briefcase and placed the flash drive in the side pocket, along with his fake passport. Nick called the front desk, and the manager on duty confirmed they would keep Nick's briefcase overnight in their safe. He took it downstairs and left it with the night manager. Maddie, the young porter, approached him as he waited for the elevator on his way back to his room. "Good evening, Mr. Martin," she said, smiling.

Nick smiled back.

"I hope you are enjoying your stay with us."

"Yes, I am so far, Maddie," Nick said. "Thanks for your help earlier. I'm afraid I was a bit jet-lagged. I've been traveling a lot, and I'm exhausted."

"Well, if there's anything else that I can do for you, and I mean anything, you can reach me at the number on this card." She pressed a midnight-blue card with *Dream Dates* prominently displayed on it into his hand. Nick slipped the card into his pocket.

"Thank you, Maddie, I will," Nick said, smiling. He had fingered her to be a college student—not a pimp.

"Have a good night," Maddie said, and she returned to her station by the door.

Chapter Thirty-Six
Boston, Massachusetts
December 2019

Nick woke up with a start the next morning and looked around the bedroom of his suite at the Hyatt. He was safe and sound back in the States; the nightmare in Russia was over. He showered, got dressed for work, and ordered room service. He grabbed the complimentary newspaper outside his hotel room, sat down on the couch, and scanned his texts and emails. There was only one text and it was from Kristen, saying that their office move to the thirty-third floor was scheduled for that morning and he should not come in until later in the afternoon. *What the fuck would he do till then?*

Nick checked his emails, but found none related to billable work. His email flow had been reduced to junk advertisements, legal notices, and office announcements. He had been cut out of the Prosperity file for weeks, and Mihkel had not sent him any new work. He considered going to his sports club to work out, but he found himself fingering Maddie's blue business card. The thought of a morning fuck was making him hard.

Nick texted the number on the card to inquire about availability. To Nick's surprise, he got an immediate reply. His date could be there within the hour.

Nick ordered coffee and was reading the *Boston Herald* when he heard a knock on his door. When he answered, a young, curvy blonde in her early twenties introduced herself as Jenna.

Jenna gave him a soft kiss on the mouth and walked past him into the suite, her ponytail swinging as she moved. She wore jeans, a short leather jacket, and running shoes; she also wore no makeup, to Nick's surprise.

Jenna threw her jacket on a chair and said, "Give me ten minutes." After a quick rinse in the shower, she reappeared—buck naked and gleaming—at the double doors to the bedroom.

"Let's do it!" She threw herself on the unmade bad. She spread her labia with her left hand and crooked her right index finger, beckoning Nick.

Nick walked to the bed, shedding his clothes on the way, and mounted Jenna.

After getting his bones properly bounced, Nick took Jenna for a long walk along the Boston Harbor trail, and they ended up at Legal Sea Foods on Long Wharf for an extended lunch. The morning with Jenna had set Nick back nearly three grand, but it had been worth it.

Nick got to work just after three, but when he stepped off the elevator on the thirty-third floor, he realized that he didn't know where his new office was located.

He walked up to Vivian's station and said, "Sorry to bother you, but I'm looking for Kristen."

"And your new office, I'm guessing," Vivian said, smiling. "Fifth door on the left. Kristen is in there now."

"Thank you," Nick said.

When he walked into his new office, Kristen looked up at him with a wide grin and, with a sweeping motion of her arms, said, "Come on in. These are your new digs."

"Looks like you're making real progress."

"Yeah, things happen fast around here when you get a promotion like this," Kristen said. "I've met with Tina in HR, and she told me about my new comp package."

"Sweet," Nick said, pleased the old Kristen was back. The move to the management floor was a promotion for them both, and she must have finally realized it.

"Tina also gave me the paperwork for your promotion. It's on your desk," Kristen said, nodding toward his new sleek and modern furniture. "Stan from IT just left. He set up your VOIP and desktop computer. You're good to go. By the way, an email about your promotion to the management committee went out overnight from Mihkel. It's very flattering. You should read it," Kristen said. "It's official: you're now one of them."

Nick forced a short laugh and opened his Outlook. Kristen had flagged Mihkel's announcement and a couple of emails from other members of the management committee congratulating him on his promotion. Nick archived them to read later.

As he scrolled through his inbox, an email from Laura's divorce attorney caught his attention. It had the predictable threatening language. *Another nail in the coffin for his marriage.*

Kristen had also red-flagged an email from Vladim, who wanted to know when Houghton & Willis was getting a comfort letter over to the underwriters.

Nick ignored the email; he had no idea what was going on with the closing, and he wanted to keep it that way.

Nick was reviewing his new compensation package when there was a timid knock on his door.

"Hey, Nick," said Stefan. "Sorry to interrupt you, but Kristen's not at her desk. Can I talk to you about something?"

"Sure, come in," Nick said, frowning. *What does this fucker want now?*

"By the way, congratulations on the promotion," Stefan said.

"Thanks. What's up?"

"We had a little problem with the Prosperity intranet last night," Stefan said nervously. "It crashed, and we lost everything. The tech guys are working on recovery right now, but it's going to take a while."

Nick's face involuntarily flushed. "What happened?"

"IT thinks it's sabotage. Someone used Paul Field's password and deleted everything. The Russians are not happy, and neither is Mihkel."

Nick resisted a smirk and said disingenuously, "Well, that's too bad."

"The good news is I had all the drafts of the prospectus on my desktop. We can file the final version as soon as we finalize the comfort letter. I prepared one for Mihkel's signature, but he refused to sign. He said to ask you." Stefan handed Nick a letter addressed to the lead underwriter.

Nick glanced at the standard "comfort" wording in the letter, which stated that nothing in the prospectus would cause Houghton & Willis to believe that it contained an untrue statement or omission that would make the disclosure misleading or inaccurate.

Nick gave Stefan a dirty look. He didn't like where this was going. Nick hadn't read the final prospectus, but he presumed it did not mention the Russian mafia backers.

"I'm not signing this fucking letter. Mihkel cut me out of the file weeks ago," Nick said. "Can you please communicate that to Mihkel for me?"

"You can tell Mihkel yourself. He's just down the hall," Stefan said sarcastically.

"Fuck you, Stefan," Nick said to Stefan's back as he walked out of Nick's office.

But Nick could not stop the wave of crushing anxiety from spreading across his chest. Nick didn't give a shit if the prospectus died—this was not one that he would take for the team.

Nick banged out an email to Mihkel, copying Stefan: *I'M NOT SIGNING THE PROSPERITY FUND'S COMFORT LETTER.*

Chapter Thirty-Seven
Boston, Massachusetts
December 2019

A few blocks from the Hyatt Regency where Nick was staying, Wolfman crouched low on the gravel rooftop overlooking a row of Beacon Hill townhouses illuminated by historic gas lights lining the street. He had carefully mounted his rifle on the stationary stand, focused the scope, and now waited patiently for his target. He only had a few moments to make the shot, and he was ready. In the distance, the brightly lit skyscrapers shimmered in the crisp, cold air. He exhaled a stream of hot breath and checked his watch again; it was 3:00 a.m. Few people were on the street at this hour. Even fewer cars were driving by, only a couple of cabs dropping off fares.

Wolfman studied the landscape. If the intelligence supplied by his client was any good, the nondescript two-story brownstone directly below him would become Alex Greene's final resting place. The building was unremarkable. It looked like every other townhouse in this upscale neighborhood.

Wolfman didn't want to kill Alex. He had tried to warn her off, but she hadn't listened.

He thought back to that night in Barcelona with her.

They had spent only five or six hours together, but he had thought about her over the years. Now he was poised to take her out. Killing her was a waste of life, but it wasn't his call. He had a job to do.

Four hours later, a black Mercedes sedan pulled up in front of the townhouse. He aimed his rifle and carefully chambered a round, yanking back on the bolt before adjusting his sniper scope one last time. The driver walked around the car to open the back door for Alex. Wolfman took a deep breath and pulled back on the trigger, but before he could shoot, he felt a gun press into the back of his head. "Put the rifle down, Joshua, and then put your hands on your head."

Joshua gently set the rifle down beside him. "Alex, so nice to see you again."

"I said put your fucking hands on your fucking head," Alex hissed.

"Come now, Alex. We both know you are not going to kill me," Joshua said, but he raised his hands, keeping his back to her.

Alex took a step back. "I wouldn't be so sure about that, Joshua, but you gave me a chance in London. I'd like to return the favor."

"Oh, we're negotiating, are we?" Joshua asked, attempting to stand up.

"Don't move," Alex said and aggressively shoved the gun into the back of Joshua's head. "Walk away from the contract, and I'll let you live."

"You know it doesn't work that way, Alex. It's either me or someone else. I would have made sure you didn't suffer."

"Talk is cheap, Joshua. I'm the one with the gun now."

"No backup, Alex?" Joshua glanced at the only door to the roof. "That's not very smart."

Hearing something rustle behind her, Alex instinctively turned her head.

That was all Joshua needed. Leaping to his feet, he whirled around and kicked Alex hard—driving her against a brick chimney and knocking the gun out of her hand.

Alex recovered quickly and launched a roundhouse kick that knocked Joshua backward.

Alex said forcefully, "I'm asking you to stand down."

"Not happening," Joshua said, driving a left cross at Alex's face.

Alex ducked and came up with an undercut, scoring a solid blow under Joshua's chin that sent him reeling.

Suddenly a shot cracked through the dark night, and Joshua dropped onto the graveled rooftop.

Alex spun around, and when she turned back, Joshua was gone.

"Where did he go?" Max said as he rushed over to the edge of the roof. "I can't believe that I missed him at such close range."

"Relax, he was a moving target," Alex said, joining Max at the edge. A zip line ran down to the adjacent rooftop. "But you get only one chance with a guy like Wolfman, and we fucked it up. Next time, he won't miss."

***

Joshua took a moment to look back. Max and Alex were standing on the edge of the roof, peering into the darkness. They hadn't spotted him. Workman couldn't keep the grin off his face. He hadn't had this much fun in years.

Chapter Thirty-Eight
Boston, Massachusetts
December 2019

It quickly became obvious to Nick that his move to the thirty-third floor would not save his bacon at Houghton. Sure, he was on the management committee, but without new billable work, he was a dead man walking. At least he was still head of the life settlement group. But Mihkel controlled the life settlement workflow, and he was pushing that work to Murphy. Maybe Murphy would throw him a bone. Nick had left Murphy several emails and voice messages, but given she was ignoring him, Nick decided that a face-to-face might be in order. He took the stairs to the thirtieth floor and knocked on her door.

Out of nowhere, Karla's assistant appeared and blocked his entry. "You can't go in there. Ms. Murphy is busy."

Nick wondered what would happen if he pushed past her and walked in. The old Nick would have done that, but now he needed Karla. "Can you tell Karla that I dropped by to speak to her?"

"Of course," the assistant said, but she remained by Karla's door until Nick was gone.

On the way to the elevator, Nick stuck his head into Stefan's office. "What's happening with the comfort letter?"

"I signed it myself."

"You can't sign it. You're not a partner," Nick said.

"That's why Mihkel made me one."

"He *what?*"

"He made me a partner," Stefan smirked.

"Mihkel can't just make you a partner, Stefan," Nick said, feeling the blood rise to his cheeks. "It has to go through the management committee. What are you even talking about?"

"I guess he can because I'm now a partner," Stefan said, his eyes glinting. "I signed it this morning and sent it over to the lead underwriter."

"That's great, Stefan," Nick said. "Just great." Trust Mihkel to make Stefan a partner to get a fucking comfort letter signed. Nick had to hand it to Mihkel. He had dodged another bullet.

"We filed the final prospectus with the SEC, and we're waiting on the final receipt. It's all good," Stefan said proudly.

Nick went back to his office and logged into the management committee intranet. There had been an emergency meeting convened by Mihkel the evening before to discuss Stefan's appointment as partner. Nick rechecked his emails: he had no meeting notification.

Nick gritted his teeth as he read the recorded minutes. All the other partners had attended in person except for Robert Houghton, who participated by phone. After confirming quorum, Mihkel informed the committee that Stefan had to be made a partner so he could sign the comfort letter to close the Prosperity offering. Only Stefan was in a position to sign it, Mihkel had explained, because there was no one else at Houghton's with personal knowledge of the disclosure in the prospectus.

Mihkel also updated the committee on the firm's exposure regarding the failure to get the consents required by the Viatical Act. Mihkel had consulted with the Russians and, rather than hold up the finalization of the prospectus and the payout of the funds raised under the prospectus, they had opted to proceed without the consents. As long as Houghton finalized the offering, the Russians would not sue them for negligence. And Mihkel had that in writing.

Nick shook his head. *No wonder he had not been invited to the meeting.*

Nick was considering his next move when Kristen walked into the office. "Vivian called. Mihkel wants to see you right now."

Mihkel was waiting for him in his office. "Sorry, buddy, there's no nice way to say this: Karla Murphy is now the head of life settlement."

Nick looked at Mihkel with disbelief. "You can't—"

"I can, and I have. Accept it and move on."

"What the fuck?"

"It's effective immediately," Mihkel said with a dismissive gesture.

"I built the life settlement practice with my sweat and blood. And you're going to put someone else in charge of my group? Does the management committee know about this?"

"Of course they know. It's been in the works for a while. It's part of our new diversity planning. We need more pussy in management," Mihkel said, laughing at his own crude joke and lighting up a Don Arturo. "Look, want some friendly advice?"

Nick seethed silently.

"Stop harassing Murphy, *comprende*? You don't need that on your record too. I can only protect you so far."

"On my record? What the fuck are you talking about, Mihkel?" *How dare this hypocritical bastard accuse me of harassing Karla.*

Mihkel turned in his chair and looked out the window. "We're done here."

Nick was dismissed.

Chapter Thirty-Nine
Boston, Massachusetts
December 2019

Back in his office, Nick stared at his blank computer screen for a few minutes. Mihkel had been planning this for a while. Karla's new role had been in the cards before he even went to Moscow. That fucker had used him in Moscow. And Murphy, that two-faced bitch, was probably in on it too. With a pounding heart, he dialed Vladim's cell.

"Hello, Mr. Martin," Vladim answered after a couple of rings. "Congratulations on closing the Prosperity Fund offering. Igor and his partners are very happy."

"They should be." The stock had opened that morning at $110 a unit, and by noon, it had risen to $134.

"So, my young friend, you didn't call me to talk about Prosperity's trading price. Have you decided to come and work for me?"

"I'm very interested, Vladim, but I need more information. I won't go back to Russia."

"Don't worry, you won't have to. I work out of Dubrovnik," he chuckled. "I am at my villa on the Adriatic right now. Come for a visit, and we can discuss your new role. I can arrange for my jet to pick you up."

Very impressive. "I have a few things to clear up, but I'll text you with my availability in the next couple of days."

"Don't wait too long, my friend," Vladim said and hung up.

Vladim's offer was looking like his only option, but Nick had unfinished business in Boston. For starters, he was waiting on the numbers for the bonus that Mihkel had promised him. Bonuses were paid at the end of January, and if Mihkel got wind that he was leaving, Nick wouldn't see a dime. Nick had no choice but to keep Vladim on the back burner until then.

Nick also had personal business to sort out. His relationship with Laura and the girls was a train wreck. He'd been back in town for a week, and Laura still hadn't let him see his daughters. He looked at his watch; it was close to 3:00 p.m.—almost the end of the school day.

Nick texted Laura: *Picking up the girls after school. Will bring them straight home.*

When he arrived at his girls' private school on the outskirts of Boston, he checked his cell, but there was nothing from Laura.

Odd, he thought. *Laura's being reasonable for once.* He went and stood by the front doors and waited for his daughters to walk out.

Neena came out first, but Nicole wasn't far behind. Nick gave each a big hug. Holding their hands, he had started walking with them toward the parking lot when the bus monitor jogged over and called out to the girls.

The girls pulled away.

Nicole, looking up at her father nervously, said, "Daddy, Mom said we have to go home on the bus."

Flustered, Nick turned to the bus monitor. "What's going on here?"

Ignoring Nick, the bus monitor said to the girls, "Neena and Nicole, can you please wait with me until Mrs. Stornoway gets here?"

Before they could answer, an overweight woman walked up to Nick and extended her hand. "I'm Principal Stornoway. I don't believe we've met."

Sensing an ambush, Nick ignored her extended hand.

"I know who you are. I'm here to pick up my daughters."

"I just got off the phone with your wife, Mr. Martin. Unless you have a court order, the girls must get on the bus."

Neena looked up at Nick. "Dad, can we please get on the bus?" She started to cry.

Nick was suckered, and he knew it. The girls were not going with him. Nick kissed them both on the forehead and said goodbye, trying not to cry himself.

Nick had just opened his car door when he heard a familiar voice call out his name. He whirled around and came face-to-face with Alex Greene.

"What the fuck are you doing here?" Nick said. "How did you find me?"

Then it dawned on him. He pulled out his cell and waved it at Alex. "You needed my new cell number, didn't you? That's how you tracked me here. It didn't fall out of my pocket, you took it."

"You're quite the detective, Nick," Alex said derisively.

Nick leaned into the SUV and opened the console between the seats.

"Your gun isn't there. I've got it," Alex said, patting her purse. "Pretty fucking desperate move. What were you going to do? Start a shootout at your kids' school?"

Nick turned, red-faced, and shouted, "What do you want from me?"

"Lower your voice for starters," Alex said, nodding in the direction of the school steps, where the principal was still conferring with the bus monitor. "I'm here to tell you I've wrapped up my investigation, and I'm leaving town."

"You're doing what?" Nick asked.

Alex reached into her Gucci bag.

Nick, fearing the worst, stepped back against the open door of his SUV.

"Relax," Alex said. "I'm not going to hurt you."

She took two stapled documents out of her bag and threw them at Nick. They landed on the ground, and Nick stooped to retrieve them. His jaw dropped as he rifled through the pages: one was Stefan's memo to Mihkel on the Viatical Act, and the other was Jennifer's letter to the Insurance Council. "How the fuck did you get these?"

"Doesn't matter," Alex said. "I'm here to tell you that the crimes committed by your Russian clients are no longer my concern. You are offside federal legislation, a little piece of legislation called the Viatical Act. Ever heard of it?" Alex said sarcastically. "Once the SEC is finished with your clients, there will be no fund."

"I fucking knew it," Nick spat out. "The only thing you care about is Basel Re's bottom line."

"That's special, coming from you, Nick—the whacker of Wall Street," Alex said, smirking. "You sat by while your colleagues and the insureds were murdered, all for your client's economic benefit. Do not even try to lecture me." She shook her head. "You're pathetic."

Nick looked away quickly, trying to control the anxiety that threatened to paralyze him.

"I've never seen these documents before," Nick lied.

"Bullshit you haven't," Alex spat out.

"Why can't you just leave me alone?"

"Stop your fucking whining."

"You can't come here and make these accusations. Who do you think you are?" Nick barked back at Alex.

"I know who I am, Mr. Martin. Who do you think *you* are?"

And without waiting for a response, Alex continued, "You know what I think? I think that you believe you are above the law."

She stepped a bit closer. "But let me make this simple for you. Your little death fund is done. Investors will never get their cash back. When this hits the street, you and your partners will be lucky to avoid jail. Consider yourself lucky I'm not going to the police."

Nick looked Alex straight in the eye. "I'm done talking to you. I want my gun back."

"I don't think so, Mr. Martin."

"I'll report you to the police," Nick said aggressively.

Alex moved even closer to Nick—they were standing only inches apart. "No, you won't, you piece of shit." She walked away and didn't look back.

244

Chapter Forty
Boston, Massachusetts
December 2019

Nick headed back to Boston and his office, still shaken by what Greene had told him at his daughters' school. If the SEC had Stefan's memo, they were all fucking history—him, Mihkel, the whole fucking firm. When he got back to the office, Nick walked right past Vivian and swung Mihkel's closed door against the wall with a resounding bang.

Mihkel looked up from his screen with a startled look on his face.

"I just got a visit from our friend Alex Greene. She knows about the Viatical Act. Greene has the fucking memo from Stefan. She says that the SEC knows that we didn't get the consents. Tell me she is full of shit."

"What the fuck are you talking about? The consents for what?"

"You know fucking what. The beneficiary consents required by the Viatical Act. Greene said that we never got the consents."

Mihkel exhaled sharply. "It's always fucking something with you, isn't it?"

"You told me that Stefan got them," Nick said.

"Yeah, Stefan told me he fucking got them. What am I supposed to do? Check his fucking work? I'm surrounded by incompetent assholes," Mihkel spat back defensively.

Then it dawned on Nick. "So that's why I couldn't find the consents in the Prosperity intranet. You didn't fucking get them!"

As soon as the words were out of his mouth, Nick knew he'd said too much. *Fuck.*

"But you were locked out of the Prosperity intranet." Mihkel paused and shook his head. "It was you, wasn't it? *You* deleted the Prosperity data."

Mihkel chortled and, forming his right hand into the shape of a gun, said, "Bang-bang, you're dead, Nick. You self-righteous son of a bitch."

Nick turned dark red. "Greene said something else, Mihkel. She said that the Russians were killing off the insureds and that we stood by and did nothing."

Mihkel jumped out of his chair, enraged. "I told you not to speak to Greene, didn't I? But you didn't fucking listen. Did you? Igor should have fucking finished you off. Now that cunt has really fucked us up."

"Greene said she's not going to the police."

"And you fucking believed her?" Mihkel dropped his gaze and shook his head.

Nick could see that he was about the blow.

"Now, go back to your fucking office and keep your goddamn mouth shut. Nothing about this to anyone, ever, understand?" Mihkel said in a low, guttural tone. "Or you're dead, and so is your entire family. I can't protect you from the Russians."

Nick returned to his hotel room, feeling very alone. His world was caving in on him. As soon as Nick was in his suite, he texted Jenna: *Time for dinner?*

Jenna responded immediately with a smiley face. She also texted: *Just dinner?*

Nick texted back a smiley face.

Jenna responded: *Booked for dinner but can accommodate an overnight. Does that work?*

He texted back: *Done.*

Jenna sent a heart emoji and confirmation: *I'll be there around ten.*

Nick sighed. Overnights were not cheap. Even though he was paying Jenna with Igor's cash, it still hurt when he handed over the $5,000 for the overnights. He had even once told Jenna that he really liked her and asked if she would be his girlfriend.

Jenna shot that proposal down. She claimed he was supposed to like her, and if he didn't, she wasn't doing her job.

Nick promised himself that once the divorce was settled and he got a "real" place, he would get a "real" girlfriend.

In the meantime, the pay-to-play with Jenna would do just fine.

Chapter Forty-One
Boston, Massachusetts
December 2019

Over the next few days, life snapped back to a semblance of normal for Nick. Not that he had much of a career left at the firm. New work was nonexistent, and the days dragged by; only lengthy sessions at the gym and time with Jenna interrupted his boredom.

Fortunately, he had arranged with the management committee to bury his time spent in London and Russia in the hundreds of pages of invoices that had been sent to the fund on closing. *That was something, at least.*

Nick had spent his career working on other people's files, and now that he had to get his own clients, he didn't know where to start. He half-heartedly developed a business plan and met with several of his partners, all of whom assured him they would keep him in mind for future work. But nothing ever came.

Nick called Vladim and put him off till January; Nick blamed the Christmas holiday chaos.

The truth was Nick was still considering his options stateside. He wanted to be a part of his daughters' lives, and a permanent move to Dubrovnik, Croatia, would make that difficult.

After the visit to his daughters' school, Nick had gotten a lot of negative attention from Laura's attorney, who'd insisted on supervised access of his daughters at a psychologist's office, which was humiliating. His own attorney advised him against agreeing to it, but his attorney didn't know about the Moscow tape.

Nick folded, and his first visit with the girls was scheduled for the upcoming Saturday.

He was in the middle of reviewing the last draft of the agreement sent over by Laura's attorney when his door flew open, and Stefan stormed into his office.

"What do you want?" Nick snapped.

"You prick," growled Stefan. "I got served a Wells Notice for the Prosperity prospectus filing."

Nick did a double take. A Wells Notice was the SEC's precursor to an enforcement action—very bad news.

"What are you talking about?" Nick asked.

"The Insurance Council filed a complaint with the SEC: they want to know why there is no disclosure in the prospectus about the Viatical Act."

"You didn't include the Viatical Act in the final prospectus?" Nick asked.

"No, Mihkel said we didn't have to," Stefan responded defensively.

"Mihkel's not a fucking securities attorney. Why would you listen to him?"

"It's his client, so I just did what he said! And cut the bullshit, you son of a bitch. How could we include a reference to the Viatical Act when you didn't get the beneficiary releases like you were supposed to do?"

"What the fuck are you talking about?" Nick yelled. "You were supposed to get the consents."

"No, Nick—Mihkel said *you* were getting the consents! We had to leave the Viatical Act out because you did not do *your* job," Stefan said, raising his voice.

Nick broke out in a cold sweat. Trying to control his anger, he said, "Stefan, listen to me. No one asked me to get the consents."

"You fucking liar!" Stefan shouted.

"How could I get them? Mihkel took me off the file."

"Bullshit! Mihkel didn't take you off the file. He took you to Moscow," Stefan said. Then, without warning, he jumped up and grabbed Nick by the lapels. "If I go down, I won't go alone!"

Nick escaped Stefan's grip and shoved him— hard. Stefan stumbled against Nick's desk and fell to the floor.

Fearing a further escalation, Nick extended his hand to help Stefan up, but Stefan scrambled to his feet on his own. "Yeah, and it gets better, fucker," Stefan huffed. "The SEC issued a trading halt for the Prosperity Fund. The fund's going down, and so is the firm."

"Lower your fucking voice. I'll talk to Mihkel and the management committee. We'll work this out. Trust me."

"Trust you? That's a joke. And don't try to fucking pull rank on me. Your management committee buddies aren't going to think you're so great when I tell them that you deleted the Prosperity intranet," Stefan jeered at Nick.

"Who said I deleted the Prosperity intranet?" Nick snapped back.

"Mihkel did. And you know what? I saw you in Jennifer's office the day after she died. IT told me her computer was wiped. That was you, wasn't it?" Stefan asked.

Nick beat Stefan to the door and blocked his exit.

"What are you saying?" Nick growled.

"Fuck you, Martin," Stefan hissed, spraying spittle all over Nick's face. "You deleted the Prosperity file using Paul's password, and you did the same for the Insurance Council files from Jennifer's computer. I'm not stupid. I've got enough to go to the FBI."

"The FBI?" Nick said, panicking. "What the fuck are you talking about? Calm down, okay?"

"Get out of my way!" Stefan shouted.

Nick stepped aside as Stefan left. It was useless. Stefan was right about one thing: Stefan would not wear this alone. Nick jogged down the hallway and, ignoring Vivian, burst into Mihkel's office. The heavy door slammed against the wall with a bang.

Mihkel jerked to attention. "What the fuck?"

"We have a big fucking problem," Nick said.

"What problem?" Mihkel asked.

"Stefan got a Wells Notice. Greene called it. The SEC has Stefan's memo. And it's addressed to you, Mihkel—not me. You're fucked too," Nick said, pressing his palms onto Mihkel's desk.

"What the fuck," muttered Mihkel.

"Stefan said that you told him to leave the Viatical Act out of the prospectus. That's on you; it has nothing to do with me."

"What? I didn't tell that stupid fuck how to do his job. The disclosure in the final prospectus was his responsibility, and he signed off on the comfort letter. Don't worry, we'll feed his ass to the SEC. I kept that incompetent bastard around for a reason."

"Stefan is not going to take the rap for this. He's out there right now blabbing to anyone who'll listen to him, including the FBI."

"I'll deal with him."

"Just like you dealt with Jennifer and Paul?" Nick yelled, his face twisting in anger. "Just so you know, I'm done covering for you."

Mihkel smirked. "Covering for me? That's a joke. You should be on the street with Stefan. You're the insurance expert on the file. You should have known about the Viatical Act, and you should have made sure that we got the consents. This is just *another* pile of your shit that I have to clean up."

"You're dirty, Mihkel, and you fucking know it. You're an ungrateful, lying bastard. And you want to know something else? Stefan's as good as accused me of killing Jennifer and Paul." Nick bunched his right hand into a fist.

"Take it easy," Mihkel said, lowering his voice. "We both know you didn't kill them."

Mihkel's words made Nick sick. *Yes, you fucker, you know I didn't do it. That's because you know who did.*

"Don't worry," Mihkel said. "I'll take care of that little prick. If Stefan values his life, he'll keep his mouth shut. Now go back to your office. I've got this," Mihkel said, waving Nick off.

About an hour after his conversation with Mihkel, Nick heard a commotion in the hallway. He stepped out of his office and saw two security guards on either side of Stefan, walking him out of Mihkel's office in the direction of the freight elevator.

Stefan wore a look of stark bewilderment on his face, but his eyes widened when he saw Nick.

"You bastard!" shrieked Stefan.

He broke free of the security guards and lunged at Nick, grabbing him by the throat.

Nick fell back on the floor, and Stefan landed heavily on him, knocking the wind out of both of them. It took both security guards to pull Stefan off Nick.

Nick jumped up off the floor. He straightened his jacket and tie, trying to regain his composure.

"Sorry about that, sir," said one of the security guards as the other hauled Stefan back toward the elevator. "Are you okay?"

"I'm fine," Nick answered curtly.

"Do you want to press charges?" asked the guard.

"No, just get him the hell out of here."

It wasn't until 6:30 p.m. that Nick finally looked outside his office door. The floor was deserted; Kristen and the other assistants had long gone home. Karla Murphy had left him an urgent message to come down to her office. It was the first time that he'd been back on the thirtieth floor since his move upstairs, and the empty offices freaked him out. His colleagues were either dead or gone.

Nick knocked lightly on Karla's door and poked his head in. "You wanted to talk to me?"

"Come in and close the door," Karla said. "What the hell happened with Stefan? I heard it got ugly. You okay?"

"I'll live, thanks," Nick replied warily, not sure where she was going with this. He didn't trust her.

Karla eyed him carefully. "What's the connection between Stefan's firing and the SEC investigation?"

Who the fuck told her about the SEC investigation?

"Best to speak to Mihkel about that."

"What's going on, Nick?"

"Talk to Mihkel," Nick said evenly. *Conniving bitch.*

"Mihkel isn't saying. I already spoke to him."

"Then you have your answer, don't you?" Nick walked out of her office.

Karla called after him, "Enjoy your fancy office on the thirty-third floor, Nick. I have a feeling you won't be there long."

Nick headed to his office with Karla's words ringing in his ears. *What does she know?* Nick knew now that he could not survive the Prosperity fiasco at the firm, that it was just a matter of time till he was on the street. He just hoped he could hold on long enough to get his January bonus.

Nick grabbed his coat and headed for the parking garage. He had arranged for another overnight with Jenna, and she was waiting for him at the Hyatt.

He felt himself harden just at the thought of rolling around with her on his king-sized bed. *They didn't call hookers "professionals" for nothing.* Nick smirked as he entered the empty elevator.

The elevator chimed as Nick stepped out into the deserted underground garage. As he turned the corner, Alex Greene emerged from behind a pillar.

"Nick, it's all starting to go down. Work with me, and you won't go to jail."

A black Mercedes SUV pulled up beside them, and Alex's bodyguard got out.

Nick looked at Alex. "I thought you were finished with the file."

"Yes, that was before the shit hit the fan with the SEC. Now it's cleanup time. Get in the car."

When Nick hesitated, Alex grabbed his arm. "I said get in."

Nick tried to shake off Alex's grip, and when that failed, he shoved Alex. Alex lost her balance and fell against the Mercedes and onto the dirty concrete floor. Nick bolted toward his SUV.

Max easily caught up with Nick, and after a brief struggle, he put Nick into a chokehold and dragged him back to the Mercedes, where Alex was still dusting off her camel-colored Max Mara coat.

"Are you okay, boss?" Max asked, gripping Nick around his neck.

"I'm fine," Alex said. "Let him go."

"I won't turn on the Russians. They'll kill me," Nick said.

Alex stared at Nick impassively. "You think I won't?"

Then she stepped forward and gave Nick an uppercut jab under his chin, followed by a hard straight-line punch in the nose. The quick one-two combo wreaked devastation: Nick's top and bottom teeth slammed together as Alex's fist smashed into his nasal bone.

Nick staggered backward. Tears welled in his eyes and blood ran from his nose and mouth. "You bitch, you broke my nose!"

"You started it. Now get in the fucking car."

Chapter Forty-Two
Boston, Massachusetts
December 2019

Nick sat in his office and looked at his watch again. It was 10:30 a.m., but Nick felt as if he had put in a full day at work. His meeting with Alex the night before had lasted till nearly dawn, and when Nick got back to his hotel, he could not sleep. It was too late for a sleeping pill, so he watched TV for a while before he showered and got dressed for work. When he arrived at the office just after 8:00 a.m., Kristen was already at her desk.

Kristen had eyed him warily. His top lip was cracked and bruised, and the skin around his eyes was slowly turning black.

Nick said nothing, went into his office, and shut his door. Alex had relayed his marching orders the night before. First, he downloaded the management committee intranet onto the petabyte storage disk she had given him. He uploaded the entire disk onto his laptop, and from his laptop, he uploaded the disk's contents to a secure site. Then he wiped the disk and erased the laptop's history.

Now, all he had to do was wait.

Within a few minutes, raised voices echoed in the hallway.

Nick got up from his desk and looked out his door. Vivian frantically rushed up to him. Two men in navy-blue windbreakers followed her.

"Mr. Martin, thank God," said Vivian. "These men say they're from the FBI. They're looking for Mr. Ivanov."

"Isn't he in?" Nick asked.

Vivian shook her head.

One of the men stepped forward. "Nick Martin?"

"Yes, I am," Nick said with a deep sigh. Alex had told him to expect this.

"I'm Special Agent Parks, FBI," said the officer, flashing his ID badge. "We have a warrant for your arrest."

"On what charges?" Nick asked, swallowing hard.

"Securities fraud." Parks locked eyes on him. "Here's your copy of the indictment," he said, handing the thirty-page document to Nick.

After Parks read him his Miranda rights, Nick asked, "Can I get my overcoat?"

"Sure," Parks said. He followed Nick into his office.

Nick put on his coat. "I'd like to avoid handcuffs."

"Sorry, that's not possible," Parks said. He handcuffed Nick and escorted him to the elevators, where they joined other FBI agents and the dozen or so management committee members who'd been rounded up.

Nick endured an extremely uncomfortable elevator ride down to the ground-floor lobby with several of his partners, and when the doors opened, they were met with a horde of media assembled in the glittering shadow of the building's giant Christmas tree.

Nick kept his head down as camera crews scrambled to capture content for the evening's headline story.

Nick and his partners were hustled into a police bus in the underground garage. As Nick worked his way to the back of the bus, he looked for Mihkel. But Mihkel wasn't there. *Fucking Mihkel. He'll get away with this, just like everything else.*

The driver carefully maneuvered through the reporters and camera crews waiting for them on the street, taking Nick and his partners to the FBI's Boston headquarters on Schroeder Street. The trip in midmorning traffic took almost an hour. Nick's partners worked their cells, and by the time they reached the police station, the parking lot was filled with BMWs, Jaguars, Bentleys, and a couple of Rolls Royces—all belonging to the attorneys' attorneys.

Nick and his partners were placed in a segregated cell area to protect them from the general inmate population. One by one, the committee members were called away to be fingerprinted and photographed before they could meet with their attorneys.

It was several hours before Nick got his turn. His attorney, Sammy Alderman, was waiting for him in the interview room. Sammy, an old buddy from law school, had been doing securities defense work for years. He was the go-to guy if the SEC came after you; he had defended some of the worst fraudsters in America. Nick knew that Sammy would do whatever it took to save his sorry ass.

With Sammy riding shotgun, Nick's three-hour interview with the FBI investigators went smoothly. Nick was taken back to his cell for his bail hearing, scheduled for the next morning.

He watched his partners shuffle back and forth from the cells to the interview rooms. *First-timers.*

The overnight in the county lockup was a walk in the park compared to his time in the Russian jail. The guards were polite, and Nick's evening meal of roast beef, gravy, mashed potatoes, and peas was edible. Instead of a shit bucket, he had a real toilet and a sink with cold *and* hot running water. *Downright civilized,* he thought.

Nick appeared before a judge the next morning with Sammy, and after a short hearing, he was released on a million-dollar bail bond.

"It's all under control," Sammy told Nick as they left the police station. He put his hand on Nick's shoulder. "I had a call with the prosecutor's office this morning. They're ready to deal."

Nick looked at his friend. "You're a lifesaver, Sammy."

"No problem. It's what I do. Can I give you a ride back to the hotel?"

"Sure," Nick said, and they climbed into Sammy's shiny Jaguar.

On the way to the hotel, Sammy turned to Nick and said, "Now, what can you tell me about that aluminum briefcase you want me to get from your safe deposit box?"

Nick fished in his pockets and took out a set of keys, which he handed to Sammy. "Here are the keys, but believe me, you don't want to open the briefcase."

"Hell, no. I'm not stupid," Sammy chuckled.

"It's all about those damn Russian clients. If it wasn't for them, none of this bullshit would've happened."

"Tell me about it," Sammy said.

So, Nick did. He told his old friend almost everything: his suspicions about the deaths of Jennifer and Paul, the untimely and accidental deaths of the policyholders, the frame-up job in Moscow, the wild business in Curaçao. But he didn't tell Sammy what was in the briefcase. That would only compromise him—and the money, of course.

Sammy whistled. "You've been a busy little bastard. Holy shit!"

"Sammy, please," Nick said.

"And you said Greene knows all this?" Sammy asked.

Nick nodded.

"Are you sure Greene will keep her mouth shut?" Sammy asked. "You'd better pray she doesn't blab."

"She won't," Nick said.

"How can you be so sure?"

"It's simple: it's not in the best interest of her client," Nick said, and he concentrated on the traffic ahead of them for a few moments before continuing. "Greene is only concerned about minimizing the reputational risk to Basel Re. She wants to keep the FBI focused on the SEC issues and not all the other shit. That's why she's making their case against the Houghton attorneys for them. It should be the easiest fucking prosecution ever."

Sammy gave Nick a concerned look. "So, who alerted the SEC in the first place?"

"According to Greene, the Insurance Council of America," Nick replied.

"But how did *they* find out?" Sammy said.

"Jennifer emailed the Insurance Council and outed the firm the same night she died." Nick looked away; he still couldn't say her name without a catch in his throat.

"Is that a coincidence?"

Nick shrugged. "She probably got frustrated with Mihkel. He told me that he called her that evening to discuss the viatical legislation. My guess is that she sent the email after that call."

Sammy shook his head. "Putting all your law firm partners in the shitter is a gutsy move, Nick."

"Yeah, and for my troubles, I'll do time and never practice law again."

"It's going to take some fast talking to get the deal you want. It would have been a hell of a lot easier if you'd called me before you agreed to testify against your partners."

"Let's just say that Greene didn't give me a choice."

"Help me out here, Nick. Why doesn't the SEC go after the Russian managers?"

"We don't have an extradition treaty with Russia. But even if we did, making a case against the Russians would be uphill. The Russians would claim that they thought everything was okay with the SEC filing. Mihkel told Igor as much. The Russians are technically liable for any misrepresentations in the disclosure, but they would have a reasonable reliance defense."

"So, the Russians will get away with everything?" Sammy asked.

"Probably. Honestly, it's the least of my concerns." Nick swallowed hard. "Look, Sammy, I'm no hero in any of this. I deserve jail. I knew something was going on, something bad, but I ignored it. I'm a coward—end of story."

They rode in silence until Sammy pulled up in front of the Hyatt Regency. "Don't worry," he said. "Ol' Sammy will take care of you."

Nick got out of the car and walked unsteadily into the hotel. A surreal logic now permeated his life. He went to his suite, took off his shoes and jacket, and lay down on the bed. He'd call Jenna in the morning.

Tonight, he felt only fatigue—extreme fatigue—and dropped off into a black, bottomless sleep.

Chapter Forty-Three
Steubenville, Ohio
December 2019

Julie Yusky stood in the parking lot of her mother's condo complex and watched as the real estate agent slapped the *Sold!* sticker on the *For Sale* sign. It had all happened so fast. Julie's mother had fallen and broken her hip, and that, combined with her growing dementia, meant she required round-the-clock care. The only way to pay for her long-term care was selling the condo.

The condo had sold quickly in an all-cash deal with an end-of-month closing. Julie had sold off most of the furniture in a yard sale and donated what didn't sell to the local Salvation Army. That pleased her mother, who was a big fan of the Sally Ann.

Julie had held on to a few keepsakes: her mother's jewelry, mostly costume; a box of old pictures; and her dad's revolver, which she had crammed into the trunk of her car, along with everything else.

Julie thanked the agent and walked to her car, where her two daughters were waiting patiently in the back seat. She finished loading the trunk and got in.

"All buckled in?" she asked.

"Yes, Mommy," said Bekka. "Where are we going?"

"We're staying at the Steubenville Motor Inn for a while. We used to go there with your dad for breakfast—remember?" Julie said, trying to sound upbeat.

It wasn't working. "Why can't we stay at Grandma's?" asked her younger daughter, Kaylie.

"Grandma's going to live in a special place for old people," Julie replied.

"I'm going to miss her," Kaylie said.

Julie looked in the rearview mirror and saw a tear rolling down Kaylie's cheek. Julie struggled to keep her own emotions in check. Her girls could not see her crying.

Julie wheezed out, "Don't worry. We'll visit Grandma soon, sweetie."

That evening, Julie made mashed potatoes and meatloaf for the girls in the motel's little kitchenette. The meal was the girls' favorite.

After putting the girls to bed at their regular time, Julie lay in the darkness, watching the flickering television with the closed captions on. Suddenly, a breaking news segment on CNN caught her eye. She turned up the volume.

"The arrests were the result of several months of investigation by the FBI and the SEC that resulted in fraud charges being laid today against the senior partners of the Boston law firm Houghton & Willis associated with the Prosperity Fund..."

Julie blinked. *Those were the crooks who talked Charlie out of our money.* A fiery wave of anger swept through her chest and stomach. The image on the television screen shifted from the reporter to a well-dressed man being led outside by agents in blue windbreakers.

"Among those indicted on charges of securities fraud was Nick Martin, a senior attorney at Houghton & Willis. Arrest warrants have also been issued for other attorneys from Houghton & Willis… As a result of today's action, the SEC has suspended trading in the Prosperity Fund—"

"Nick Martin! That's him!"

Bekka raised her head. "What's wrong, Mom?"

Julie turned the sound down and stroked Bekka's hair. "Go back to sleep, sweetie. It's nothing—thought I saw someone your dad used to know."

Nick Martin is a con man. Julie had always known that, but now it was on CNN for the whole world to see.

Chapter Forty-Four
Boston, Massachusetts
December 2019

As they drove to their early morning meeting with District Attorney Amanda Basheer, Nick told Sammy his news: Houghton had terminated him from the partnership. According to the brusque email, all his accounts and his security passes were suspended, effective immediately. Nick was instructed to courier both his cell phone and laptop to the office at his earliest convenience.

The termination was devastating, even though Nick expected it. He had spent most of the past ten years in the office, and it had defined him. *All those years for nothing,* he thought. And now he was not even getting his bonus.

"I know it's tough, but you need to focus on the meeting with the DA. If that goes badly, you could be looking at twenty years," Sammy admonished him.

"Understood."

"Basheer is meeting with us personally. That speaks volumes about how important this prosecution is to her political career," Sammy said. "A successful conviction will ensure her reelection next spring."

"Is that supposed to make me feel better?" Nick asked. "You're making me very nervous, Sammy."

Basheer's ruthlessness was legendary. *She was not to be fucked with.*

"Don't be nervous. Just keep your mouth shut, and you'll be fine," Sammy said.

"Any word about Mihkel?" Nick asked.

"They haven't found him yet, and maybe that's to our advantage," Sammy said. He then added, "If you can give them a lead—"

"Nope." Nick shook his head. "I've got nothing, but I have a feeling that the all-knowing, all-seeing Alex Greene might be able to assist."

After Sammy parked in the lot for the Dorchester Center on Washington Street, he turned to Nick and said, "Remember, I will do the talking. You say nothing, okay?"

"Of course," Nick said.

"Let's go in then," said Sammy.

It took them twenty minutes to get through security, and by the time they arrived at Basheer's office, they were late. Not off to a great start.

Basheer's assistant gave them a dirty look and asked them to wait in the hallway. When they were finally ushered—thirty minutes later—through the double wooden doors into the DA's office, Basheer stood up to greet them.

"Hello, Amanda," Sammy said.

"Hello, Sammy."

Basheer's ballooning linen dress, Doc Martins, and purple buzz cut belied her thirty-plus years at the bar and her fourth term as Suffolk County's elected District Attorney.

"It's great seeing you again. You're looking well," Sammy said with a toothy smile and a sparkle in his eye.

"Please have a seat," Basheer said, ignoring Sammy's compliment and pointing to a pair of chairs on the other side of the table. "I believe you know everyone here."

Nick nodded and looked past the table occupied by suits from the DA's office and Special Agent Parks from the FBI; Alex Greene was leaning against one of the window ledges.

They locked eyes for an instant, and Alex half-smiled at Nick. He did not smile back.

"Who invited Greene?" Nick whispered in Sammy's ear.

Sammy shrugged.

Basheer looked over at Alex and said, "Perhaps Ms. Greene would like to join us at the table."

Alex sat down on Basheer's immediate right.

Basheer pulled on her ear. Her office was silent as they waited for her carefully formed words. "I understand that, in exchange for a reduced sentence, Mr. Martin is prepared to cooperate with us on the securities fraud charges against Mr. Mihkel Ivanov and Mr. Stefan Popescu. In addition, Mr. Martin is willing to assist us with the charges of aiding and abetting securities fraud against other Houghton partners."

Sammy put his hands on the table and said earnestly, "Amanda, let's call a spade a spade. I think we can agree that you don't have a case against the Houghton attorneys without Mr. Martin's cooperation."

"Don't get ahead of yourself, Sammy," Basheer said.

"Understood. Let me put this another way," Sammy said in a more deferential tone. "My client is prepared to take responsibility for his failure to blow the whistle on his partners in a timely manner. Mr. Martin was taken off the file by Mr. Ivanov several weeks ago and was under the mistaken belief that the compliance issues related to the Viatical Act and the misleading disclosure in the prospectus were being addressed."

Sammy looked around the table. "After being informed otherwise by Mr. Stefan Popescu, Mr. Martin immediately confronted Mr. Ivanov with this knowledge. Mr. Ivanov admitted to Mr. Martin that the disclosure in the Prosperity Fund prospectus was incomplete. Mr. Ivanov also told Mr. Martin that the management committee was aware of all actions taken on the Prosperity Fund file and that they approved these actions."

"Can I stop you there, Sammy? We both know Mr. Martin's recounting of conversations among Mr. Ivanov and his partners is hearsay; therefore, it is inadmissible in court. You'll have to do better than that," Basheer said.

Sammy moistened his lips before continuing. "Mr. Martin has documentation in the form of minutes from the management meetings where these matters were discussed."

"How were the documents obtained?" Basheer asked.

"As a managing partner, Mr. Martin had access to a password-protected intranet only accessible to committee members. He downloaded the documents from the network." Sammy paused to let that sink in. "I have been informed by Mr. Martin that he was not involved, either directly or indirectly, in drafting the final prospectus for the Prosperity Fund, nor did he participate, either directly or indirectly, in any communications with the SEC regarding the final prospectus."

Sammy paused again for effect. "But Mr. Martin acknowledges that he should have come forward earlier and reported what he knew to the SEC. Mr. Martin deeply regrets this decision. He is now prepared to assume responsibility for his actions, or—to be more accurate—for his failure to take action."

Basheer put up her right hand and chuckled. "Sammy, you had me at recorded minutes. What is your client looking for in exchange?"

Sammy took a breath before continuing. "In light of these extenuating circumstances, and given Mr. Martin's current cooperation, we are of the view that the appropriate punishment is two years in jail to be served in a low-security prison near Boston so Mr. Martin can remain close to his children. These events have already ruined my client's life. Mr. Martin's biggest mistake was trusting his partners at Houghton & Willis."

Basheer exchanged a glance with Greene before responding. "Normally, we'd ask for eighteen to twenty-five years. You're going to have to knock my socks off to get that kind of deal for your client." Basheer paused. "Now, if Mr. Martin had information that would support other charges, like conspiracy to commit murder, we *might* be open to two years. Lots of dead bodies around this file—including two Houghton attorneys."

Nick face fell. Did Basheer say conspiracy to commit murder? *Where the fuck was that coming from?*

Worry crossed Sammy's face. "May I have a few minutes with my client?"

"Yes, of course," Basheer replied. "Agent Parks, can you please escort these gentlemen to an interview room?"

Once they were seated in the windowless interview room and behind closed doors, Sammy said, "Basheer may be fishing, but she knows something. Either Greene gave the FBI a heads-up or someone there has been doing their homework."

"I can't believe Greene would raise the wrongful deaths," Nick said. "It's counter to the interests of Basel Re and a public relations nightmare."

Nick continued, dropping his voice even lower. "And I don't think she'll talk about what happened in Moscow. She's done her job, and now she's out."

"All I know is that you, my friend, are on very, very fragile ground if they proceed on any murder charges. You've had a good idea about what was going on for months, yet you did nothing, said nothing," Sammy said.

Nick looked at Sammy and said, "Okay, okay, I get it. I fucked up."

Sammy nodded and said, "You need to stay silent on the conspiracy to commit murder. It's your only choice."

Sammy stood up. "I'll ask for a meeting without Greene present. If Basheer won't agree to the two years on the securities fraud charges, then we'll take our chances in court."

Nick's eyes widened. "Sammy, I trust you with my life. Please don't fuck this up."

"Relax, piece of cake. Just don't talk to anyone."

"Yeah, sure, but first, I need to use the gents," Nick said, and he followed Sammy out the door and down the empty hallway.

Nick sidled up to one of the urinals and flipped out his dick. He was finishing up when he heard the door open. He glanced over his shoulder and saw Greene's reflection in the sink mirror.

"What the fuck?" Nick said, shoving his dick back in his pants midstream.

Alex's heels clicked on the tiled floors as she approached him. "I don't know how you sleep at night."

"What more do you want from me?" Nick huffed.

"How about a little fucking remorse? And for the record, I didn't discuss the wrongful deaths with Basheer. It never came up," Alex said and walked out.

Nick believed Greene, but he hoped to never see her again.

Sammy returned to the interview room an hour later with a big smile on his face. "Okay, my friend, the deal is done. Basheer blinked—she went for the two years. The prospect of a successful prosecution of the Houghton attorneys was too much to pass up. There were so many fucking boners around that table, it was positively levitating. I couldn't fucking believe it."

Nick couldn't stop himself from smiling. "You are a fucking miracle worker. No one else could have gotten me that deal."

Sammy chuckled. "Yeah, I'm one fuck of a superstar negotiator. I told Basheer that if she proceeded with the conspiracy to murder charges, we would go to trial, and you would be a hostile witness. Bottom line is that the FBI are lazy fuckers. They'll go with a sure thing any day of the week. Basheer was fishing when she raised those murder charges. I called her on it, and she backed off."

Sammy, grinning from ear to ear, slapped Nick on the back and said, "We did it. Now let's get back in there and paper the fucker. Basheer is waiting for us."

By the time they left Basheer's office, Nick had signed the settlement agreement: in exchange for his testimony against his partners, Basheer would recommend a two-year sentence.

They were charging him with the lesser offense of knowingly filing a document with the SEC containing a material misrepresentation, which was a misdemeanor and not a felony charge. Nick's sentence would be served at a low-security jail, and he'd be given time to put his house in order before starting the sentence.

Nick texted Jenna after Sammy dropped him off at the Hyatt, but all he got back was a *No can do* and an inverted smiley face emoji.

He wasn't surprised. Since he'd been arrested, Jenna was always busy, even when he offered to double her already outrageous fee. Tonight was no different. Nick guessed that even hookers had standards. *Go figure.*

In an even more desperate move, Nick called Kristen and invited her out for dinner. Nick had not seen Kristen since the day he was arrested. He had learned through the grapevine that another law firm had scooped her up.

Predictably, she declined his invite.

Nick thought she could have come up with something more original than "I'm tied up with my parents." He knew Kristen was estranged from her parents, who lived in Denmark. It would have felt better if she had just told him to fuck off.

Nick's cell rang. *What now?* Sighing, he reached for his phone. "Nick Martin."

"Mr. Martin, this is Detective Cece. Remember me?"

Nick certainly did remember him. "Yes, how can I help you, Detective?"

"Well, sir, the body count around your law firm keeps growing. We found one of your colleagues in an abandoned warehouse in South Boston."

"One of my colleagues?" Nick asked, his brow furrowing. *Could it be Mihkel? Could I be that lucky?* "Who is it?"

"Stefan Popescu," Cece answered.

Nick felt a chill run up his body. "What happened?"

"A security guard found him in his car with a hose leading from the exhaust pipe into the window. He'd been there for a couple of days—carbon monoxide poisoning."

Nick felt his stomach muscles clench. "I can't believe it." But that actually wasn't true. *In fact, Mihkel predicted it.*

"One thing bothers me," Cece continued. "Based on the autopsy, the coroner is leaning toward a finding of suicide. But why would Popescu kill himself in that warehouse? Why not at home?"

Nick said nothing.

Cece asked, "Do you know anyone who might want to harm Popescu?"

Nick could think of two dozen disgraced attorneys who might want Stefan dead. But he didn't say that. "I don't know anybody who would want to harm him. However, I do know that Stefan was dismissed from the firm."

"Do you know why he was fired?"

"I understand he was terminated because he was being investigated by the SEC for securities fraud," Nick answered, espousing the firm's official party line.

"I see. And that bothered Popescu?" Cece pushed.

"Yeah, you could say that. Stefan's job was everything to him, and he didn't take it well."

"What do you mean?" Cece asked.

Nick instantly regretted raising Stefan's distress at being fired. He wasn't going to tell Cece that Stefan tried to strangle him, but he also didn't want to minimize what happened. Cece could easily talk to someone else at the firm.

"I just meant his dismissal was sudden, and Stefan was upset. He had to be forcefully removed from the office. A very tough day for all of us."

"Well, that fills in some of the blanks. Appreciate your help," Cece said and hung up.

Nick sat back and stared into space. *That fucking Mihkel.* How many people had died because of him and his fucking Russian clients? *He hoped the fucker burned in hell.* But as much as he hated to admit it, Stefan's death helped him. With Stefan dead, there was no one left to contradict Nick's version of events.

It made Nick feel sick, but there it was.

Chapter Forty-Five
Boston, Massachusetts
January 2020

It had not been difficult for Alex to find Mihkel after he made the mistake of calling Vivian for an update. Max was able to locate Mihkel on the sailboat moored at the Palm Harbor Marina and they flew down to Palm Beach to pick him up.

Alex, wearing a black turtleneck, jeans, and black trainers, crept toward the moored sailboat with Max three steps behind her. The floating dock shifted slightly under her feet and creaked as she moved along, and the lights of Palm Beach twinkled on the shoreline, their reflection dancing in the still waters of the marina.

Alex counted off the berth numbers as she passed. 111…112…113. She smiled when she reached number 113.

This should be it. She sized up the boat. *Decent size. At least a 30-footer.* Alex motioned for Max to stand guard on the dock, and she pulled her 9mm Glock automatic from its shoulder harness. Flicking off the safety lock, she stepped aboard the sailboat. The buzz from a television below had muffled her approach.

She looked down into the open hatch and called out, "Mihkel Ivanov!"

When there was no response, she slowly descended the stairs to the lower deck and called out again. There was a stirring noise and the sound of shattering glass.

"You okay?" asked Max in her earpiece, ready to help.

"I'm fine. He's here," she said softly into her microphone. Alex carefully opened the gallery door with her pistol drawn. The smell from a lit Don Arturo wafted up toward her. "Mihkel Ivanov?" she asked.

"Who the fuck wants to know?" said Mihkel, sprawled across the couch in a dirty gray tracksuit with a half dozen empty liquor bottles on the coffee table in front of him. A cigar burned on a tinfoil plate, and the remains of a dozen take-out dinners were strewn across the couch and the floor. "Are you the hooker the agency sent over?" Mihkel said as he leered at Alex.

"No, I'm not," Alex said as she scanned the room for weapons. When she saw none, she slid her pistol back into its holster. She walked over and turned off the TV.

"Aww, why didja do that?" Mihkel said, raising his glass and squinting at her. "Do I know you?"

"Yes and no." Alex found a chair among the debris in the cabin and pulled it up to the couch where Mihkel was sitting. "We need to talk."

Mihkel, eyes glazed over, cocked his head sideways and said, "Can we fuck first?"

Capturing Mihkel and delivering him to the FBI was the last task for Alex in an extraordinarily complex case. With her usual deftness, Alex had managed to keep herself and Basel Re out of the spotlight, even though the securities fraud charges against Houghton's managing partners made headlines around the world and lit up the blogosphere for months.

The SEC's cease-trade order ended up gutting the Prosperity Fund. By the time the SEC put a trustee in bankruptcy in place to oversee Prosperity's windup, the Russians had cleaned out the fund's bank accounts. At the peak, the fund's market cap had been nearly a billion dollars, but after the enforcement action, the units were soon rendered worthless; the investors lost everything.

No criminal charges were ever laid against Igor Dimitrov or Vladim Bulgarin. Foreign nationals were beyond the jurisdictional reach of the US courts. All the Houghton attorneys on the management committee, except Mihkel, had made a deal with Basheer. Not that Basheer would have had any trouble getting convictions against the Houghton attorneys. A team of thirty-five investigators from the FBI had served the Houghton law firm with a series of warrants the day after Nick finalized his deal with Basheer. The documents and recordings they'd recovered were more than enough to support the charges laid. But in the end, a lengthy and costly trial process was avoided by the plea deal. Basheer agreed to withdraw the charges after the attorneys agreed to contribute ten million dollars each to a fund for the benefit of the Prosperity investors. Basheer had wanted to send a message to the Street, and so she did. The media attention she got from the case was priceless.

Houghton & Willis quietly filed for Chapter 11 after a billion-dollar class action lawsuit on behalf of the investors was certified against them.

All the US partners declared personal bankruptcy, and the Massachusetts Board of Bar Overseers suspended their practicing licenses.

However, the partners were not out of pocket: they'd long ago "judgment proofed" their assets, holding them in either family trusts with their spouses and children as beneficiaries or in offshore trusts beyond the reach of the US courts.

When Houghton's Boston office closed, hundreds of Houghton attorneys found themselves on the street, looking for new positions. Houghton's clients were cherry-picked by its competitors, and the international firm changed its name to VPP International to distance itself from the fiasco in the United States.

Karla Murphy sailed through the disaster without a scratch to her reputation. She resigned from the firm the day the scandal broke and immediately bagged a lucrative equity partner position across the street at Wares & Wares LLP. She took Houghton's entire life settlement practice, valued at over a hundred million dollars, with her. Within months, Wares & Wares was rebranded to Wares & Murphy.

Chapter Forty-Six
Boston, Massachusetts, and Paris, France
March 2020

Alex flew first-class commercial to Boston in early March to attend Mihkel Ivanov's trial. Her attendance was not required, but she wanted to witness his prosecution. More importantly, she wanted to be ready to do damage control should anything come out that could hurt her client.

Alex sat in the courtroom on the first day of the trial and watched the comings and goings of the attorneys, police, court officials, and media as she waited for the judge to arrive. As far as Alex could determine, no one from Mihkel's family was there, nor were any of his former partners.

She sighed a breath of relief when she discovered that the press was not there in the numbers that she had expected.

Mihkel had elected for a trial by judge alone; putting his future in the hands of a jury of his peers was not in his best interests. A jury would view him, an affluent attorney accused of a white-collar crime, more harshly than a judge of the same profession and class. The judge assigned to the trial was an experienced commercial trial judge named Beatrice Singh. Judge Singh had cut her teeth at the SEC as a corporate finance attorney and then did a stint at a major Wall Street law firm before being appointed to the federal court by the George W. Bush administration. She was a tough, no-bull judge who had a unique insight into the capital markets.

The booming voice of the court clerk broke into Alex's thoughts. "All rise, Her Honor Judge Singh attending."

Alex stood along with the other people in the courtroom and waited for the circus that is the American trial system to begin.

After Judge Singh made her preliminary opening remarks, the attorney heading Mihkel's defense team rose and asked to make a preliminary motion to the court.

Addressing the judge directly, Walter Lire said, "We object to the unlawful flight charges being tried at the same time as the securities fraud charges. To do so would be extremely prejudicial to Mr. Ivanov's chance for a fair trial."

"Your Honor," Amanda Basheer said, rising to her feet. "It's essential to the prosecution's case that the charges are all tried together."

"I object!" Lire said. "Trying the unlawful flight charges and the securities fraud charges together is unprecedented."

"That's utter nonsense, Your Honor," replied Basheer. "The charges of unlawful flight to avoid prosecution speak to Mihkel Ivanov's guilty mind."

"My client's constitutional rights are not nonsense," Lire said.

Basheer leaned on her desk and said, "My learned friend forgets that this is not a jury trial."

The packed courtroom detonated in excited conversation, and Justice Singh slammed down her gavel.

"Order! Order!" Judge Singh said at the top of her voice. "I will have order, or I will have this courtroom cleared!"

Judge Singh waited for silence before she continued.

"I agree with Ms. Basheer. Motion denied. Call your first witness, Ms. District Attorney."

"Thank you, Your Honor," Basheer said. "The State of Massachusetts calls Mr. Nicholas Martin as its first witness."

Nick swallowed the lump in his throat as he walked to the stand. He could feel Mihkel's glare boring into the back of his head. Nick was sworn in by the judge, and he took his seat in the elevated witness box.

Basheer stood up and began her examination. "Mr. Martin, what position did you hold with Houghton & Willis LLP?"

"I was a partner and the head of the life settlement group practice."

"Are you still at the law firm?"

"No, the partnership was dissolved last year."

"What is your current position?" Basheer asked.

"I'm currently unemployed," Nick replied.

Nick's testimony went forward from there. He had been well-rehearsed by Basheer, and his evidence came out coherently with damning precision. Under the careful direction of Basheer, Nick connected the dots, providing the factual background to support the State's case.

However, the cross-examination by Lire did not go as smoothly for Nick.

"Mr. Martin," Lire began. "Is it true that you were the partner in charge of the Prosperity Fund file and that Mihkel Ivanov was the relationship attorney?"

"Yes, that was true until Mihkel Ivanov denied me access to the Prosperity intranet. He did that to me in late October of last year. By early November, I was off the case file altogether."

Mihkel's attempts to keep him out of the loop on the Prosperity file were now saving Nick's bacon.

"Did you hack into Houghton's document management system and delete all of the files related to the Prosperity Fund?" Lire asked.

"I object!" Basheer stood up. "Relevance?"

"Your Honor," Lire said, addressing the judge. "My learned friend will soon see the relevancy of my current line of questioning if Your Honor would allow me to continue."

"Mr. Martin, you will answer the question. Objection overruled," Judge Singh said, turning to Nick for a response.

"Yes, I went into the document management system using Paul Field's username and password and deleted the Prosperity files." Nick winced. It sounded much worse when he said it out loud.

"Were you still working on the Prosperity file at this time?" Lire asked.

"I was not," Nick responded.

"So, let me get this straight, Mr. Martin. You hacked into the Prosperity intranet using your recently deceased partner's username and password after you were taken off the file. Was it your usual practice to hack into password-protected intranets?"

"No, sir, it was not."

"Why did you do so in this case?"

Nick couldn't believe his luck. Lire was doing everything he could to impugn Nick's credibility in the eyes of the judge, but he had asked him an open-ended question. *Dumb move for a seasoned litigator.*

"I had reason to believe that I was being cut out of the file because of irregularities in the prospectus process." Nick leaned forward. "I wanted to find out if my assessment was accurate."

Lire stood up and asked for a sidebar with Basheer and the judge. The two attorneys approached the bench.

Nick could overhear them despite the hushed tones.

"Your Honor, Mr. Martin is speaking of matters that are subject to solicitor-client privilege. As far as I know, that privilege has not been waived by Mr. Bulgarin, Mr. Dimitrov, or any other official able to do so on behalf of the fund. Please correct me if I am wrong," Lire said.

Basheer handed a letter to the judge.

"What do I have here, Ms. Basheer?" the judge asked, glancing at the letter.

"It's a letter from the Prosperity Fund bankruptcy trustee waiving privilege on behalf of the Prosperity Fund for the purposes of these proceedings, Your Honor," Basheer answered. "We provided a copy of the letter to Mr. Lire's offices several days ago."

Lire, turning red, said, "Your Honor, I have not seen the waiver."

Basheer, without missing a beat, handed a second copy to Lire and said, "Here is a copy for your records."

"Can we resume the proceedings?" Judge Singh asked.

"Yes, we can, Your Honor," Lire said, sounding disheartened. "And thank you for your indulgence."

Basheer and Lire returned to their respective tables, and Lire continued his cross-examination.

"Is it true that you downloaded all the data off the Prosperity intranet site before you deleted the files?" Lire asked, recovering quickly.

"Yes, I did." There was no way to sugarcoat that.

"You did what, Mr. Martin?" Lire pushed.

"I downloaded all of the Prosperity intranet's data to an external drive before deleting the data from the network," Nick repeated, and then he paused before continuing. "I deleted the data because I was afraid that Mr. Ivanov was trying to frame me for his own wrongdoings."

Lire, who had been looking at his notes, jerked his head to attention. "I object, Your Honor. I ask that the last part of Mr. Martin's answer be struck from the record. The witness is answering a question that I did not ask."

Judge Singh frowned at Nick and said, "Mr. Martin, please restrict your answers to the questions asked."

Turning back to Lire, she said, "Objection is sustained. The clerk will strike that last sentence from the record."

Lire pressed on, "Is it not true that you deleted all of the data on the Prosperity intranet to cover up your participation in the fraud for which Mr. Ivanov is currently being tried?"

"No, that is not true," Nick responded.

Sensing Nick's hesitation, Basheer jumped up. "Mr. Lire is fishing. We object to his line of questioning."

"Objection sustained," Judge Singh ruled. "Mr. Lire, where are you going with this? Mr. Ivanov is on trial here—not Mr. Martin. You will abstain from an open fishing expedition in my court."

"Is it not true, Mr. Martin, that you deleted all of the data on the Prosperity intranet to cover up your own failure to obtain the consents required by the Viatical Act?" Lire asked.

"No, that is not true," Nick said.

There was a pause as Lire went over his notes again.

After Lire conferred briefly with Mihkel, he asked, "Mr. Martin, when did you become aware of the Viatical Act and the requirement to obtain the beneficiary consents?"

Nick took a deep breath. It was the day that Paul and Jennifer died. He would never forget that date. If Lire pushed him on the date, it would have implicated him at a much earlier time than he had disclosed to the court.

But before Nick could answer, Mihkel tugged on Lire's arm, and Lire asked the judge for a few moments with his client. After a brief whispered exchange, Lire stood up and said, "Thank you, Your Honor. No further questions at this time, but we reserve the right to a re-cross of Mr. Martin should further evidence come out."

Nick felt sorry for Lire. Lire could nail his ass if he had free rein to drill down on the details of what Nick knew and when he knew it. But Mihkel wouldn't let him.

After obtaining permission from Judge Singh for a re-direct, Basheer asked, "Mr. Martin, can you tell the court why you deleted the data off the Prosperity intranet?"

Nick thought for a moment. Basheer had not prepared him for this question. He knew that he couldn't tell the truth. No one, including Mihkel, wanted that.

"It was an accident," Nick sputtered. "I thought that I was deleting Paul Field's account. I accidentally deleted the entire Prosperity intranet."

"I have no further questions for Mr. Martin," Basheer said and sat down.

"Do you wish a re-cross, Mr. Lire?" Judge Singh asked.

The courtroom was quiet.

For a nanosecond, Nick locked eyes with Mihkel sitting at the counsel desk beside Lire.

Nick had just saved both of their asses, and Mihkel knew it. Mihkel leaned over and whispered in Lire's ear.

Lire stood up and said, "We do not wish a re-cross, Your Honor. If it pleases the court, I would like a few minutes to confer with my client."

Singh looked at the clock on the wall and said, "Why don't we break for lunch? See you back here at two o'clock sharp. Mr. Martin, you are dismissed until after the break."

Nick got up and glared at Mihkel as he walked by the counsel tables. *You can't touch me now, you asshole,* Nick thought. *You did your worst and I'm still here. So, fuck you.*

When they returned after the recess, Lire shocked everyone in the courtroom, including Nick, by asking Judge Singh for an adjournment to work out a deal with Basheer's office.

"Is your client changing his plea, Mr. Lire?"

"Not at this time, Your Honor. My client would appreciate the opportunity to have discussions with the District Attorney. A change in plea may come out of that."

"Is this acceptable to the District Attorney?" Judge Singh asked Basheer. "It is highly irregular at this stage of the trial, as I am sure you are aware."

"The State is in agreement, Your Honor."

"In these circumstances, I am prepared to grant a short adjournment."

The parties involved did not take long to hammer out an agreement. After they presented the deal the next morning, Judge Singh allowed Mihkel to change his plea to guilty and adjourned the case for sentencing.
***

Alex sat in the second row of the courtroom the day Mihkel Ivanov was sentenced. Out of the corner of her eye, she saw Nick Martin sitting across the aisle from her.

He stared stonily ahead, refusing to even acknowledge her presence.

Judge Singh surveyed the media-packed courtroom before she began, "Thank you, Ms. Basheer and Mr. Lire, for your submissions on sentencing. Ms. Basheer's office has requested that this court stay the unlawful flight charges, and while I assume that you have no objection to that, Mr. Lire, I am duty bound to ask."

Lire stood up and said, "Your Honor, we have no objection to the stay on the unlawful flight charges."

Judge Singh continued, "Mr. Ivanov, can you please stand up for sentencing?"

Mihkel noisily pushed his chair back and stood with his arms hanging by his sides. He had put on several pounds and was busting out of his suit.

"Mr. Ivanov, it is my understanding that you have agreed to the plea arrangement worked out between your attorney and the District Attorney. Is that accurate?"

"Yes, Your Honor, I have agreed to the plea arrangement," Mihkel said.

"Ms. Basheer has recommended a prison sentence of six to eight years. Your counsel has indicated satisfaction with the proposed sentence range. Are you aware of that, Mr. Ivanov?"

"Yes, Your Honor," Mihkel replied again.

The judge looked directly at Mihkel. "Mr. Ivanov, I have considered the District Attorney's recommendation, and it is my decision that six to eight years is too low."

Alex leaned forward to listen.

"This has been a very troubling case. I have never seen such greed. Thousands of investors have lost hundreds of millions of dollars because of your actions—or should I say inactions—and the actions of your clients. Your clients would not have perpetrated the fraud without your advice, direction, and assistance," Judge Singh said. "For these reasons, I sentence you to ten years in jail."

There was a gasp in the audience, and Mihkel seemed to teeter for a moment on his feet. Lire put a hand on Mihkel's arm to steady him.

The judge cleared her throat before continuing. "I regret that there are certain parties living beyond the borders of the United States whom justice will not reach; no doubt they have done so with your assistance and guidance, Mr. Ivanov. I wish that these individuals, the promoters of the Prosperity Fund, had been brought before this bench to answer for the fraud that they have perpetrated on honest, hard-working Americans, but I despair of that ever happening.

"Your sentence, Mr. Ivanov, is intended to impress upon the so-called gatekeepers in the public markets—the accountants, attorneys, brokers, and investment bankers who participate and enable their clients to orchestrate these enormous frauds—that they will be held personally and criminally liable for their actions.

"Attorneys cannot look the other way—or be willfully blind—to the criminal and quasi-criminal activities of their clients and expect to avoid the long arm of the law under the ruse that they were acting on instructions from their clients. On that imperfect note, these proceedings are now closed." Judge Singh motioned to the sheriff and said, "Take Mr. Ivanov to the cells."

Imperfect, indeed. Alex frowned as she watched the sheriff take Ivanov away. Mihkel's face was unreadable.

Alex momentarily locked eyes with Judge Singh, and they exchanged a barely perceptible nod as Singh rose to leave the courtroom.

Judge Singh's precedent-setting decision got the attention of attorneys, both nationally and internationally. Law students would study the decision into perpetuity for one reason and one reason alone: the SEC would go after not only bad actors but also their attorneys.

Holding attorneys responsible for the actions of their clients was a game-changer. The upshot was that law firms could no longer ignore the bad conduct of their clients. Judge Singh's decision made it clear that the justice system would not tolerate the attorneys' willful blindness of their clients' wrongful activities.

Chapter Forty-Seven
Paris, France
March 2020

When Alex got back to Paris after Mihkel's sentencing, she met with Guttmann for their usual postmortem session. These sessions were need-to-know. Guttmann would never know how close Alex came to being killed, nor would she ever share her suspicions about the deaths of the Houghton attorneys and the insureds. It would only put Guttmann in an awkward position vis-à-vis his superiors. He would have an obligation to disclose the revelations up the corporate chain, and at the end of the day, the disclosure would make no impact on the outcome for Basel Re. Alex had done her job and taken care of all of that. It was a game she played with Guttmann: he asked for and she gave him the information that he required to do his job—no more, no less.

Unfortunately, the financial outcome achieved by Alex on the Prosperity file had not been a win-win for Basel Re. The original purchases of the life insurance policies by the Prosperity Fund were null and void because of her efforts, but the death benefits still had to be paid. That meant that beneficiaries like Julie Yusky would receive payouts on the death of their loved ones, and for Alex at least, there was some justice in that.

But Basel Re was grateful that Alex had managed to minimize the damage to Basel Re's good name. Neither the suspicious circumstances of the insureds' deaths nor the fund's relationship to the Russian mafia ever became public. "It's all here, Karl," Alex said as she slid the slim blue folder across Guttmann's broad mahogany desk. "Everything you need for your internal reporting."

"Thank you, Alex," Guttmann said. "This was a terrible business, and now it is done."

"This is one file I am happy to put behind me," Alex said. "Did you sort out my compensation package?"

"I did, and I think you will be very pleased with your payout." Karl slid a copy of a wire transfer across his desk.

Alex picked it up and glanced at the number at the bottom of the page. She grinned. "Thank you, Karl."

"So, ready to take on another file?" asked Guttmann.

"First," Alex replied, "I need to catch up on a few personal matters."

"Your renovations to Hanna's bedroom suite?" Guttmann asked.

"You're obsessed with my renovations, Karl," Alex said, and they both laughed. "It's not only the renovations—it's Hanna herself," Alex said, sitting back in her seat. "She seems to need more and more attention, and frankly, I have neither the inclination nor the time to spend with her."

Karl adjusted his glasses.

"I think," Alex continued, "it's time for boarding school. It's what my grandmother did with my sister and me when we were Hanna's age."

"I might be able to help you with that," Karl offered. "I sent my daughters to the Institut Le Rosey in Switzerland. It's pricey but worth it."

That was unexpected. Alex knew Guttmann was married, but she had no idea that he had children.

"Le Rosey has two campuses, one for the summer in Rolle, Switzerland, and one for the winter in Gstaad. The curriculum includes mountain climbing and equestrian. She would be boarding with the daughters of billionaires and royalty. My girls loved it, and I think Hanna would too."

"Well, that would solve a problem for me," Alex said. "I've met someone that I'd like to get closer to, and having Hanna around makes that difficult."

"I don't believe it. Is the independent Ms. Greene settling down with one man?" Guttmann teased.

"Who said it was a man?" Alex teased back, and they both laughed.

***

With the Prosperity investigation behind her, the pattern of Alex's days in Paris resumed their normal routine. That meant catching up on her sleep, indulging in long, relaxing breakfasts, and shopping at her favorite haunts in Paris. Alex also took advantage of her downtime to fulfill a promise she'd made to Sophie before Christmas.

Sophie was losing patience with Hanna. According to Sophie, Hanna's thirteenth birthday the previous July had changed everything. Hanna started the summer as a compliant and pleasant twelve-year-old child and emerged as an argumentative and defiant adolescent who came and went as she pleased, skipping school at will, and hanging out with a "bad" crowd.

In Sophie's view, a little more "guidance" from Alex would be helpful, and they agreed that it might be time for a private boarding school like the Institut Le Rosey. The private lycée that Olivier attended would provide neither the structure nor the stimulation that Hanna obviously needed. Alex knew they would be putting a lot of faith in the boarding school experience to keep Hanna on the straight and narrow. It hadn't exactly worked for Alex's sister, Meagan, and Hanna may not fare any better. But Alex had no other option. If she played her cards right, she could enroll Hanna at Le Rosey for the fall session.

So, one sunny day in March, Alex invited Hanna out for lunch at Caretta on the Place des Vosges in the Marais, with the express intention of raising Hanna's recent recalcitrant behavior and broaching the boarding school idea. But before Alex could read Hanna the riot act, Hanna surprised Alex with a peremptory question: "Auntie Lex, have you ever killed anyone?"

Alex choked on the Chassagne Montrachet Blanc the waiter had poured for her. "Why would you ask me that?"

But Alex knew the answer: Hanna was smart—scary smart. She was also extremely inquisitive. Hanna knew about Alex's gun collection, her martial arts training, and Max's role as security. Hanna had seen Alex coming home bruised after more than one "business" trip. Sophie and the kids had even visited Alex in the hospital on a few occasions after an assignment had gone awry.

"Why not?" Hanna responded. "You obviously have a dangerous job. You have a gun in your bag right now. I've seen you fight. You're like Nancy Drew on steroids."

Alex's jaw dropped.

"I think it's cool," Hanna continued, "but we live together and…" Hanna paused and leaned forward. She put her hand on Alex's arm and said warmly, "You're my Auntie Lex. I just want to get to know you better."

Alex was dumbfounded. Sophie wasn't kidding when she said that Hanna had grown up quickly. She had the self-confidence and panache of a twenty-five-year-old. But that didn't mean Alex was going to give her a straight answer.

"Can we change the subject?" Alex asked, looking around. "This is not the place to drill down on my kill rate." And they both burst out laughing.

"Agreed," Hanna said, eyeing her empty glass. "Can I have some wine? Sophie lets me have some at dinner."

"You know that sixteen is the legal drinking age here," Alex said, hoping that would be the end of it.

"Auntie Lex, if it makes you uncomfortable, I'll skip the wine, but I would like an answer to my question."

Alex laughed. Hanna was good: at thirteen, she'd already honed her negotiating skills, boxing Alex into a corner. Alex guessed that Hanna knew she was about to get some "guidance" and had turned the tables on her.

When the waiter returned with their salads, Alex asked him to pour Hanna some wine.

"*Un peu*," Alex said, indicating a small amount with her thumb and index finger.

Hanna smiled broadly as she picked up her glass and said, "*Salute*." She took a small sip before eating her Monégasque salad.

Alex considered it a draw: Hanna got her wine, and she avoided Hanna's question. She'd save the "guidance" for another day.

Alex sighed heavily. "My dear Hanna, you have grown up. Whatever will I do with you?"

Hanna smiled and shrugged.

Smiling back, Alex decided to leave the boarding school conversation for another day.

Just as they were making plans to visit a couple of Hanna's favorite boutiques in the area, Alex's cell pinged—a text from Hugo Babin inviting her to dinner that evening at the Café des Initiés.

Alex could not hide the look of surprise on her face when she saw the text. She hadn't seen Hugo since their night together last November. Hugo's response to an earlier text from Alex had been clipped; he was out of town and would get back to her. Now he was inviting her to dinner that same evening. It was short notice, but Alex wanted to see him.

She texted Hugo: *See you there.*

Sensing something was up, Hanna asked, "A new assignment, Auntie Lex?"

"Something like that," Alex said slyly. The last thing she wanted was to have a discussion with Hanna about her sex life.

"Oh, it's a date," Hanna said immediately.

Alex laughed. "Do you want to shop or not?" she asked, sliding her cell into her Hermès shoulder bag.

***

When Alex walked into the Café des Initiés at precisely 9:30 p.m., Hugo was waiting for her. She loved that Hugo was not just on time, but early. *So un-Parisian.* Punctuality was important to Alex, and she had met a kindred spirit in Hugo.

She slid in beside him on the upholstered bench and said, "*Quel plaisir de te revoir.*"

Hugo leaned over and gave her a soft kiss on the mouth. "You look amazing."

Hugo is good. Alex was wearing one of her recent purchases from the Lanvin ready-to-wear collection: a black, belted midi dress with a square neckline.

"Thank you. I'm glad you like it," Alex said with a crooked smile. Alex could feel the warmth of Hugo's leg pressed up against hers.

The waiter appeared with a bottle of Léon Beyer Comtes d'Eguisheim, and he poured Alex a glass.

"I've taken the liberty of ordering wine," Hugo said.

A bit presumptuous. But as it was the same wine that Hugo had paid for all those months ago when they first met, she would let it go.

"I was out of town for a few weeks," Hugo said.

"No need to explain—we all have busy lives."

"Yes, we do," Hugo said as their waiter stepped forward to take their order.

Alex handed the unopened menu back to the waiter. "I'll have the *entrecôte* grilled medium rare with the asparagus starter." It was one of her favorites.

Hugo quickly glanced at the menu, and then said to the waiter, "*J'aurai le même.*"

"I have a confession to make," Alex said as the waiter left the table. "I finally Googled you."

Hugo laughed. "I'm flattered."

"You have your own Wikipedia profile. I'm impressed."

"Well, you shouldn't be," Hugo said. "The Collège de France arranged it."

"Is that where they teach Lacanian psychoanalysis?"

"You are a quick study, my dear," Hugo said.

Alex didn't like the tone of sarcasm in his voice. And she didn't like men calling her "dear." "Dear" was a term reserved for wives and mothers. But she'd let it go this time. "I was reading up on Jacques Lacan," she continued, "and found his views interesting—and confusing."

Hugo smiled at Alex, apparently amused by her unsophisticated foray into Lacanian theory.

Alex continued, "I am especially interested in Lacan's work on the need to distinguish desire from need and demand. He says that desire is neither the need for satisfaction nor the demand that it be met but the difference that results from the subtraction of the first from the second. That's pretty heavy."

"Heavy indeed. I'll have to include the Wikipedia page with my Collège de France course reading list." Hugo chuckled. "You are referring to Lacan's view that desire can never be satisfied; it is constant in its pressure and eternal. You'll have to drop by one of my lectures and learn more."

Alex nodded. "I would like that."

"As would I," Hugo replied as the waiter brought their food.

They continued their discussion over dinner, and once they'd finished eating, Alex said, "It's funny that you texted me today. I was thinking about you this morning."

"And what were you thinking?"

"I wondered what you would make of my recent dream."

Hugo took another sip of his wine. "I'd love to hear about your dream."

"I've had the dream before, but it was years ago." A troubled look flashed across her face.

"I'm in a dark and dirty basement," Alex said. "When I try to leave, the doorway keeps getting smaller and smaller, and I can't get out."

"How old are you in the dream?" Hugo asked.

"When I walk into the room, I am ten or eleven, and when I try to get out, I am an adult."

Hugo nodded knowingly. "Is there someone in the room with you?"

Alex cast a sharp look at Hugo; his ease of analysis was irritating. *Was she really that predictable?* "Yes, there is a man in the room. I'm trying to get away from him."

Hugo cleared his throat. "Is it always the same man?"

"Yes, it's the same man." Alex suddenly realized that their waiter was standing by, waiting for them to pay. Alex reached into her purse, took out a credit card, and placed it on top of the bill without looking.

"The man—it's my father. Maybe my grandmother was right about him. He's an evil bastard who ruined my mother's life." Alex felt an involuntary shudder run through her body.

Hugo sat back in his chair. "Does the dream trigger anything else from your childhood?"

Alex thought for a moment and said, "Yeah, the dream reminds me of my mother's apartment in New York."

Hugo nodded at her the way all shrinks do when they're in active listening mode.

"My mom," Alex continued, "was breaking bad at the time, and our grandmother had cut her off. The only place my mother could afford to live was a one-bedroom basement apartment in Chinatown. It had a small window that opened to a loading dock at the back of the building.

"My mom locked my sister and me in that room whenever she went out. I tried to escape once, but the window was too small." Alex paused. "I have no idea how this memory relates to my father, though. He was nowhere in sight."

Alex looked at Hugo and could see he had already formed a theory. Instead of sharing, he played with his wine glass.

Alex wasn't going to let him off the hook. "Hugo, is it that easy? Is it just a reversion to my childhood experiences in that basement apartment in Chinatown?"

"I am going to think about what you've told me." He squeezed her hand. The psychoanalysis session was over.

"That's fine. Take your time. I wanted to tell you, and now I have," Alex replied.

Alex could feel the warmth of Hugo's hand on the inside of her thigh. She moved her hand up his thigh and over his hardening penis and shuddered for a second time that evening.

Chapter Forty-Eight
Greater Boston, Massachusetts
May–September 2020

On the first of May, Nick voluntarily surrendered himself to the Bolderstock Correctional Center, a minimum-security federal prison. It wasn't exactly hard time at Bolderstock. The institution imprisoned nonviolent offenders, which meant no ten-foot, razor wire–topped fences and no prison guards watching the inmates' every move. Nick's cell was austere but more than adequate—with a wall-mounted TV above his toilet! *Beats doing time in Russia,* he thought.

After watching daytime TV for a couple weeks, Nick started a legal aid clinic in the prison library, holding court most afternoons from two to four. He spent many hours listening to his fellow inmates, many convicted felons of white-collar crimes, as they recounted the details of the frauds they had perpetrated. The scams were pretty clever—but not clever enough to avoid getting caught.

When he wasn't giving free legal advice, Nick took advantage of the jail's well-equipped gym and its outdoor basketball and tennis courts.

Nick found the experience oddly peaceful; the debacle at Houghton & Willis was over, and he was doing his time, paying back society for his wrongs.

There was one downside: Nick hadn't seen his girls since the day he'd tried to pick them up from school. His attorney had obtained a court order requiring Laura to bring the girls to the jail once a week for an hourlong visit, but Laura ignored the order.

Nick had let it go. *Laura had the Moscow tapes.*

Six months after he was incarcerated, Nick was given early release, and on the first of September, he stepped out of the jail onto Western Street and into the early fall sunshine. Judge Singh had not included a supervised release order in Nick's sentence, so he was free and clear when his feet hit the pavement.

Nick put on his Wayfarer glasses and looked up and down the deserted street for the cab that would take him—and his briefcase of cash—to Sammy Alderman's law office. He spotted a cab driving up the street and waved it over, but before Nick could get in, a CNN truck drove up.

A reporter and a camerawoman jumped out and rushed up to Nick.

"Mr. Martin, what do you have to say to all the investors who lost hundreds of millions of dollars when the Prosperity Fund went bust?" the reporter asked earnestly.

Nick didn't answer. He put up his hand to shield his face from the camera and jumped into the cab. He had resolved to put Prosperity behind him when he got out of jail, but it looked like the press wouldn't let him off that easily.

The reporter and the camerawoman ran back to the truck and followed the taxi to the steps of Sammy's law office. When Nick arrived, Sammy quickly ushered him into the building and went back to give a brief statement to the CNN reporter.

"Mr. Martin has served his time and has no further comment. He asks that he be allowed to reunite with his family and be left in peace."

Two hours later, CNN—still reporting live outside Sammy's office—was none the wiser when Nick was bundled into the trunk of a car in the underground garage, and Sammy's assistant, serving as the getaway driver, sped down the street. The assistant dropped Nick off at a townhouse in Cambridge, where Nick could hide out for a few days. The townhouse had been prearranged and was a short-term solution. Vladim—God love him— still wanted him, and he'd soon be off to Dubrovnik; however, he wanted to see his girls before he left. The decision to move offshore had not been a difficult one. Nick really had no other options: the Massachusetts Board of Bar Overseers had given him a lifetime ban from practicing law.

He called Laura's landline and cell. Both numbers were out of order. He sent her an email, but it bounced back. He put a call in to Laura's attorney. The attorney didn't call him back, but she did send a lengthy text indicating Laura wished to postpone contact with the girls till things calmed down. Laura had worked hard over the last six months to shelter the girls from Nick's legal problems, and she wanted to keep it that way.

Nick texted back to ask about arranging phone calls with his daughters.

While waiting for a reply, his doorbell rang.

He looked out the window and saw the CNN truck parked outside. So much for Sammy's assurances that the townhouse was a secure location.

Ignoring the doorbell, Nick turned on CNN and watched in horror as the reporter did a live news segment outside his front door. Within minutes, a panel of legal commentators had sliced and diced the Prosperity affair for the umpteenth time in light of Nick's early release. It didn't take long before his location hit the news and the other media outlets lined the block.

Chapter Forty-Nine
Steubenville, Ohio
September 2020

Julie Yusky was watching CNN with her best friend, Myrtle Simpson, when the segment on Nick and the Prosperity Fund came on. Julie and the girls had moved in with Myrtle a few months back. Myrtle was single and lived in a big old house that she had inherited from her mother. The arrangement worked for everyone. Myrtle liked the company, and the rent was low enough that Julie had cash at the end of the month to top up the girls' college education fund. When the segment was over, Julie went up to her bedroom and Googled "Nick Martin CNN video." Dozens of hits came up, including links to other TV stations. After reviewing several links, Julie found the one that she wanted.

The CNN reporters were camped outside a townhouse with the house number "144," but no street name was listed.

Then Julie remembered that she had seen a *For Sale* sign on a house across the street when the CNN cameraman had panned the area.

She went back to the segment, found the sign, froze the screen, and wrote down the contact information.

She called and asked the agent to send her a link to the listing. It arrived within minutes. Nick Martin was staying at 144 Dana Street in Cambridge, Massachusetts. Julie did a Google Map search; he was only six hours away.

Julie packed a small bag and went downstairs to talk to Myrtle. Julie explained that she had to make a short trip and would be back tomorrow. *Would Myrtle watch the girls?*

Myrtle could see that something was up; however, she didn't ask where Julie was going, and Julie didn't offer the information.

Julie went back upstairs and said goodnight to the girls. She told them Myrtle would get them off to school in the morning. When Julie saw the worried look on her girls' faces, she said, "Don't worry, I'll be back by the time you get home from school."

Julie knew they both wanted iPhones, but she had been saving that for Christmas. "Maybe I'll get you those iPhones that you want," Julie said teasingly.

Both girls perked up considerably when they heard that. Julie kissed them on their foreheads, turned out the light, and quietly left their bedroom.

Downstairs, Myrtle handed Julie a slip of paper. "You got a second notice from the post office. It's a registered letter from someone called Basel. If you don't pick it up by the day after tomorrow, the post office will send it back."

"Thanks. I'll pick it up tomorrow," Julie said. *Tonight, she had some unfinished business with Mr. Martin.*

Chapter Fifty
Cambridge, Massachusetts
September 2020

As soon as Nick saw that the media was not going to leave him alone, he got on the phone with Vladim. Nick explained that all the publicity was making him very nervous. He and Mihkel had been the faces of the Prosperity fraud in the US, and they both had received dozens of death threats on social media. It was only a matter of time before one of them tracked Nick down. He needed to disappear—and fast.

Vladim called him back within a few minutes; the arrangements had been made. One of Vladim's jets would be waiting for Nick just after midnight at Hanscom Field, a small airport for private aircraft outside of Boston.

Nick fell asleep while watching TV with the briefcase on his lap and a Glock from Sammy by his side.

A call around midnight broke Nick's sleep. Vladim's jet had arrived. It was a forty-minute drive, and Nick had made arrangements for a limo service to be on standby.

Nick texted the company and received confirmation that the limo would be there in ten minutes. He looked out the window and felt relieved: the media trucks were gone, and the street was quiet.

Nick grabbed Igor's cash, shoved the pistol into his pocket, and went outside to wait.

After ten minutes, Nick texted the limo service again.

The dispatcher relayed the driver would be there in another ten minutes.

Gripping the battered aluminum briefcase, Nick nervously looked down the one-way street and wondered if he should go back into the townhouse to wait. Then he heard someone call out his name.

Nick looked in the direction of the voice. A woman was approaching from the sidewalk. *How had he missed her?* "Mr. Martin. Nick Martin?" the woman called out again. In the dim light, she looked to be in her thirties.

"Yeah," Nick said, cautiously resting his hand against the gun in his trouser pocket. "Can I help you, miss?"

"The name is Yusky. Julie Yusky," she said.

Nick frowned; the name sounded familiar.

"Yes, you can help me. You can tell me why you took my husband's insurance policy and then had him killed."

"What? I, erm, I don't know what you're talking about," Nick stammered.

"His name was Charlie Yusky," the woman said. Her voice warbled. "Don't tell me you can't remember him."

"Yes—Charlie Yusky, of course," Nick said, licking his suddenly dry lips. "You have to believe me, ma'am. I had nothing to do with his death."

"Alex Greene told me what happened," Julie said, her voice cracking. She took a revolver out of her bag, pointed it at Nick, and cocked it.

Fucking Greene. She was the source of everything that was shit in his life.

"Alex Greene told you I killed your husband?" Nick said, playing for time. "I'm sorry, but she was wrong. Please put the gun down."

Julie's hand shook with the weight of the gun. "You're lying," she said, tears streaming down her face. "You think just because you're out of jail you're innocent? My Charlie's dead! Our house is gone!"

She shook her head and kept the gun trained on Nick. "My girls and I have nothing now, I can't even afford decent housing. Do you know what it's like to lose everything?"

Nick stole a quick glance down the street. Still no limo.

"Look, I'd like to help you—" he started.

"We lost everything because of you!" Julie cried out. "I lost my husband. My girls lost their father!" Her voice was full of pain. "We lost everything!"

"I understand, but—"

"You understand?" Julie spat out. "You understand what it means to be poor? You get out of jail, and you move right into this fancy house. Don't insult me. I'm not stupid." She pointed the revolver at Nick. The gun gleamed in the streetlight as it wavered uncertainly in her shaking hand.

"Please be careful with that gun," Nick said, his eyes locked on the barrel.

"Don't tell me to be careful!" Julie shouted back.

"Times have been tough for many people, Mrs. Yusky," said Nick. His mouth had gone dry. "If—if you don't put that gun away, I'm going to have to call the police."

"Go right ahead. Then you can tell the police how you killed Charlie," Julie said, waving the gun at him.

"Look. I have money in this briefcase," Nick said.

He lifted the aluminum briefcase for Julie to see. "You can have it all. It's not traceable. It's nearly two million."

"I don't want your money. I want my life back!" Julie lifted her left arm to wipe away the tears.

In that moment, Nick pulled out his Glock. "Look, I don't want to hurt you, but I will if I have to."

"I'm not afraid of you!" Julie shrilled and stumbled backward. She missed the curb and fell against the trunk of a parked car.

Her father's gun went off with an ear-piercing crack. One red-hot punch struck Nick in the chest.

Nick staggered back and dropped the Glock and the aluminum case. The case skidded across the sidewalk and onto the street behind Julie.

Julie and Nick made eye contact for an instant, each looking equally horrified. Then Nick's legs crumpled beneath him, and he dropped to the ground.

Julie Yusky stared for a few moments at Nick's body. Blood pooled under his chest, and his eyes stared blankly at the dark sky.

Julie's heart was pounding, and her ears were ringing from the sound of the blast. She could not believe what she had done. She only wanted to make him understand what he had done to her family.

She looked around. Someone must have heard the gunfire, but the street was quiet; the windows in the houses remained dark. It was an accident, a terrible accident, and her girls needed her.

Julie jammed her warm gun into the pocket of her coat and turned toward her car, nearly tripping over the metal briefcase at her feet.

She picked up the briefcase, threw it into the back seat of her car, and drove off.

Chapter Fifty-One
Outside Moscow, Russia, and Cote d'Azur, France
August 2020

Wolfman crouched low just outside the stone wall surrounding Igor Dimitrov's *dacha*. Igor had not been happy when Wolfman refused to honor his contract to kill Alex, and in retaliation, Igor had tried to put a contract on Wolfman. But Igor was having trouble finding an assassin who would go after Wolfman. Word quickly got back to Wolfman, and he decided to take offensive action.

A guard carrying an AK-47 passed by Wolfman on the other side of the wall, focusing on the ground in front of him instead of paying attention to what was going on around him. *Probably dreaming of what he would do when he got off shift. Tonight, that would cost him his life,* Wolfman thought. Wolfman raised his silenced Walther PPK automatic pistol and aimed it at the guard. He squeezed the trigger, and the guard's head exploded.

Then Wolfman scaled the wall and ran to the body, dragging it out of sight. Nearby, an owl, the only witness to the killing, hooted.

Wolfman sprinted across the lawn and slipped through the unlocked French doors.

As he crept down the darkened hallway, he heard voices coming through the closed doors of a nearby room.

Wolfman inhaled and kicked the doors in with one of his well-worn army boots.

Igor Dimitrov lay sprawled on a couch before a roaring fireplace. His unzipped pants revealed a small, flaccid penis lying languidly up against his fleshy thigh. Kneeling on the floor in front of Igor was a naked prepubescent girl. She looked up at Wolfman for an instant and then dropped her head in shame.

Igor's eyes flashed with recognition. "What the fuck are you doing here?" he screamed.

Without answering, and leveling his pistol at Igor, Wolfman walked over to the Russian girl and helped her to her feet. "*Ukhodi.*"

Terrified, the girl rushed out the door.

"You should have left me alone," Wolfman said, moving closer to Igor.

"You touch me, and you're a dead man!" Igor shouted, spittle spraying from his mouth as he scrambled to find his gun.

"*Nyet.* You're the dead man," Wolfman said, and he shot Igor between the eyes.
***

A day after the hit, Joshua Workman drove his silver '63 Jaguar XK-E convertible along the highway that hugged France's hilly Mediterranean coastline. Enjoying the warm breeze rushing through his hair, he raced the vintage car up the steeply graded hill to the small mountaintop village of Eze. Joshua had his custom-made .50 BMG silenced sniper rifle in the car's trunk for a contract the next day in Monaco, but tonight was all pleasure.

Joshua pulled up to the parking lot at the base of the village and handed his keys to an attendant at the gate.

He grabbed his black dinner jacket off the passenger seat, slung it over his shoulder, and walked up the steep, cobblestone walkway to the Château Eza. Joshua loved the village with its winding, narrow streets, charming sidewalk cafés, and stunning views of Monaco to the east and Nice to the west. There was no other village like it on the planet.

When he reached the Château Eza, he put on his jacket and walked across the opulent lobby to its hillside bar overlooking the Mediterranean Sea. The view was spectacular. A full moon shone down on the calm, sparkling waters, and lights twinkled up and down the coast.

Joshua smiled when he saw a dark-haired woman sitting at a table facing the water. She was immaculately dressed in a black, mesh-paneled Mugler midi dress and four-inch-high, black Louboutin heels. He walked up behind her and whispered into her ear, "Hello, Meagan."

She looked up, smiling, and pulled his face down for a long, lingering kiss.

Joshua glanced over at the bottle of Dom Perignon '56 icing in a silver bucket and the two half-filled glasses and said, "My darling, you waited for me."

"Of course, *liebling*, don't I always?" was her husky reply, and she raised her glass in a toast.

When she smiled, Joshua thought she looked like Alex's twin.

Epilogue

Startled, Alex sat up in bed and looked around her. The moon was shining into her bedroom through the patio doors facing the endless expanse of a Parisian cityscape. The TV had gone into sleep mode. She had fallen asleep again to the endless rumblings of the CNN reporters. *Better than a sleeping pill.*

Alex clicked the TV off and plumped her pillows. Snuggled under her feather duvet, she soon drifted off.

The bedside clock showed 2:30 a.m. when Alex's eyes fluttered open again. *Someone's in the room.*

She slowly reached for the .45 Colt automatic she kept strapped to her bed frame. She felt for its familiar solid mass.

She froze. *Gone.*

Alex sucked in her breath and called out, "Who's there? What do you want?"

"Alex, it's me," said a familiar voice.

Goosebumps ran up and down Alex's arms. Hanna was in the bedroom suite next to hers, and Alex didn't want to wake her.

When Alex switched on the bedside light, she met the Wolfman's unblinking gaze. *How had he gotten past her security system?*

"What are you doing here?" Alex said, slipping out of bed.

She pulled a robe over her silk teddy, keeping her eyes riveted on her intruder.

"I'm here to say that you don't have to worry about Igor anymore."

"That's old news. Why are you really here, Joshua?"

"Maybe I just wanted to see you again."

"Try the fucking phone next time," Alex said, still not convinced she and Hanna were out of danger.

"Think of it this way: I just did you a favor. If I can get in here, you need to get better security," Joshua said.

Alex had no choice but to play along. He'd caught her at her most vulnerable. "Okay, okay, you got me. But now you're going to leave," Alex said, walking past him to the bedroom door. She opened it for him. "Let's go."

Joshua followed her down the hallway until they reached the next door, which had been left ajar. He stopped. "Seriously, Alex, you need to be more careful. I could have hurt you or Hanna."

Alex's knees weakened. *How does he know Hanna's name?* She grabbed his arm and hissed, "I will kill you with my bare hands if you don't keep on walking."

Joshua smiled at her and continued down the hallway.

When they got to the elevator, the doors were open. Alex couldn't believe it. She turned to face him. "You used the elevator to get in here?"

Joshua stepped forward and tried to touch Alex's hair. Alex slapped his hand. "Answer my fucking question." Joshua shook his head and stepped into the elevator.

He pressed the ground-floor button, and as the door closed between them, he said, "I'm not here to hurt either of you; it's just a warning. You need better security."

When the elevator door closed, Alex turned and ran down the hallway to Hanna's bedroom.

She threw open the door and rushed to her niece's bedside. She let out a huge breath when she saw Hanna sleeping peacefully in the moonlight.

Alex dropped to her knees on the floor beside Hanna's bed, swallowing the scream that rose in her throat. *How dare he—how fucking dare he!* He had been too close; it could never happen again.

Joshua was right. She needed better security.

She also needed him dead.